HUNTED

THE SHORTEN CHRONICLES BOOK 5

ROSALIND TATE

Hunted
The Shorten Chronicles Book 5

*In the first and second books of the Shorten Chronicles, **Stranded** and **Escape**, Sophie and her beloved dog, Charlotte, fall into a parallel universe, a century back in time. Sophie struggles to adapt to living in Shorten Manor but the heir to the estate, Freddy Lacey, is besotted. At the end of Escape, Sophie, Charlotte, and Hugo manage to return to the 21st century. Sophie and Hugo confess their love for each other, act on their feelings and sleep together, but then Freddy turns up. He's followed them through time.*

*In the third book of the series, **Exile**, Freddy finds out that Sophie is with Hugo. In despair, he dashes recklessly across universes, and they all find themselves in a terrifying medieval kingdom. Charlotte's DNA is enhanced, giving her a human lifespan and an advanced understanding of language. Sophie acquires a temporary, deadly power and trapped in a bear pit, she and Freddy give into temptation to fend off the bitter cold. When they finally return to modern London, Sophie discovers she's pregnant.*

*In **Intermezzo**, a fun, rom-com novella (exclusive to Rosalind's Fantasy Bookshop: https://bookshop.rosalindtate.com), Sophie marries Hugo but gives birth to Freddy's child, Bella. Freddy and Sophie become platonic friends. Charlotte the labradoodle accepts this unusual state of affairs with aplomb, adores the new baby and, with her enhanced DNA, listens to audiobooks featuring canine sidekicks.*

*In the fourth book of the series, **Defiance**, Freddy insists on taking Bella to his family in Shorten. As a civil war rages, Freddy falls in love with Clarissa. Janus, the Roman god whose ship enables them to travel between universes, tricks Sophie and Freddy into* *returning to modern London without their daughter. If they are ever to see Bella or Clarissa again, they need Hugo and Charlotte's help to track down the only artefact that can kill Janus: his walking staff.*

Hunted *is the penultimate book in the* **Shorten Chronicles.**

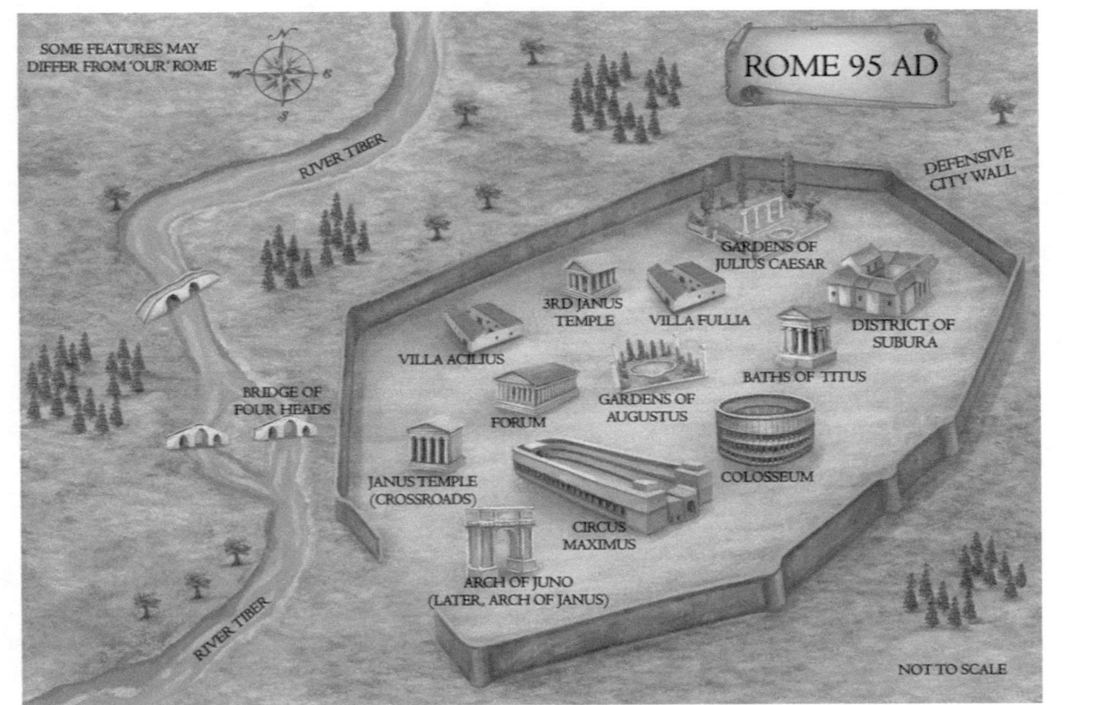

SOME FEATURES MAY
DIFFER FROM 'OUR' ROME
ROME 95 AD
RIVER TIBER
DEFENSIVE
CITY WALL
GARDENS OF
JULIUS CAESAR
3RD JANUS
TEMPLE
VILLA FULLIA
DISTRICT OF
SUBURA
VILLA ACILIUS
BATHS OF TITUS
BRIDGE OF
FOUR HEADS
FORUM
GARDENS OF
AUGUSTUS
JANUS TEMPLE
(CROSSROADS)
COLOSSEUM
CIRCUS
MAXIMUS
ARCH OF JUNO
(LATER, ARCH OF JANUS)
RIVER TIBER
NOT TO SCALE

Fortune and love favour the brave.
Ovid
(43 BC – 17 AD)

CHAPTER 1

The air above Euston Road in London shimmered, summer-greasy with petrol and diesel fumes. Pedestrians, mostly tourists, dawdled or looked at Google Maps on their phones, ignoring the car horns of motorists stuck in traffic and distant sirens.

Sophie hurried along the pavement towards the British Library, her mind full of her baby daughter, a parallel universe away. Bella's serious blue eyes, her wobbly, determined stumbling, her contented gurgling… Sophie stumbled, barely keeping her balance, and Hugo grabbed her hand.

'I know this is hard,' he said. 'Let's just hope the sketch is in the book.'

Sophie avoided his gaze. If the obscure textbook had the sketch of Janus' walking staff, copied from the physical object, there was a chance, a small chance, they could track it down. The walking staff was the only way to end the two-faced Roman god who'd cut them off from Bella. And Sophie couldn't, wouldn't accept she'd never see her daughter again.

They reached the British Library entrance. The tall red-brick arch was brutalist and angular. Hugo took off his Tilley sun hat and wiped his brow. 'This might be a hidden portal.'

What they called a 'portal' was Janus' ship, a vessel that travelled between universes. For millennia, the ship's software had prevented Janus from harming or interfering with travellers but yesterday, Janus had altered that software, preventing them from crossing universes.

A youth strolled past them through the arch and headed across the courtyard that fronted the library.

'Come on,' said Sophie. 'Not every arch is a portal.' They stepped together into the courtyard, Sophie's flip-flops slapping on the granite paving slabs. Not far from the arch was a huge bronze statue of a kneeling figure. They walked past it, followed a path lined with neat flowerbeds and garden benches, and came to the library.

In different circumstances, this would have been a fascinating day out. On its nine floors and five additional levels underground, the library stored every British book published in the last four centuries, as well as much older works.

They'd confirmed online that *Classical Myths and Legends: A Convenient Guide* was stored here. The same book had been hidden in a grand house in a parallel universe, Shorten Manor. That book had included a sketch of Janus' walking staff, drawn from the real thing in 1889. If the sketch was in the book in the library, then the staff had also been in this universe, and might have survived until now.

But the British Library edition might not have it. Parallel universes, however similar, had tiny differences.

Inside, they were met by cold air-conditioning and shivered as they passed through airport-style security before joining tourists taking selfies in the grand foyer.

'Wow,' said Sophie. The architecture on the outside might be modern and ugly, but the inside resembled a *Harry Potter* film set. Multiple floors spiralled up around a glass tower of books, as tall as the building.

The author of *Classical Myths and Legends* was George Herbert, a pseudonym for H. G. Wells. Back when they'd first crossed universes and found themselves in Shorten Manor, they'd figured out that Wells, who'd penned such classic novels as *The Time Machine* and *The War of the Worlds*, had travelled to parallel universes.

They headed towards an information booth. *Classical Myths and Legends* wasn't available to the casual browser. To order the book, they needed Reader Passes.

From the booth, they were directed down a corridor to a room filled with workstations. At each station, a library employee sat behind a screen, grilling an applicant as to why they wanted a Reader Pass.

The woman behind the front desk looked up. 'Have you already joined online?'

Sophie searched for the reference numbers on her phone and read them out. They gave over their passports and driving licences.

After a cursory glance, the woman returned their ID, and pointed to high stools in front of a row of computers. 'Sign in please, and wait to be called.'

As they tapped on the chunky keyboards, Hugo whispered, 'A face-to-face interview seems over the top for Reader Passes. It's like being vetted for MI5.'

Sophie nodded, shivering in her shorts and T-shirt.

When they were called to a workstation, they sat on hard chairs.

'Purpose of visit?' asked Workstation Guy, or should that be guard?

'Pleasure,' said Sophie. 'We're into old books.'

'Then you're in the right place. Our oldest item is an

inscribed Egyptian stone from 3,600 years ago, praising Osiris, god of the underworld.'

'Do you have any Roman texts that reference Janus?' said Hugo.

'We have digitised Roman tablets. I don't know whether any refer to Janus. Interesting god. Master of time and all that.'

Statues from antiquity portrayed Janus with two faces looking in opposite directions, towards the past and the future. The faces were mostly male, clean-shaven or bearded. Once worshipped in ancient Rome, Janus had the status of a myth. Shame he was real. The thought of him made Sophie shudder—

'Can I see your ID?'

They'd already shown their documents, but they handed them over. Workstation Guy copied their info onto his screen. 'You order books via the Reading Room's computers. Laptops and phones are allowed, and you can take photos.' He gave them back their ID. 'No drinks or food. Store your bags in the library lockers.'

There were more rules and info, but Sophie stopped listening. The library had their details. If they were caught stealing the book, they'd have criminal records. She swallowed. If they took on Janus and lost, a criminal record wouldn't matter. They'd be dead.

A camera on the workstation screen recorded their headshots for the Reader Passes, and the guy watched them sign their cards.

The lockers were down another corridor. Sophie put her bag in one but struggled to follow the instructions to create a passcode, her mind on Bella. She finally sorted it, half an eye on the uniformed security guard. 'Stealing the book isn't an option,' she whispered to Hugo. 'We'll just have to take photos.'

The Humanities Reading Room on the first floor had oak double doors with inlaid square glass panels and long vertical handles made of shiny brass. Sophie pulled open the right door and Hugo followed her in. They paused for a moment, looking around.

There were no windows, but clever lighting made the expansive space airy and bright. Two security guards were seated by the door. Further inside, manned by a librarian with red spectacles, was a booth with a black and white sign: *Book Requests.* Further along was an enquiries desk and another librarian, and there were rows of connected desks, every other workspace with a built-in screen and keyboard. About half were occupied with people reading, clicking keyboards on laptops, or scribbling notes. Beyond the desks were bookcases, freestanding or against the wall.

'Do you need help?' asked a security guard.

'We're fine, thank you,' said Sophie.

They found the nearest vacant desk and computer. Sophie signed in and ordered the book. A message popped up. *Waiting time 70 minutes.*

Hugo sighed. 'No point hanging around here.'

Outside the Reading Room, Sophie phoned Freddy who was waiting in a teashop down the road. An illegal alien with no ID and no way of acquiring any, Freddy could never have a Reader Pass. Disenfranchised by time travel as well as geography, he'd been born in 1904. 'It won't be delivered for over an hour,' she told him.

'Understood,' said Freddy. 'Charlotte loves the teashop. I've ordered her a sausage sandwich and Earl Grey tea.' Charlotte was Sophie's brown labradoodle and despite her unusual talents, also didn't qualify for a Reader Pass. The library allowed emotional-support dogs, but Charlotte had declined to dress up in a fluorescent jacket.

Sophie chewed her lip. 'The sketch might not be in the book.'

'It has to be.' Freddy ended the call.

He sounded as tense as she was. Sophie exhaled, wishing this over. If there was no sketch, their baby was lost forever, but this waiting and not knowing was almost worse. Her friendship with Bella's father was now platonic. Which was fortunate, as she'd married Hugo.

'Let's get a coffee.' Hugo put his arm through hers and they walked along another passage into a bustling café.

The glass tower of books was right beside the café and this close up, the height and scale of it was even more impressive. No wonder requesting a book took a while. They ordered coffees and at the edge of the café, Sophie looked down over a rail. Between them and the tower was a lethal hundred-foot drop to the ground floor.

Sitting down with her back to the rail, Sophie touched her T-shirt where Bella's key-rattle hung from its necklace chain and jutted out under the cotton. Picked up from the floor in the Manor, the last time she'd been with her daughter.

Hugo looked at her over his mug. 'Bella's safe in Shorten.'

He often read her thoughts, which was comforting rather than creepy. But she couldn't be reassured about this. 'We can't know that. How can we?' They couldn't see Bella, never mind keep her safe.

'Anne and Clarissa will protect Bella with their lives,' added Hugo.

Anne Lacey, Freddy's mother, was the fiercest granny in any universe, and Clarissa was Freddy's fiancée, who he might never see again.

Hugo reached across the table and held her hand, and Sophie smiled at him, grateful beyond measure for whatever accident or fate had brought them together.

'If there was no chance we can end him, Janus wouldn't have cut us off,' said Sophie, reassuring herself. The walking staff would reset Janus' ship, sending the ship — and Janus — back to factory settings. Janus would no longer be sentient, just an obedient algorithm. They could travel safely to Shorten Manor, be reunited with their loved ones, and she'd hold her baby again.

Hugo squeezed her hand. He'd brave anything, and she would too.

CHAPTER 2

An hour later, in the Humanities Reading Room, Sophie and Hugo approached the booth.

'We ordered *Myths and Legends: A Convenient Guide*, by George Herbert,' said Sophie.

The librarian with the red glasses pushed a book wrapped in tissue paper under the partition glass, and Sophie gingerly accepted it.

They headed to a back row desk, sat down, and Sophie placed the pocket-sized book on the table. Hugo stared at it.

'Putting this off won't change the answer.' Sophie peeled away the tissue paper. The cover was a yucky yellow-brown, and plain except for the title in fancy black font, and H. G. Wells' first names reversed: *George Herbert*. The binding was new and stiff, and squeaked when she opened it.

'The edition in Shorten was the same,' said Hugo. 'Unread, forgotten.' He'd come across the book in the library in Freddy's home.

'Why would it have been in the Manor?' said Sophie.

'Wells visited the pub in the nearby village. Perhaps he left it there?'

'By accident?'

'Possibly. And somebody from the Manor found it.'

Sophie opened the first page. *Fitzroy Publishing 1889.*

'There was a chapter in the Shorten book that listed Greek and Roman gods, including Janus,' said Hugo. 'The sketch was after that.'

Sophie carefully turned another page. 'Oh.'

Underneath the heading, *Mythical Symbols Reimagined,* was a drawing of a long key. It was grey, apart from a green heart at the tip of the handle that had a hollowed-out centre containing a gold figure T. The T stood for tempus or time. The end of the limbs touching the circle represented the past, present, and future.

Sophie read the caption. *Janus' key symbolises the Roman god's protection of doors, gates, paths, and thresholds.*

Below the key was the walking staff, drawn in the same style, shaded with tiny strokes. But it had depth, the shape and proportions so well done, it appeared to be standing up from the page. Most of the staff was a textured, rich brown, like oak, and the design of the head matched the key: green and heart-shaped, with the three gold limbs of the T joined to the inner rim. *Janus' walking staff indicates his knowledge, guiding the way,* said the caption.

Relief and joy surged through Sophie, and she beamed at Hugo, seeing the same emotions on his face. She messaged Freddy and he replied with dancing emojis.

Hugo pointed to where someone had scrawled *June 1889* and *I. M.* 'The initials stand for Isabel Mary, Wells' first wife. I should have realised before.' He tapped on his phone. 'She was an artist. Drew illustrations for textbooks and worked as a photograph retoucher.'

'Retoucher?' asked Sophie.

'Making photographs prettier. The job required hands-on skill and an eye for detail.'

'Isabel didn't have the gene,' said Sophie, patting the illustration with her forefinger. 'Saw it just as a walking staff.'

Only individuals with the gene could see the device beneath the illusion. The gene was inherited from a race that built ships that crossed universes, the 'builders,' as Sophie called them. The builders had visited many worlds and interacted with the locals. Sophie's dog, Charlotte, had the gene, as did Freddy. Hugo, though, didn't have it. He'd never see the device, couldn't operate it, and could only travel between universes in their company.

'I wonder what it really looks like, what you would see? What Wells saw.' Hugo scrolled on his phone and peered at a sepia photo he'd recently downloaded. Staring at the camera was a podgy middle-aged H. G. Wells, in a dark suit, a pale shirt, and a bow tie. His drooping moustache was theatrical, stretching all the way to the bottom of his face.

Sophie shivered, the hairs on her forearms standing up. 'Having the same rare gene as a literary genius is … unnerving.' She exhaled. 'Let's do this.'

She photographed the book cover and Hugo turned the pages, keeping them flat as she recorded the whole book. With only fifty pages, it didn't take long.

'I've researched Wells to death, feel as if I know him,' said Hugo. 'He was driven, ambitious, and had an extremely high opinion of himself—'

'Justifiably, writing those wonderful novels.' Sophie shut the book.

'When this was published, he'd only written a short story.'

Sophie checked her photos. 'All good.' An illogical reluctance to return the book to the stacks came over her but she picked it up and took it to the booth.

~

Outside the library, they walked across the bright courtyard and Sophie put on her sunglasses. 'Now, we find the walking staff.' The sketch was only the first step. She pictured Bella, her resolve strengthening. I'm coming for you, baby. No matter what it takes.

They came to the massive statue and Hugo removed his shades to read the plaque. 'Sir Isaac Newton. Measuring the universe with a pair of compasses.'

Sophie moved closer to it. Parts of the body were bolted together. Representing armour? Or was he supposed to be mechanical and robotic? Her mind skittered to Janus, to before he was sentient. In ancient Rome, to impress the locals, the builders had summoned him out of his ship. A creature of advanced technology, would he have looked like this? Half machine, half human?

Hugo's phone pinged. 'Lovely photos from Scotland.' His parents and the family dog were on holiday there.

Other people's ordinary happy lives continued, but there wasn't space in Sophie's brain to think about them. 'Let's get back to Freddy.'

They crossed the road, stepped into the teashop, and Freddy waved from a corner table. Charlotte barked a greeting and so did her devoted companion, Jack the retriever.

'I'll buy cold lemonades.' Hugo went to the counter.

Sophie sat beside Freddy and stroked the dogs. Charlotte had been given a water bowl by the teashop, but she was drinking tea from another bowl. Jack, being a regular dog, preferred water.

'You won't believe how many auction sites there are.' Freddy closed his laptop. 'Specialist sales, collections, house clearances…'

Hugo set down the lemonades. 'Shouldn't we start with

Wells' descendants? He had four children. One might have inherited the staff and passed it down?'

Freddy patted Sophie's hand. 'Already gone through all that,' he said, his expression grim. 'Tracking down the staff will be a formidable task.'

*H*ugo's home in London was spacious, the back garden walled and private, and Sophie carried the printed-off photos of *Myths and Legends* out onto the sun-dappled terrace. A faint breeze ruffled the blossom on the apple tree, releasing a delicate flowery scent. The dog-eared photos fluttered but were securely stapled together, the sketch on top.

Jack didn't stir under the table and Freddy didn't look up from his laptop, likely following another dead-end lead. Their painstaking online searches over five days suggested the walking staff hadn't survived from 1889 to the present day. The only mention of a heart-shaped carving and a figure T related to Janus' key — not his staff. Hope and determination had given way to despondency and rising panic as search after search had proved fruitless. Sophie touched Bella's key-rattle chain around her neck. Keep going.

Charlotte, sleek and cooler after a groom, was seated between Hugo and Freddy, reading a second-hand paperback, *Heroic Dogs*.

'It's a shame Charlotte can't use a phone or a computer,'

said Hugo. 'She could have helped.' Charlotte displayed her large front paws, then returned to *Heroic Dogs*. She understood English and knew their plan but couldn't talk. That would have been weird.

Hugo turned a paperback page. 'There are machines that can do this.' He scrolled on his phone and turned the screen to show her.

Charlotte gave Hugo her unnerving, human-like nod and he smiled. 'I'll buy it.'

The cool breeze died away and Freddy opened an unfamiliar browser on his laptop. Despite being relatively new to the 21st century, he'd embraced its technology. 'Time to investigate the dark web.'

Hugo raised his eyebrows.

'Where criminals and terrorists hang out?' said Sophie. 'Why would the staff be there?'

'If a lowlife with the gene has it, they might believe it's worth something,' said Freddy. 'May have sold it. Could be a record of that?'

Charlotte watched the screen as Freddy delved into bad places, and Sophie moved to distract her. But then hesitated. Charlotte was five in dog-years, the human equivalent of thirty-five. She could handle nasty stuff.

Hugo was scrolling, frowning at his phone. Sophie glanced at hers. *No match for requested item.* She brushed a tendril of hair from her forehead and sighed.

'It must be in a private house, or long ago discarded.' Freddy closed his laptop.

Sophie pictured the staff in landfill, fighting back tears. 'After all this time, it would be dented and scraped. No one would think it had any value.'

'The appearance of the walking staff's an illusion,' said Hugo. 'It would look brand new.'

'Of course.' Sophie wiped her eyes, annoyed with herself

for not realising. Though if they had found it, possessing the gene, she wouldn't have seen a pristine walking staff. Neither would Freddy.

Freddy got to his feet, his face shuttered, and walked around the garden. Jack ran in circles around Freddy's feet, trying to cheer him, but Charlotte stayed at the table, her expression sombre.

Sophie longed to comfort him, but her emotional well was empty, drained by despair. Hugo covered her hand with his. He loved Bella, but Sophie's bond with her child was beyond love, a relentless blood tie that knew no limits. Her hopes of watching Bella change from a baby to a toddler, cherishing her milestones, was now a dream, not a plan, and the future stretched out, bleak and dark.

Freddy returned to the terrace. He flicked through *Myths and Legends* as if he wanted to tear it to bits. 'Odd little book.' His tone had a bitter edge.

Wallowing in self-pity wasn't helping. Sophie dragged her brain into action. 'Why would Wells publish the sketch in a humdrum textbook? He'd witnessed the walking staff summoning Janus out in ancient Rome!'

Freddy nodded. 'Memorable enough that he took the staff as a souvenir.'

'And why didn't Wells use his usual pen name to write a novel about Janus being summoned?' said Sophie. 'Would have made an awesome story.'

'Perhaps Janus ordered him not to take the staff and when that didn't work, he told Wells to keep it secret?' said Hugo. 'Janus wouldn't have wanted the device attracting attention, falling into the wrong hands.'

'Our hands.' Freddy sat down and rapped his knuckles on the table. 'We can't know what relationship Wells *thought* he had with Janus, but if Janus ordered Wells, all the versions of him, to return the staff, he surely would have done.'

'Given what I've read, I don't believe they would,' said Hugo. 'In the 19ᵗʰ century, there weren't respected scientific theories to support the idea of parallel universes. After he stumbled into Janus' ship, Wells probably worried he was going mad or dreaming. But the staff looked different to him, compared to the illusion his wife and others saw. It confirmed he crossed universes for real, travelled in time. Far more precious than just a souvenir.'

Charlotte's gaze was on the pages of *Myths and Legends*. A new breeze was ruffling the pages, lifting the corners and making the sketch ripple.

'The unremarkable textbook could have allowed Wells to publish something about the staff on his own terms?' said Hugo. 'Consistent with his stubborn character.'

'And never marketing it,' said Sophie. 'Keeping on Janus' good side.'

'He doesn't have a good side,' said Freddy.

Despite the summer sunshine, Sophie shivered. 'Janus must have been incandescent that he couldn't stop Wells taking the last surviving walking staff.' In the 6ᵗʰ century AD, the builders had changed how they conducted anthropological research. Once they stopped interacting with the locals, they'd dismantled the staffs.

Hugo stared out at the garden. 'Janus cut us off because I discovered *Myths and Legends* in Shorten, and he knew we'd find the same sketch here.' Janus could see the past, present, and future in multiple universes. 'He knows whether the staff survived from the 19ᵗʰ century until now — or hasn't.'

'I see where you're going with this.' Sophie sat up straighter. 'Why cut us off if the staff hasn't survived? We do find it.'

'I can't see how,' said Freddy.

Hugo drove his hand through his hair. 'Let's take a break, start fresh tomorrow.'

'We'd only be putting off the inevitable.' Freddy steepled his fingers, reminding Sophie of his father. 'This is over. We should travel to Shorten, get back to Bella and Clarissa in Juno. Take our chances.'

Sophie said nothing, dread sliding down her spine. Juno was Janus' sister ship, but less advanced. Janus' ship changed to blend in with its surroundings, appearing as a fancy lift, and while crossing universes over weeks or months, it protected travellers from the passage of time. Most travellers remained oblivious, believing mere minutes had passed. Juno's passengers, though, suffered harrowing, protracted journeys. Some had starved to death.

Hugo stood up from the table. 'You'd be taking a hell of a risk.'

Sophie noted he'd said, 'you,' not 'we.' Shorten would never be home for Hugo. It would destroy him to be separated from her, but he wouldn't go with them. He met her eyes and seeing his distress and unable to hide hers, she dropped her gaze. Bella had to come first.

She drew a long, slow breath. 'There must be another way.'

Charlotte was still considering the drawing. If she came up with an idea, though, she couldn't share it.

Sophie stared at the sketch, wondering for the nth time what the device really looked like. Stolen from ancient Rome, only to be lost forever. Ancient Rome... She slapped her head. 'The walking staff's lost here, but it's not lost in time.' Picturing Janus towering over buildings and people, a hybrid monster of flesh and metal, she ignored a twinge of fear. 'The staff summoned Janus in ancient Rome. That's where we need to go.'

'Yes!' Freddy's eyes lit up. 'A universe where time passes much more slowly than here. Where it's two thousand years ago.'

'Slow down.' Hugo pushed his fringe off his brow. 'If you found Janus' staff in Rome, to reset him, you'd have to cross universes again to a place and date where he's sentient and been summoned by somebody he hasn't cut off. Not to mention risking two trips in Juno.'

'What's happened on previous crossings doesn't change the odds for each subsequent journey, the same as tossing a coin,' said Freddy. 'You know this.'

'Knowing is one thing.' Hugo's mouth compressed into a grim line. 'Believing it, trusting in it, is too difficult.'

He was overlooking a crucial fact they could trust. 'Janus cut *us* off,' said Sophie. 'This version of us. Because we cross safely and end him.'

'You'd better be right about that.' Hugo stared at the table. 'Or you'll die trying.'

'Sophie's logic is sound,' said Freddy.

She shot him a quizzical glance. He sounded impressed, or was he just surprised?

'Hugo, we need you with us,' said Freddy.

The words hung in the air and Hugo scrutinised Sophie's pensive face. After what seemed an age, he nodded.

CHAPTER 4

Two weeks after abandoning their search for the walking staff in this world, they drove in Hugo's car to Derbyshire, to the university where they'd first crossed universes. Before he'd cut them off, Janus' ship had appeared in the students' union, where the universe had a weak spot and least resistance. The best location to call Juno.

Hugo indicated and changed lanes on the motorway, slowing in heavy traffic. While Jack snoozed and Charlotte had on her headphones, listening to an audiobook, Sophie read *Latin for Dummies*. She wanted to at least nail the basics. *Salve* meant hello. *Vale* meant goodbye.

For the last fortnight, they'd spent every waking moment researching ancient Rome. Hugo had scrutinised academic tomes and textbooks, and Sophie read novels by history professors. She'd even unearthed a book claiming to be a time travellers' guide. A good joke for the author and handy for the real thing.

'I've found another article about Janus.' Freddy scrolled on his phone. 'He intervened in the rape of the Sabine women.'

'Doesn't sound nice,' said Sophie.

'In August, 750 BC, Janus prevented the Sabine men from reclaiming their women,' read Freddy. *'He set off a volcanic cascade of scalding water.'*

'Random,' said Sophie. 'What's the context?'

'The Romans had kidnapped the women because they didn't have enough of their own.'

Sophie shook her head. Bizarre to think of something like that happening today.

'If Janus was summoned out in corporeal form in 750 BC,' said Hugo, 'the builders must have been conducting mythological research for a thousand years. Mind-boggling.'

'Hopefully, Rome later on will be more civilised,' said Sophie. 'Less kidnapping.' They were planning to visit the 1st century AD, when Janus appeared at his annual festival.

Hugo signalled and turned off the motorway. 'You should buy a leather-style bikini. Women wore them in wrestling contests.'

Sophie rolled her eyes. He'd unearthed many outlandish anecdotes, some of which she suspected were Hugo-fantasies. She went back to her phrase book, trying to memorise more words. Hugo and Freddy were way ahead of her, had studied the language at school. Freddy could recite in Latin how Roman men should practise 'virtue' and be nice to people. Charlotte, though, had struggled with Latin, so Hugo had bought her an audiobook, an adventure tale narrated in English and set in ancient Rome. It had spies and swords and despite dogs not featuring, Charlotte loved it.

In the university car park, everyone got out of the car except Hugo, who drove to a hypermarket to buy food and water for the crossing. The campus had no trees, and no other shade, and the sun was soon burning Sophie's legs and feet. She loosened the straps of her sandals and swigged water from her flask. Freddy downed half of his and the dogs slurped from a dog-travel device that poured into a shallow bowl.

They hurried towards the concrete tower block. Originally painted to resemble Lego bricks, the tower's crude colours were faded and crumbling. Over the entrance was a tatty sign in red letters: *STUDENTS' UNION AND ACCOMMODATION.*

Inside, they scurried through the large hall, past two grey lifts. Only one hosted ships from other universes.

Out of term-time, with no undergraduates, the students' union was deserted. Their friends would be here, though. Elliot and Lorna were post-grads, lived here all year round. They'd befriended Freddy when he first arrived. They knew about Shorten and Bella, and Janus' ship, but not about the walking staff or Juno.

The security door which led to their flat was locked, and Freddy messaged Elliot.

Elliot unlocked it. He smiled at Freddy and hugged Sophie.

In the flat's neat sitting room, Lorna stood up from the sofa, Fudge by her side. Lorna was partially sighted, and Fudge was her guide dog. Jack bounded up to Fudge who put up with being inspected. Charlotte kept her distance, understanding Fudge was on duty.

'This is a surprise,' said Lorna. 'Has Janus relented?'

'No.' Sophie's answer sounded bitter. Janus would never relent. She explained how they planned to cross in Juno and steal the staff to reset him.

Lorna shuddered. 'You could die in Juno?'

'We're taking enough supplies,' said Freddy.

Sophie felt the outline of the key-rattle on her T-shirt. Stay strong. Her phone beeped and she jumped. 'Hugo's here.'

Elliot helped them unload the car and they transferred everything into the flat. He grimaced at the piles of food cans, protein bars, and bottled water.

Freddy's brow furrowed. 'I appreciate this is an inconvenience.'

'I'm afraid there are two more carloads to collect,' said Hugo. 'Freddy, I'd appreciate some help.'

After they left, Elliot said, 'There's an abandoned shopping trolley behind the library. That'll help with unloading.'

Two hours later, the flat was so crammed with supplies, it was difficult to walk around the furniture. In addition to all the food, there were also three heavy holdalls they'd brought from London, crucial survival gear in case Juno didn't land in ancient Rome.

Hugo's phone rang. 'It's Lucy.'

Lucy had crossed universes to Shorten years ago and recently travelled back.

Freddy looked at his lap, half worried, half embarrassed for Lucy. During the civil war in Shorten, she'd been attacked by one of the militia and fallen pregnant. As a single parent, she'd kept her condition secret but now she was safe in modern London, Sophie had shared Lucy's secret, not wanting Freddy to be taken by surprise. 'She wants the baby,' Sophie whispered to him. 'Be happy for her.'

Freddy nodded. He also knew the true nature of Lucy and Tiana's relationship and — surprisingly — had taken the revelation in his stride.

Hugo put Lucy on FaceTime and speaker.

'Three weeks till I'm due.' Lucy's face was pink and sweaty.

Her partner came into view. Tiana had also travelled to

Shorten and returned with Lucy. Sophie remembered their last — brief — phone conversation. Newly cut off from Bella, she'd been too distraught to chat.

'Do you know the baby's gender?' Freddy had been astounded in the hospital here when he'd seen Bella's ultrasound scan. And though an ordinary enough question, his voice betrayed his feelings. Half dwelling on his own daughter, he couldn't completely focus on the couple's happiness.

'It's a girl!' Tiana's Californian twang was shrill with excitement.

'Any tips for the birth?' asked Lucy.

Remembering the agonising contractions, Sophie said, 'Ask for an epidural.'

'On it.' Tiana winked at her partner. 'Before everything kicks off, can we touch base, meet for lunch?'

Hugo stepped up to the plate and summarised why they couldn't. Lucy and Tiana listened with dawning horror. 'The thing is,' said Hugo, 'Janus can only be reset if he's summoned, so he's cut off everyone we know who crosses universes. Including you.'

Tiana glanced down, maybe hiding her relief. She had no wish to leave the 21st century.

But Lucy looked stricken. 'We might never get back to Shorten.' She'd loved being head gardener, would always yearn to return. 'Keep safe.' Lucy's voice broke and she ended the call.

'You're not alone in crossing universes,' said Elliot.

'I used to think we were lucky,' said Freddy, 'but we're cursed.'

Charlotte nodded, and Elliot did a double take. They'd concealed her talents, fearing word would get out and she'd end up prodded in a lab. Charlotte trotted around the cans and slabs of water and stood beside Elliot, signalling her secret could be shared. Sophie recounted how Charlotte's

DNA had been altered by the builder in medieval Georgia, including giving her a human lifespan.

Elliot and Lorna gawped and stared at Charlotte, who blinked solemnly.

Then Lorna's expression became wistful, and she cuddled Fudge. 'How wonderful.'

CHAPTER 5

$\mathcal{J}$ust before midnight, the university's security guard left the tower block to patrol elsewhere. Half an hour later, in front of the lifts, Sophie parked the last trolley-load of food cans and water bottles and set down her holdall crammed with survival gear. Janus had subverted travellers' instructions when he could, selecting dangerous places and times for his own amusement. Juno wasn't sentient, so shouldn't mess with their requested destination, but if she did, they were prepared.

'How come you're not taking the sword you brought back from the medieval place?' asked Elliot.

The blade was in Hugo's basement, stored in its scabbard and wrapped in blankets. 'It's incredibly heavy,' said Sophie. 'Not practical.'

'More to the point,' said Hugo, 'having a sword in ancient Rome without permission could get us executed.' Their research had revealed that civilians were prohibited from holding weapons of any sort within the city boundaries, but they'd still packed kitchen knives in sheaths. Travelling entirely unarmed into the past would be crazy.

Elliot surveyed their supplies. 'How big is Juno? Will all this fit in?'

Sophie bit her lip. 'We don't know.'

Hugo put his arms around her and pulled her close. 'If the ship hasn't room, we shouldn't cross.'

If they didn't travel, this was over. Charlotte was trembling, and Sophie hugged her, then patted Jack. Sophie had dearly wanted Charlotte to stay safe with Lorna and Elliot, but Charlotte had been adamant she was coming, so Jack was crossing too.

Sophie straightened and stared at the lifts. 'Juno.'

Nothing happened.

Freddy read from his notebook. 'Lucina, Mater, Regina, Curitis, Moneta, Caprotina, Tutula, Fluonia, Fluviona, Februalis, Juno of Falerii.'

The goddess the ship was named after had countless titles. 'Juno,' repeated Sophie. The lift where Juno should have appeared remained grey. 'We need your help.' Sophie's voice cracked. 'Queen of the gods, you alone can help us. Patron of Rome, we beseech you. We must travel.'

Freddy repeated her words in hesitant Latin.

'Janus has cut us off from our beloved baby daughter.' Sophie swallowed down tears. 'Only you can reunite us.'

A clank sounded from one of the lifts. Grinding. Then the lift disappeared, leaving an elevator-sized hole. Sophie and Freddy gasped, and Charlotte scurried backwards.

'What are you seeing?' asked Hugo.

'Hugo, Elliot, Lorna, Jack, Fudge,' said Sophie. Speaking individuals' names aloud had let them see Janus' ship. Even Lorna had 'seen' it, the image projected into her brain.

'The lift's still grey,' said Hugo.

Elliot folded his arms. 'Yep.'

'A black void,' said Freddy.

Charlotte stared at the dark hole and gave a single bark. A

moment later, there was a humming noise and the blackness faded, changing into red bricks that rippled like water. The bricks separated into two columns that curved and joined at the top.

'A Roman arch,' said Freddy, 'with the keystone at the apex.'

Sophie took a cautious step closer. 'Through the arch, there's a courtyard with a tree and a fountain.'

'I'm seeing the modern lift,' said Hugo.

'And me,' said Elliot.

Lorna frowned. 'No different from the usual. A fuzzy outline.'

So, unlike Janus' ship, Juno didn't reveal herself to individuals without the gene, and for those with the gene, she couldn't camouflage her appearance to blend into her surroundings. Sophie pushed the shopping cart forward. 'Let's test what happens to this.' The front wheels squeaked as they passed under the arch. 'Whatever's there, it's supporting the weight.' She pushed until the whole cart was inside except for the handle she was holding. Giving it a final shove, she stepped back. It trundled forwards, the wheels complaining, and stopped.

'What's happening?' said Hugo.

Freddy's forehead creased. 'The trolley's run into a tree.'

Sophie raised her chin. 'We can only test this if I go in.'

'No.' Hugo gripped her arm. 'Juno hasn't been heard of for millennia. What if you can't get out again?'

'The leaves on the tree are rustling,' said Sophie, 'and a woman's speaking in Latin.' The tone was matronly, authoritative.

'I can hear her,' said Freddy. 'Roughly translated, enter the sacred grove and travel.'

Charlotte whined, and Hugo tightened his hold on Sophie's arm.

'Juno, will we survive the crossing?' Sophie asked.

A soft click and the woman spoke in English. 'Eighty per cent of travellers have crossed and lived.'

Which meant twenty per cent didn't.

'When did you last cross universes with travellers who didn't land safely?' said Freddy.

'By your measurement of time,' said the voice, 'four weeks and seven hours ago.'

'Who were they?' said Sophie.

'Freddy and Sophie Lacey, and a canine, Charlotte.'

Sophie gasped. Had she misheard? Sophie *Lacey*? Another version of her who'd married Freddy? 'Please check their identities.'

'Done.'

Freddy's face crumpled and Charlotte backed further away from the arch.

'What's the voice saying?' said Hugo.

'That she transported versions of me, Charlotte, and Freddy a few weeks ago. And we … I mean, they died.' Sophie struggled to take that in. Not her, not Freddy and Charlotte, but so much like them, likely indistinguishable. The same thoughts, the same feelings, the same hopes and dreams, desperate to see their Bella. And they'd paid a terrible price.

'If the other versions of you were travelling in Juno, Janus must have cut them off too,' said Hugo. 'Each of us is just one version of countless almost identical individuals. We've no greater chance of surviving this than them.'

Freddy gulped, and the old dread enveloped Sophie, turning her legs to jelly. The certainty that they were special, that they would reset Janus, had got her this far. She sat down on her holdall.

'Juno, where were those travellers trying to get to?' Freddy struggled to keep his tone even.

'Universe 422, variant ending 23944886556677.'

422 was the numeric designation the builders had given to Freddy's home universe.

Sophie gulped. 'There are many versions of Shorten.'

'We stop now.' Hugo's lips flattened into a grim line. 'Bella might not be in some ... or many versions of Shorten. How many crossings would it take to find out?'

Freddy paled.

Sophie glanced at them, then back at the brick arch. This was a turning point, and a one-off. If she had time to rationally consider, the risk would eat away at her, sap her resolve. She should at least test if the ship was safe. Sophie stood up and drew a deep breath. 'I'm going in, but I'll come straight back.'

Hugo made to stop her, but she brushed him off and walked through the arch.

She turned around. 'Can you see me?'

'Yes.' Freddy screwed up his eyes. 'Is it a real courtyard?'

The area was harshly lit, though how was a mystery. She dipped her hand into the fountain. The water spilling from the spout was an illusion, as was the basin. Circling the courtyard were dark-green Roman pillars. Fake. She bent down and tried to touch red geraniums in full bloom, a glorious riot of flowers spilling out over an urn, but her fingers passed through them. Presumably, the sweet breeze cooling her skin wasn't genuine either. She laid her palm on a long stone seat. Solid. She sat down. 'Some of this is real, most isn't.' She cleared her throat. 'Juno, please show the actual inside of the ship.'

A click and the courtyard dissolved. Sophie was sitting on a metal bench in a vast cargo plane. Impossible to gauge its size. Hard, flip-down seats lined barrel-shaped walls, and the rest of the space was empty, except for more benches and the full shopping cart. Brown boxes tied onto wall racks were piled up high and into the distance.

Sophie scurried out through the arch and described it.

'Should we stay, or should we go?' said Freddy.

Hugo sighed. 'What does your gut tell you?'

Sophie imagined cradling Bella, kissing her face, inhaling her baby-scent, hearing her infectious giggle. It was now or never. She hauled her holdall onto her shoulders. 'We go.'

CHAPTER 6

Sophie ferried the supplies into Juno using the trolley, and Hugo, Freddy and Elliot staggered in carrying food cans and water bottles. Freddy put his on the floor and left to get more but Elliot, seeing the cargo bay for the first time as he crossed the threshold, nearly dropped his cans. He lowered them down, straightened, and stared around. 'You're not fazed by this?' he asked Sophie.

Since this mad adventure started, she'd learned to go with the flow. 'I've seen amazing stuff, so I guess new amazing stuff is less surprising.' And stressed witless about Bella, even an awesome spaceship was just a means to an end.

'Juno's bigger than I expected.' Hugo set down a slab of water.

Charlotte was staying by the exit, her expression set and serious. She knew the risk they were taking. Beside her, happily ignorant, Jack wagged his tail.

Once the supplies were in, Elliot shook hands with Hugo and Freddy, and hugged Sophie.

Elliot took a last look around and stepped outside. Lorna was waiting with Fudge.

'Don't worry, I'm not crossing universes,' said Elliot. 'Well, not today.'

Lorna smiled in relief.

Sophie waved goodbye and for a moment her resolution slipped. She pushed down a whisper of fear. 'Juno, we're ready to travel.'

The exit that looked like a Roman arch filled in, became part of the ship's metal wall.

'State your destination number,' said Juno.

'We don't know the number,' said Hugo.

Sophie's thoughts turned to the other versions of them who'd died in this ship. 'Juno, does our choice of destination affect the length of the crossing?'

'No.'

'Please explain,' said Freddy.

'Only activity in the black hole affects the duration of crossings. Destinations are irrelevant.'

So, this should be straightforward. 'We wish to go to a universe which most closely resembles our own, number 666,' said Sophie, citing the builder's designation for this universe. 'But one that's two thousand years behind ours, where it's the 1st century AD.'

'Which variant of 666 do you require?' said Juno.

Freddy swallowed. 'How many are there?'

'Over 2.5 billion in my database,' said Juno.

Sophie struggled to take that in.

'What's the variant number of the universe where you picked us up?' asked Hugo.

Silence.

Right. Like Janus, this ship ignored travellers without the gene unless told otherwise. 'Juno, answer Hugo Harrington as you would me,' said Sophie.

'That variant ends in 3026958930284.'

'Can you repeat that, so I can write it down?' Hugo fished out his notebook and pencil.

'The full variant is 10,013 digits. Do you require that?'

'Just the last numbers.' Hugo scribbled them down.

'Juno, select a universe closest to that variant,' said Freddy, 'and the city of Rome, a few days before Janus is summoned out in corporeal form.'

Click. 'There are many. Narrow your criteria.'

'A variant where there are no natural disasters,' said Hugo.

'There are fewer.'

'And humans are kind to each other,' said Sophie, 'and kind to other species.'

'No universes fit that description.'

'What?' Sophie frowned.

'None at all?' said Freddy.

'No.'

'Then the nearest fit,' said Sophie, 'where we are most likely to survive.'

Click. 'Juno selects variant ending 0798849478145. The 5th day of August, 95 AD.'

The height of an Italian summer. They wouldn't need the cloaks they'd packed. 'Juno, why was Janus' festival held in August and not January?' said Sophie. The month of January was named after him.

'By the 1st century, the festival was conducted when the emperor was out of the city, at his country residence. Previously, emperors sought to use it for their own purposes.' Click. 'Juno cannot travel until your cargo is secured beyond the red line.'

Further inside the ship, red lines marked the floor, with long belts riveted to the walls. Sophie sighed. Carrying everything down there would take a while.

Charlotte watched them impassively, unable to help, and

Jack dozed. It took half an hour to move the supplies and the holdalls and clip on the ties. They lay the trolley on its side to tie it down. Sophie stretched and wiggled her shoulders, muscles aching.

'Now, you must secure yourselves,' said Juno.

They strapped Jack onto a flip-down seat, then Charlotte, and everyone else belted up.

Click. And humming, like the purr of a distant engine.

Sophie was shaking. Don't think about our other versions that died. Don't—

The ship lurched forward and spiralled down so fast she blacked out.

CHAPTER 7

When Sophie recovered consciousness in Juno, she was consumed with unbridled panic. The ship was spinning, and Hugo and Freddy's faces were white and strained. Charlotte and Jack's eyes were wide open with terror.

'G-forces that fighter pilots train for, or astronauts,' muttered Hugo. 'I never thought I'd say this, but in Janus' ship, we had it easy.'

Sophie focused on not throwing up.

'We must take inspiration from the Stoics,' said Freddy.

'Agreed,' said Hugo. 'Go with it.'

Finally, the ship finished spiralling, though the humming continued. 'You may leave the seats,' said Juno.

Freddy and Hugo unfastened their straps and Sophie undid the dogs' belts and her own. The dogs huddled near Sophie, trembling from being thrown around, and she stroked them.

'Can we have the courtyard?' said Freddy. 'It's restful.'

Metal benches turned into long stone seats, and the fountain appeared with the illusion of water and its soothing flow. The red geraniums in the urn materialised, as did the olive tree. Graceful green columns stood in a surrounding circle, and the rest of the cargo bay was lost to sight.

The floor was now paving stones. Sophie tapped a tile with her foot. It gave a little, springy. She bent and touched it with one finger. Cold, like steel.

Sophie sat down and Charlotte jumped up and settled beside her. Jack curled up by Charlotte. Over the ship's humming, the tree branches rustled in the manufactured breeze, but the air smelled sterile, and it was far too hot. 'Juno, change the temperature to twenty-two centigrade?'

'Done.'

'Juno, what is the median crossing time?' said Freddy, sitting beside Hugo. Freddy had a degree in maths.

'Seventeen hours and four minutes.'

'What's median mean again?' said Sophie.

'The middle, excluding outliers,' said Freddy. 'So, for example, disregarding crossings that take under an hour or over three months.'

'We should learn as much as possible about the builders,' said Hugo.

Sophie nodded. Any insight into their technology and culture could be helpful, might be vital. Their anthropological team in Rome would be setting up the Festival of Janus, and they'd be summoning him with the walking staff. 'Juno, when did you leave your builders?'

'Juno has been away for two thousand, one hundred and forty-six years, seven months and eight days.'

'Why weren't you decommissioned?' said Freddy. 'When your first travellers died?'

'A builder took Juno for his own ends.'

'Juno, what do you know about your sister ship, Janus?' said Hugo.

'Designed like Juno, but with unknown changes.'

Sophie exhaled. Not helpful. But Juno's lack of sentience, of personality, was a refreshing change from Janus. Juno supplied facts with no hidden agenda.

'Since you left, have you had any contact with Janus' ship?' said Hugo.

'No.'

'Or with your builders?' added Hugo.

'Juno's automated systems communicate with their air traffic databases.'

Freddy's brow creased. 'Please explain.'

'Necessary to ensure that landings are unimpeded by other vessels.'

There were other ships? The mind boggled.

'You've had no other contact with the builders?' said Hugo.

'No.'

Hugo looked glum.

'Why does that matter?' Sophie asked him.

'Juno's database hasn't been updated in two millennia, may be unreliable.'

Sophie's stone seat was elegant and curved, solid and smooth to the touch. Juno's technology might be ancient, but it still worked, and data she'd collected from before she left the builders could still be accurate. Juno's summoning routine, how she acted amongst the locals in Rome, could closely mirror how Janus conducted himself. Both deities had been loved but also feared. 'Juno, when you walked in Rome, what did you do?'

'Juno didn't walk in Rome.'

Sophie sighed with frustration.

But Freddy leaned forward. 'Do you store a device that would summon you and reset the ship?'

Sophie held her breath.

'Juno does not.'

Charlotte shuffled closer to Sophie on their seat and put her head on her mistress' lap. Time to ask a question of more immediate concern. 'Do you do anything for travellers if they run out of food and water?'

'If they experience discomfort, Juno induces sleep.'

'That should be reassuring,' said Hugo, 'but it isn't.'

Charlotte nodded, but for Sophie, Juno's answer brought relief. Their other versions didn't suffer at the end. Neither would they.

Freddy stared at the fountain. 'Can you heal injuries?'

'No. However, Juno has basic medical equipment.'

Sophie pictured the racks in the cargo bay, outside the courtyard illusion. The boxes stretched as far as the eye could see. 'Juno, do you have any items that could help us after we leave the ship? Protect us?'

'Please specify the threat.'

'Individuals who mean us harm,' said Hugo.

'Juno does have such an item.'

Sophie raised her eyebrows. Result.

'Please show us,' said Freddy.

The courtyard became the cargo bay. A light was flashing some way down the ship, and they went towards it, the dogs sprinting ahead. Beneath the light, on a rack level with Sophie's waist, was a bronze box labelled in the builders' language. Sophie cautiously unclipped the lid and opened it. Charlotte stood on her hind legs to see what it was.

Nestled on a blue velvet cushion was a pendant. The heavy red gem had depths and shadows and the chain was burnished gold. Familiar, and unnerving. Sophie had used a pendant like this in the medieval realm, but this device might not be the same. She should check. 'Juno, this puts the wearer a nano-second back in time, makes them invisible to others?'

'It does,' said Juno.

Long ago, the builders' research teams had worn them to

observe the locals, up close and personal. The pendant in medieval Georgia had saved Sophie's life, all their lives, and might again. 'Juno, can we borrow it?'

'All stores are available to travellers.'

Freddy felt the ruby stone. 'Does too much use trap the wearer in the past?' They'd been warned that it did.

'Safe usage times vary, depending on an individual's DNA.'

Charlotte dropped to all fours, away from the pendant, and Sophie imagined being trapped forever in a silent twilight. How long had she worn it before? How long had Freddy worn it? She couldn't remember. 'Is there a maximum recommended limit?'

'Over ten hours per wearer per device is problematic.'

'So, if you've used a similar item before, that doesn't reduce the hours you can safely wear this?' asked Freddy.

'Correct.'

'We should take it in turns to carry it,' said Freddy to Sophie.

Hugo examined the pendant. It wouldn't work for him. 'Only in a dire emergency. Promise me.'

Sophie picked it up by its chain. 'I promise.' Wearing this, she'd felt half-alive and horribly alone.

'Let's explore,' said Hugo.

They walked further down the vessel, their sandals clicking on the metal floor, and the sound echoed, loud over the ship's humming. When they entered a new section, it lit up and went dark as they left it. But there was nothing new to see, just more racks and boxes. They turned around and retraced their steps.

Between the racking was a lime-green curtain protruding out of the wall. Sophie tugged aside the material, revealing a scrubbed bench with a hole and a copper mirror over a basin. She touched the basin with her forefinger and pushed her leg against the bench. Solid. Scraps of fabric, stacked on a shelf — the equivalent of toilet paper — were also real. She pulled the tap handle on the sink, but no water came out. Just a green light that presumably sanitised your hands. Charlotte could use the loo. Jack, though, would just wee in the bay. 'Juno, how do you dispose of substances that pose a threat of disease?'

'The matter is collected and released into space.'

As if he'd been given permission, Jack relieved himself. Everyone scurried away from the pool, but a soft click made them look back. Jack's pee was gone.

Hugo looked intrigued. 'Juno, how—'

'Don't ask,' said Sophie. Bodies would be removed by the same method and, sometimes, ignorance was bliss.

'Juno, can you recycle urine to make fresh water?' asked Hugo.

'Juno cannot.'

Logical, or none of her passengers would have died. Sophie grimaced. They could drink their own urine to keep hydrated, but within a day or so it would be undrinkable, too loaded with minerals and other nasties.

Freddy went over to his holdall and dug out a notebook and pencil. 'Juno, if the builders' team in Rome have a base, what's their address?'

'Foraggi Street. The villa Acilius.'

Hugo took a map from his holdall. 'Is the base near any well-known monuments?'

'The villa is one third of the way along Foraggi Street from the south, and is north of the Forum.'

'Got it.' Hugo marked the spot with a pencil. 'It's not visible to the locals?'

'The entrance appears identical to adjacent dwellings,' said Juno.

Sophie stashed the pendant in her holdall, fitting it inside a sock, then she dug out Charlotte's paperback and the page turner machine. Once *Heroic Dogs* was set up at the bookmarked page, Sophie switched on the device, and Charlotte lay on her front to read.

'I'm not confident about speaking Latin.' Understatement. Sophie opened her phrase book.

'Can't hurt to work on it.' Freddy studied his notes. 'Juno, please give us the courtyard again.'

Sophie tried to learn more words but couldn't focus. She tried to picture Bella, but the ship's hum and the pitter-patter of the pretend fountain were too distracting. The fountain, the geraniums, and the olive tree… The illusions were the last thing the other Sophie had seen.

To distract herself, she walked out of the courtyard. She returned with a slab of bottles, finding solace in its weight, and set it on the floor.

Hugo frowned. 'We must ration the water.'

'Juno, the most recent travellers who didn't survive the crossing, did they bring supplies on board?' said Freddy.

'They did.'

'How much?' said Hugo.

'One laden trolley.'

Why hadn't they brought more? Sophie winced. She'd never know why the other Sophie had made the decisions she did. Try not to dwell on it.

'Juno, repeat the information you gave to them,' said Freddy, his tone determinedly business-like.

'Verbatim or summaries?'

'Summaries,' said Freddy.

'To establish the optimal variant of universe 422 as a destination, Juno listed the availability of foods, including coffee, chocolate, and ice cream. Juno chose the most suitable variant.'

'Did those travellers make any more choices,' said Sophie, 'different from ours?'

'They decided on an environment conducive to sleeping.'

'You mean beds?' said Freddy. 'That would be nice.'

The courtyard became a room, stone seats morphing into beds. Narrow, with metal legs, they had no headboard, thin mattresses, and firm-looking pillows. On the walls and ceiling were frescoes of children in a villa, and the goddess Juno in a blue layered robe. A kind and motherly Juno, but Sophie shuddered. *This* was the last thing their other versions had seen.

Freddy seemed pensive, maybe thinking the same. 'Juno, what's your longest ever crossing?'

'One hundred and fifty-three days.'

'If we restrict ourselves to a bottle of water each per day,' said Freddy, 'we have enough.'

'Juno, why weren't Jack and the other me on the previous crossing?' said Hugo.

'Unknown.'

Sophie kissed him tenderly on the mouth and when she drew back, she felt stronger. 'They made different choices.'

CHAPTER 8

'Juno has landed at your destination.'

Sophie breathed a heart-felt sigh of relief. The crossing to ancient Rome had taken less than twenty-four hours. She'd slept fitfully, finished her ration of food and water, and hadn't improved her Latin. Boredom had warred with fear.

They gathered by the exit and stared through the red-brick arch. The air outside was sweet with the scent of dew and promised a scorching August day. Beyond deserted scrubland and a silent road was a classical temple, half-shrouded in dawn mist.

Sophie plaited her fair hair and wound the plait around her head. She put on the plain linen dress she'd bought on eBay. Maybe she should have worn a loincloth underneath? But big pants were more practical. Anyway, if she were exposed in her underwear, likely there'd be more pressing issues than modesty.

She went into Juno's loo and did an appearance-check in the mirror. Bella's key-rattle necklace was hardly noticeable under the dress. She came out and sat down in the make-believe courtyard to fasten her sandals. Hugo and Freddy looked cool in their simple tunics. They'd found them online, surplus costumes from *Plebs*, a TV show set in ancient Rome.

Sophie clipped Jack's lead onto his collar. He was perky, keen to explore. Charlotte, though, was subdued. She knew that Romans treated dogs as family members, honouring them in tombs and epitaphs, but she was also aware they could be cruel.

They'd brought large satchels and Sophie secured hers over her chest. It held a flask, the dogs' water container, and other essentials, including a knife in its sheath, maps of Rome and a pencil, and the time-turner pendant. Apparently, Romans wore flip-flops, so she'd packed hers. Dull brown plastic, they were convincing fake leather, even up close. She'd also managed to fit in a good supply of tea bags as well as upmarket coffee. Modern Italy was famous for its coffee, but there'd be none in 95 AD, and little luxuries were vital for morale.

Freddy fastened his satchel. 'Juno, where are we in the city?'

'The Arch of Juno.'

'Logical,' said Hugo. 'When was it built?'

'147 BC.'

'Juno, the arch didn't come up in our research,' said Hugo. 'Do you know why?'

'Travellers say the Arch of Juno was dismantled. Replaced by the Arch of Janus in the 4th century AD.'

Shame the Arch of Juno was lost to history. Despite Juno's life-threatening limitations, her software had brought them safely here.

Hugo made a note on his map. 'Juno, you'll keep our food and modern clothes and holdalls safe?'

'Done.'

Freddy paused on the threshold. 'Juno, when we say your name again, you'll pick us up?'

'Done.'

Jack bounded out onto scruffy grass. Everyone else stepped out more cautiously. Birds were chattering in nearby trees and cows were grazing on rough ground, not bothered by them or the ship.

More rural than she'd expected. Sophie turned around.

Juno's entrance was still open, the ship nestled inside a chunky, four-sided arch. Square and three storeys high, the arch's flat roof was supported by thick corner pillars. Juno the goddess was depicted all over the outside of the structure, on the pillars and on triangular friezes fronting the roof on each side. The caring mother figure was the same as in the ship's bedroom illusion, but the arch had many other images, including Juno the skilled huntress and Juno the warrior. In the hunting and battle scenes, the goddess wore an emerald belted gown, a gold diadem, and held a short, grey spear, ready to throw.

The sun was rising behind the arch and its rays danced on the folds of Juno's green battledress and on her diadem. Sophie's 'time-travelling' book had said buildings had been brightly painted. Juno's arch was gaudy and glorious.

'How are you seeing the colours?' Sophie asked Hugo. In Shorten, lacking the gene, he'd seen colours as faded and washed-out.

'Almost the same as at home, but more intense.' He pointed at his map where he'd written *Juno* next to Janus' arch. 'We're here, by the river Tiber. The builders' headquarters in the city is walking distance.'

Hopefully, the walking staff would be there, their way back to Bella.

'And this is the famous defensive wall.' Hugo gestured at a thirty-feet high wall off to their left and right, flanking a gap that gave access to the river. To the south and the north, the wall followed the Tiber before encircling Rome.

Charlotte raised her chin, alert, and Jack was exploring with his nose, finding scents that humans couldn't. Sophie took out her map and scribbled a cross next to Juno's arch. When this all started, back in Shorten, when they'd believed they'd stepped through a portal, not into a ship, they'd thought locations to cross universes were rare. But they'd surely been wrong? 'There might be landing sites in most countries,' said Sophie.

'Seems likely,' said Freddy, 'given the mind-boggling number of universes.'

A grinding sound came from Juno's arch. They all looked back.

The ship had gone, flattened vegetation the only indication it had ever been there. A cow wandered over to the crushed plants and chewed on a thistle. Sophie pushed away a flutter of unease. When they called her, Juno would return.

They headed towards the river, crossing a stone-paved road. There were gaps between the stones for wagon wheels, a tricky stumbling hazard. The road was cambered for drainage, and flanked by a footpath, worn smooth from the passage of many feet.

The wall loomed up closer in the grey of dawn, mysterious and formidable, and Sophie shivered as they walked through the gap.

'This would stop an invading army,' said Freddy.

Hugo nodded. 'Brick-faced concrete.'

They reached the temple they'd seen from the ship. The Tiber was lapping at the bank beside it and Sophie sniffed. Rotting meat and other things she couldn't identify. She breathed through her mouth.

Freddy's lips twisted. 'I wouldn't want to take a dip in there.'

The temple was rectangular, with an elegant portico and steps leading up to the podium and entrance. Its fluted columns were painted scarlet at the bottom and stark white higher up. Below the red-tiled roof was a frieze that was mostly blue, with white boats and green fish.

Hugo consulted the list of monuments marked on his map. *'Dedicated to the god, Portunus.'* There were countless minor gods. 'He protects harbours and ports.'

'I know this isn't our history, our ancient Rome,' said Freddy, 'but this temple's how I imagined it, except for how it's painted.'

Hugo chewed his lip. 'Two weeks' study doesn't make us classics professors.'

They kept to the riverbank and soon came to another temple, smaller and circular. As the dogs sniffed at the marble steps, Sophie checked her map. *'The Temple of Hercules. Survives intact into modern times.* I wonder if the other gods are a myth or real like Janus?'

'I've learned to keep an open mind,' said Freddy.

Hugo stared at the Temple of Hercules. 'Janus feels closer here. I worry he's plotting something.'

'He can't hurt us,' said Freddy. 'He's trapped in his ship—'

Charlotte growled and Jack barked.

Three men dressed in brown tunics emerged from behind the temple. They moved as one, carrying swords with two-foot-long blades. On their wrists were tattoos and, on their belts, ornaments clinked as they walked. The tallest shouted in Latin.

Charlotte frowned, trying to understand the words, and Freddy paled. 'They want our money and, um, Sophie.' He stepped in front of Sophie. So did Hugo.

The men spread out. Well-practised thieves and would-be rapists.

Charlotte circled them, growling, and the men shot her

assessing looks. Jack just barked. Hugo and Freddy rummaged in their satchels, but kitchen knives were toys compared to the thugs' blades. Sophie fumbled for her knife, but her fingers found the pendant instead. This counted as a dire emergency.

Freddy yelled something.

'I'll scare the hell out of them.' Sophie couldn't physically interact wearing the pendant, but she could freak people out. She drew a deep breath and slipped it over her head. The gold chain was cold against her neck and the tourmaline gem hung heavy beside the key-rattle. Her friends and the robbers faded, became a colourless video, and she was alone, seeing and feeling, but unable to touch, or smell, or hear. She'd experienced this before, but the isolation, the misery, was overwhelming. If ghosts existed, were they stuck in this grey, hopeless world forever?

The biggest guy had stopped in his tracks, his mouth open, staring in her direction.

Put on a convincing show and get this done. Sophie ran invisibly past Charlotte, Hugo and Freddy, and the thugs, and keeping her distance, she snatched off the pendant. The world was in colour and the river was sloshing again.

'Salve.' Sophie drew out the greeting, mock-friendly and creepy.

The men whirled around.

She did a ghostly wail and swayed from side to side, the movement slow and spooky. The men put their hands over their ears. She put on the pendant. Gone from their sight but she could see them. After a moment frozen in terror, the ruffians charged away down the road, faded, sepia men running for their lives.

Sophie wrenched off the pendant, letting it dangle from her hand, and savoured the sunshine and birdsong. Freddy shouted after the thugs, but none of them so much as paused.

Sophie dropped the pendant in her satchel and patted the dogs who were nuzzling into her legs.

Freddy exhaled. 'That was close.'

Hugo enveloped Sophie in a thankful bear hug. 'The sun will be fully up soon,' he said. 'Until then, let's keep out of sight.'

'These trees are hopeless for hiding,' said Freddy. The ones on the riverbank only had branches at the top, shaped like umbrellas.

They hurried to the Temple of Hercules and Freddy tried the entrance door, but it was locked. Fortunately, the pillars encircling the temple were enormous and perfect for hiding.

Sophie took a swig from her water flask. 'Freddy, what did you shout at them?'

'Juno haunts this place, and I threw in a Roman curse. Sons of dogs.'

'That's *so* lame,' said Sophie. 'I'd happily be a child of a dog.' She patted Charlotte. 'You did good with the growling.'

Charlotte tilted her head, acknowledging the compliment.

alf an hour after they'd taken refuge at the Temple of Hercules, the dogs barked, hearing a faint noise from up the road. Couldn't be the thugs. They'd fled in the opposite direction. The murmur grew louder, more distinct: talking, laughter, and clanking metal. Men were on the road, carrying buckets and axes. Charlotte knew to keep quiet now, and somehow, she'd got Jack to copy her. The men strolled past their hiding place.

'Watchmen,' whispered Hugo. 'Leaving the city after a night shift.'

Sophie nodded, remembering their research. These men were firefighters, called Vigiles, the nearest equivalent of modern emergency services. They wore light armour over red knee-length kilts, sandals that fastened up past their ankles, and round brass helmets that dipped down at the back, covering their necks.

More people came onto the road, heading in the opposite direction from the watchmen. Women strolling in groups, their voices clear and shrill. They wore short tunics or longer dresses. Bracelets dangled on their wrists and their flip-flops clacked on the pavement. Most were dark-haired and brown-eyed, but others reflected heritage from the furthest reaches of the empire. Skin tones of Ethiopian black contrasted with others who were pale and freckled. A few had natural blonde hair. The hairstyles of others were more yellow, looked dyed. Behind them was a trail of men in belted tunics.

'No impressive togas?' said Sophie.

'These are ordinary folk going to work,' said Freddy. 'Togas were only worn on formal occasions and according to Quintilian, they were a huge fuss. If a man moved around too much, they fell off.'

'Who's Quintilian?' Sophie asked him.

'He was a teacher, taught rhetoric.'

Hugo glanced down at his map. 'We follow the road north to the builders' base.'

With any luck, they might find the walking staff within a day. Sophie pictured Bella, and she stood up, a spring in her step. She attached Charlotte's lead for appearance's sake.

Freddy kept hold of Jack's. 'I'm not sure the Romans walked dogs on leads.'

'I don't think he'd run off,' said Hugo, 'but better safe than sorry.'

They stepped down as nonchalantly as they could from the temple and set off towards the city. To their left, a lone man pushed a small boat onto the river, jumped into the craft, and paddled. On the distant bank, mules were pulling barges, the water creaming out from their hulls, buffeting the man's boat.

A clip-clop sound of a horse came from up ahead. The horse's mane was smooth and glossy, and the rider's tunic had gilt edging. The rider dismounted onto a tall stone at the edge of the road. Without stirrups, dismounting was tricky.

The thoroughfare was getting busy. A plump matron in

an orange silk gown passed them, cradling a tiny dog. Her hair was pinned up in perfect waves, a hairstyle that had to involve extensions, and was barely covered by a floaty long scarf over her dress. Young girls were waving wooden batons to clear a gap in the crowd for her. The woman's intense perfume, heavy and sweet, wafted into Sophie's nose and she coughed.

The matron glanced at Sophie and tut-tutted before continuing her promenade up the road.

Sophie frowned. Either her hair or her clothes were wrong.

A cart pulled by two horses was pushing against the flow of traffic, prompting annoyed shouts from pedestrians. Big wagons could only enter the city at night. This one was late leaving. As it passed, the stench made Sophie cover her mouth.

'Must be from cesspits,' said Hugo. 'The poor don't have plumbing.'

They reached a crossroads. Opposite was a vast three-storey building, each floor with windows the same shape as the Roman-arch in Juno's ship. And like the temples by the river, it had a red tiled roof.

Sophie and Freddy stood in a huddle around Hugo so he could discreetly read his printed map.

'That's a theatre,' said Hugo. 'A temple to Janus should be close by, next to a vegetable market. Let's check it out.'

Sophie shook her head. They shouldn't get distracted. 'We should go straight to the builders' base.'

'We don't know whether they have loads of walking staffs and we can just take one, or whether it's expensive field equipment and locked in a safe,' said Hugo. 'Janus is the focus of their mythological research. His temple might give us more info about the staff?'

'You're right.' On the raised pavement were paler stones

marking the advised route over the junction, and Sophie kept to the path. As they hurried across, they were hampered by darting children, groups of teenagers, and an elderly man leading a pony. This city was home to a million people. She should have expected the main streets to be busy.

A litter carried by four male slaves in scarlet tunics cut in front of them. A youth was sitting in it, frowning in concentration, and scribbling on a wax tablet.

Sophie mentally pinched herself. They were really here in ancient Rome! She shot Hugo and Freddy a wicked grin. 'You could carry me in a litter.'

Hugo rolled his eyes and Freddy made a face.

Okay, not going to happen.

They veered past a dismounting stone, skirted the grand theatre, and got caught up in a noisy crowd at the vegetable market. Keeping to the pavement, they turned left, and entered a deserted, tree-lined square. At the far end was another temple.

'There it is,' said Hugo. 'Dedicated to Janus.'

Sophie squinted at it, missing her shades. The lower third of its columns were deep green, the other two-thirds gold. Different from the riverside temples. Wide steps climbed to the entrance where six columns held up an emerald façade, edged with shimmering gold. Pictured on the façade were a cornucopia horn, sheaves of grain, and a flower with raised, yellow petals. 'The flower's the same as the mirror frame that covered the ceiling in the golden lift.' Part of the original Janus brand?

Before the temple was a rectangular altar on a platform, also approached by steps. On it, a flame burned, reeking of rotten eggs.

Hugo wrinkled his nose. 'Sulphur. Burns away evil and disease.'

'If you say so,' said Freddy.

'The Romans didn't have chimneys,' said Hugo. 'That's why sacrificial altars are *outside* temples.'

'As well as no stirrups,' said Sophie. 'Surprising, given their engineering feats with aqueducts and arches.'

'I suspect there'll be other surprises, hopefully nice ones,' said Hugo. 'And even on a flying visit, we may solve another more important historical mystery.'

'What do you mean?' asked Freddy.

'Given how many temples to Janus there were supposed to have been in Rome, the scarcity of archaeological evidence is odd,' said Hugo. 'This is the only site where evidence survives into modern times.'

They climbed the temple steps and passed between the pillars, leaving the sunshine behind. A door on the right had a narrow, oblong gap above a keyhole, resembling a post box, and no handle. Freddy gave it a push, but it was locked. The door straight ahead had a gilt knob. Sophie turned it and the door swung open.

The air smelled of incense, burning wood and tangy citrus. Off to the side, on a shabby wooden table, was a half-eaten wrap and a beaker. There were no windows. Wavering light came from flaming torches, high up on sconces, and there was a hushed silence, the same as churches at home.

A stooping man in a green tunic was sweeping the stone floor. He bowed and muttered.

'You're too early,' translated Freddy. 'The ceremony starts later.'

In the middle of the temple was an eight-foot statue, and Sophie's jaw dropped. Carved in marble was a young man with Italian good looks. Unlike classical figures in modern museums, this statue wasn't white. It was painted and the colours were in-your-face vibrant. His eyes were a startling blue-green, and his Caucasian face expressed purpose and power. His square jaw had a hint of stubble, and his lips looked surprisingly soft. Inlaid symbols decorated his breast-plate armour and underneath the armour was a red, elbow-length jerkin. A scarlet cloak swirled about his shoulders, leather cuffs encased his forearms, and on his feet were sturdy brown boots. An armoured kilt fell in regimented folds to his knees.

Jack gave the statue a cursory glance, but Hugo, Freddy, and Charlotte were staring, as gobsmacked as Sophie. This wasn't the Roman god who controlled time, or even a god who guided travellers through doors and across universes. This was a fantasy Janus, one Hollywood would dream up.

Sophie circled around the statue. Okay, this she had expected. There was a different face on the rear. Late thirties, with darker skin. More jaded, but just as fit.

A pace away was a free-standing stone slab, a foot wide and four feet tall. Set in the top was a mosaic of a key. On the other side of the statue was a slab of identical size, depicting the walking staff. The base of the key and the top of the staff were green hearts and they both had the gold figure of a T in the centre.

Sophie's breath hitched. They exactly matched the sketch in Wells' book, *Myths and Legends*, right down to the textured, oak-brown of the stick.

The attendant leaned on his broom, spoke, and Freddy repeated his words back to him.

'What are you saying?' asked Sophie.

'Health and great joy,' said Freddy. 'It's a standard greeting.'

'You're doing good,' said Hugo.

The attendant pointed at Charlotte and Jack and asked a question. Hugo stepped in front of the dogs and vigorously shook his head.

'He's asking if they're our sacrifices.' Freddy screwed up his face.

Charlotte moved closer to Sophie. 'I didn't realise they sacrificed dogs.' She felt sick.

'Don't go there.' Hugo gazed at the statue. 'Perhaps this is how the corporeal version looks when he's summoned?'

'From Janus' voice in his ship, I'd imagined him older,' said Freddy, 'with a biblical white beard.'

'The Janus we spoke with *is* older,' said Hugo. 'By two thousand years.'

Sophie moved nearer to the statue. It might react, do something, if someone with the gene touched it? But her fingers only met cold marble.

CHAPTER 10

Outside Janus' temple, Sophie took a moment to feel the sun on her face. Jack sniffed and Charlotte wrinkled her nose at the rotten eggs smell from the altar.

Sophie bent down, patted Jack, and the skin between her shoulder blades itched. The slightest sensation, there for just a moment, but familiar. The square was still deserted. She glanced back at the temple. Looking out of there was impossible. No windows.

'What is it?' said Hugo.

'That creepy feeling when someone's watching you.' She shot him a nervous smile. 'Put it down to Janus' statue.'

'When he's summoned during the festival, he'll be an algorithm, as lifeless as marble,' said Hugo.

Sophie shaded her eyes. She needed to remember that. If Janus materialised in this sunny square right now, he'd be a puppet, performing to order for the builders.

'How far is it to the headquarters?' said Freddy.

Hugo peered at his map. 'About an hour's walk.'

'Won't be pleasant in this heat,' said Freddy. 'We should fortify ourselves. Get some breakfast.'

The crush of customers at the vegetable market had gone. Freddy led the way inside and Sophie waited for her sight to adjust to the relative gloom. Customers were browsing stalls that filled the warehouse, haggling with sellers. The stalls were decorated with garlands of herbs and flowers and tantalising aromas layered the air, but less tantalising was a different scent. Many shoppers had yet to visit the baths.

The first stall displayed garlic and onions and olives, stored in separate glass jars with red lids. Another had kale, broccoli, and asparagus. The next had red bowls of lettuce and carrots and peas. The Romans were really into red. And the range of produce was surprising: celery, radishes, turnips, beets, and leeks. There were also many varieties of plant bulbs.

'It's all so fresh,' said Sophie, breathing in sweet coriander.

'But nothing tasty for breakfast,' said Freddy.

Charlotte was assessing the wares on the largest stall, her head tilting as she sniffed, and she was getting odd looks. Time to leave.

From the market, they entered a narrow street where two-storey shops cast the road into shade. Shopkeepers were unfolding wooden shutters with a clatter, others setting out goods on the pavement, leaving even less space to walk. Most of the shops had the same sign. Green fumes spiralling out of a clear bottle.

They paused at a pink counter displaying red and blue glassware. Half sunk into the countertop, the vessels had delicate bronze handles and cork stoppers. The storekeeper spoke, and Freddy put out his arm. The woman dabbed a perfume sample on his wrist, and Freddy sniffed. 'A bit like Hugo's aftershave. Tangy.'

'It's clear why perfume's so popular.' Hugo held his nose as a gang of small boys ran past.

'Do you think they're slaves?' Sophie hoped they weren't.

'Apparently, for every citizen, there are six to ten slaves.' Hugo stepped aside to avoid a young girl in a hurry. 'This is incredible … if a bit overwhelming.'

'Most people are talking Latin but too quickly,' said Freddy. 'And there are other languages I can't understand at all.'

'We might have to pretend we're foreign and gesture,' said Sophie.

'We don't have to *pretend* to be foreign,' said Freddy. 'We're as foreign as you can get.'

The dogs were keeping close, Jack near Freddy and Charlotte near Sophie, her lead slack. Neither were fans of crowded spaces. Sophie scanned the noisy, bustling street. Enjoy it, take it all in.

'This "starting early" chimes with what we've read.' Freddy swerved around a woman erecting a table. 'Working in the morning and relaxing in the afternoon.'

Hugo glanced at his map. 'This way.'

They cut down a less busy street, then another. High walls lined the curving road on both sides, the lower third of the walls painted red. At irregular intervals, there were closed doors made of wood or metal.

Hugo frowned. 'No street names.'

They passed a blacksmith's forge, then a workshop where a man was hitting plates of copper with a hammer. Across the road was a larger building. It was fronted by a long stone basin, half full of stinking yellow liquid. A teenager strode up to it. He lifted the hem of his tunic, relieved himself, and sauntered into the building.

'This place is a laundry.' Hugo approached the basin and lifted his tunic. 'Get paid to pee.'

Freddy joined him. Jack was uninterested, Charlotte seemed intrigued, and Sophie averted her gaze, illogically embarrassed. The ammonia in urine dissolved grease and dirt, so was used to clean floors and pavements as well as clothes. The ultimate natural cleaning product.

A small child ran out, gave Freddy and Hugo a coin, and ran inside again.

The child's earnest expression reminded Sophie of her daughter. Every child was unique but, in some ways, all small children were alike. Bella's blue velvet dress, her mischievous eyes. Kissing Bella on her brow … *Be good till I get back*. She'd assumed she'd be gone an hour, two at the most. Bella would be steadier on her feet by now. Had she learned more words?

'The child must be from the family who run the place,' said Freddy.

'More likely a slave,' said Hugo.

In the next street was a five-storey block of flats with a takeaway on the ground floor. Families were queueing to buy breakfast. By the storefront was a brick oven, sending out a delicious aroma of baking bread.

Sophie gazed at the café sign. A big letter 'C' and smaller writing within a red border. Below that was a drawing of what looked like a pizza.

'Caesar's … something,' said Freddy.

Hugo sat on the edge of a water trough opposite the take-away. He studied his map, then stared up at the flats. 'This should be Foraggi Street and the popina selling snacks should be the researchers' headquarters.'

Popinas were what fast-food joints, cafés, and bars were called here. 'Maybe it's disguised?' Sophie joined the queue. 'Charlotte, can you sense a barrier?' Charlotte shook her head.

Inside the popina was a skinny man sitting at a table eating a bread wrap. At a nearby counter, a small boy was standing on a built-in step, helping himself to nuts and olives.

'I thought everyone had meals reclining on couches?' said Sophie.

'Only the rich did that,' said Hugo, 'at dinner parties.'

They reached the front of the queue. The sides of the serving counter were painted with red carrots, white goats jumping about, and pink pigs. Sophie touched it. 'No barrier. No disguise.' The popina was just a shop. Her heart sank. If they couldn't find the headquarters, they couldn't find the walking staff. They'd failed at the first hurdle. She patted Charlotte who was nuzzling her legs. 'How can we track it down?'

'We can't.' Freddy looked glum.

'I'm sorry,' said Hugo. 'I'm out of ideas.'

Sophie sighed. Eat breakfast. Maybe that would help her think of something?

Beside the counter on a mini altar were statuettes, merry men holding goblets. 'That's Mercury, the god of commerce,' said Freddy, pointing. 'And Bacchus.'

Set in the countertop were sunken red bowls, flush with the surface, their lids off. There was steaming meat and vegetables, a stack of still-warm flatbreads, and a murky brown sauce with a tart, fishy smell. A free-standing amphora, as tall as the counter, held red wine. Also on the counter, was a phallic-shaped candle lamp, alight and flickering in the bright sunshine. Sophie knew from their research there'd be a lot of phallus images, but this was ... odd.

The red-faced man behind the counter said the formal greeting. He had bags under his eyes and pockmarked skin. Freddy repeated it back to him. They dug out low denomination copper coins from their satchels, that Hugo had bought for a pittance online. The ancient coins were cheap because so many survived into modern times.

Freddy pointed at skewers of beef, Sophie selected

sausages for the dogs, and beans and lentils with a boiled egg for herself. Hugo chose pork flavoured with the sauce. The shopkeeper wrapped their choices in bread, then picked up a chunky grey glass, gesturing at the wine.

'Not on an empty stomach,' said Freddy. The shopkeeper muttered and gestured at a tap on the wall. Freddy shook his head. 'Even watered down.' The shopkeeper talked and winked.

They sat on the trough to eat. 'His girls will be around later,' said Freddy. 'I presume he meant … you know.'

Sophie smiled at him. They'd had a baby together, but he was never explicit about intimate things. Part of his charm.

Hugo filled his flask from the trough. 'These are connected to the mains. Should be fine to drink.'

Sophie topped up the dogs' plastic shallow dish. They drank it all, and she filled it again. She added water to her own flask and risked a bite of beans and lentils. Well-cooked, mildly fragrant, and enhanced by the soft-boiled egg, olive oil, oregano, and garlic. Who knew the street food here would be so yummy? She fed the dogs their sausages.

'I suppose the river's too polluted for fish?' said Freddy.

'Fish has to be imported, so expensive.' Hugo bit into his pork wrap. 'Wow! Spicy.' He swigged water. 'The famous fish sauce.' He took a second bite. 'Delicious.'

'I'm glad the popina wasn't selling dormice,' Freddy said with a grimace.

'Ordinary people didn't eat mice,' said Hugo, between mouthfuls. 'Another dinner party thing.'

Sophie's mind was on Bella. 'We must search for the headquarters, street by street.'

'Even if it takes months,' said Freddy, 'or years.'

'The research team could have left the city altogether,' said Hugo.

Sophie finished her wrap. 'But if they've moved within

Rome and not too long ago… Freddy, ask the popina guy if he knows where they went?'

The queue had gone. Freddy went over to the counter and spoke to the shopkeeper in halting Latin. The shopkeeper talked fast, and the only word Sophie recognised was *Nero*.

Freddy returned and screwed up his face. 'These flats were built when Nero was emperor, thirty years ago. Hugo, you were right about Juno's database being out of date.' His lower lip wobbled. 'This is hopeless.'

'It's not hopeless, Freddy,' said Sophie, fired up by breakfast. 'Ask him about the Festival of Janus. If the research team's still here, they'll be organising it.'

They all went to the counter. Freddy talked and the guy's answers grew louder, accompanied by animated gestures. 'The date of the festival hasn't been announced,' translated Freddy. 'But he's prepared and will set up a stall near the river.'

The shopkeeper stirred the dishes on the counter, put lids over the bowls, and continued talking.

'He saw Janus last year,' said Freddy. 'Janus appeared as a beautiful woman, and he loves her.'

'He doesn't seem the gullible type,' said Hugo. 'And he seems to believe what he's saying.'

Sophie nodded. 'If Janus was summoned twelve months ago, that suggests the builders haven't left Rome, just moved premises.'

'We need to find somewhere to stay.' Freddy talked in hesitant Latin, and the shopkeeper spoke and pointed upwards. 'He has a spare room.'

'These tenement blocks were death traps,' said Hugo.

Sophie squinted up at the tenement. With each storey, the windows got smaller. 'Only one night.'

They followed the shopkeeper along the road and up a

steep staircase on the outside of the flats. The chatter of residents inside sounded clearly through the wall. Pots banged and there was a strong smell of cooking. As they climbed, the shopkeeper shouted, sounded angry.

'People weren't supposed to cook,' said Hugo. 'Fire hazard.'

They reached the top and went in. Across a tiny landing, the shopkeeper threw open a door with a flourish.

The space was more like a musty cupboard than a room and the ceiling was so low, Hugo and Freddy had to stoop to go in. A mattress took up most of the floor and the dogs backed away from it. A hole under the eaves served as a window that overlooked an internal courtyard crisscrossed with washing lines.

Scratching came from the roof. Presumably, the rats were included in the price.

Hugo smiled politely at the shopkeeper and Freddy spoke. The shopkeeper shrugged and set off down the stairs.

'I told him it was unsuitable,' said Freddy, displaying his capacity for understatement.

Back down on the street, Freddy asked the shopkeeper if he knew where they could find a town house to rent. The shopkeeper answered, and Sophie caught a word she understood.

Forum.

CHAPTER 11

The temples in the Forum were six storeys high but their columns had a familiar colour scheme: red at the bottom and the remainder stark white. Most looked brand new, but some were being renovated. Near the entrance to the square, a temple was covered in scaffolding, and bangs and thuds came from men working on the roof. Alongside the temples were commercial arcades, gaudy and resplendent in blues and golds and pinks. The largest was a vibrant green.

Traders were hawking their wares, their cries carrying across the whole sunlit square. Watchmen guarding temples chatted to each other. Litters swayed, small carts clattered, and teenagers gossiped in doorways. In porticoes, families and couples were playing dice and drinking wine. With no coffee or proper tea, the poor souls had to drink wine.

Freddy was keeping Jack on a short lead and Sophie held Charlotte's. Jack was unfazed, unaware of the iconic nature of this place, but Charlotte's eyes were wide, taking it all in. Making her way through the crowd, Sophie caught whiffs of body odour and traces of perfume worn by men as well as women: delicate and flowery, or intense and spicy. Contrasting cooking smells came from restaurants and cafés and the dogs were manically sniffing, in scent heaven.

Sophie's mouth was open, and she shut it, hoping to appear nonchalant. She wasn't the only one overawed. People were gawping, listening to earnest guides talking over each other and pointing at buildings. Many were clutching tablets with red frames. She glanced over at one. Judging by the map, a guide to the Forum. Who knew? Tourists visited this Rome, just as they would in the future.

Freddy was scanning the square, his face slack with wonder, but Hugo moved the strap of his satchel on his chest, seemed distracted.

Sophie knew that expression. 'Enjoy the moment. Stop thinking about Janus.'

'I wasn't, not directly. I was thinking about tourism.' Hugo shaded his eyes with his hand. 'There could be other travellers that cross universes, for pleasure?'

Sophie shrugged. 'We've never met anyone else in Janus or Juno.'

Freddy dragged his attention from the Forum to their conversation. 'Janus' vessel could be as big as Juno, perhaps bigger?'

'It could carry travellers in silos,' said Hugo, 'each with a different illusion of a room?'

'I suppose,' said Sophie. They'd only seen the inside of the lift.

'They could be right here,' said Hugo, 'and we wouldn't know.'

'Like us,' said Sophie, 'blending in fine.' She'd worried they'd attract unwelcome attention, strolling with the dogs, but wealthy matrons and youths in gilded tunics were carrying lapdogs, and pets on leads included an ostrich and a baby tiger.

'H. G. Wells must have come here to the 1st century, when he took the walking staff home to the 19th,' said Freddy. 'We should keep an eye out. I'd love to meet him.'

Picturing Wells' outrageous moustache, Sophie gazed at the crowd. Most men were clean-shaven.

They strolled to the centre of the square, to a raised stage with columns but no roof. This was the Rostra where men made speeches. Only men. Obviously. Sticking out from the base of the stage in a horizontal row were prows of ships tipped with bronze. They were carved with the heads of different animals, including a boar and a lion. Hugo examined each one in turn. The paintwork was varnished and immaculate.

Sophie stood with her back to the Rostra next to Freddy. She tried to commit the busy Forum to memory. The glory that was Rome!

A woman and toddler dawdled past, the mother holding the child's hand. Freddy's face shuttered.

'We'll see her again.' Sophie squeezed his arm.

Freddy swallowed. 'A kind time traveller would bring perambulators here.'

They needed to keep busy and on task. Sophie unfolded her map of the Forum. Public buildings in the 1st century were named, but not individual shops or services. If they couldn't find somewhere to rent, they'd be sleeping rough. 'Let's search systematically for estate agents. Start on this side of the square.'

'Janus' other temple was supposed to be near the shopping precinct.' Hugo pointed across the Forum. 'It might have more info about the walking staff?'

Sophie frowned. 'Didn't archaeologists find zero evidence for that temple?'

Freddy was perusing his map. 'No harm in looking.'

They navigated the square, skirted the shopping

precinct, and stopped in their tracks. There was a temple. Dwarfed by the surrounding buildings, it was rectangular, with golden arched double doors, open at both ends. External green and gold pillars supported a flat roof with gilded tiles, and underneath the roof, a frieze featured the same imagery as the temple by the crossroads: sheaves of grain, horn-shaped baskets overflowing with nuts and grapes, and the gold-petalled flower. Under the frieze, on each side, was a long, grated window, sealed with grey glass.

On top of the roof, in the centre, was a four-headed bust statue, a third of the height of the structure. The statue's faces looked east, west, north, and south: one had a beard, two were clean-shaven, and the other was female with a tall, elaborate hairstyle.

People were going in and exiting at the far side in a steady stream, most of them excited tourists. Two watchmen flanked the doors. They were standing to attention, buckets at their feet. Prepared to put out fires as well as maintain order.

'It's similar to the picture we found online,' said Freddy. The 21st century sketch had been based on a Roman coin.

'The coin didn't have the statue on the roof,' said Hugo.

'The artist got most of the building correct, if not the colours,' said Sophie. This temple was mostly green, not red.

Hugo returned his map to his satchel. 'It must be built over the black stone.'

'Black stone?' Sophie had missed that in her research.

'Dug up here in Victorian times, dating from 500 BC,' said Hugo. 'The surviving hieroglyphics mention a king and there's a curse on anyone disturbing the stone.'

'Did the archaeologists start dying, like with Tutankhamun?' Sophie asked him, half-joking.

'I don't think so.'

They joined the queue into the temple, and Hugo grabbed Sophie's hand. His palm was sweaty, and he'd tensed up.

'What's the matter?' she asked him, putting away her map.

'An uneasy feeling.'

'Curses are hogwash, and this is just a temple,' said Freddy. 'Janus isn't there.'

'I know.' Hugo took a swig from his water flask.

Inside, the tourists' chatter died away, switched to awed muttering. The incense lingering in the air was the same as in the previous Janus temple, woody with a touch of orange zest. The glass in the overhead grilled window was thick and opaque, making the interior dim.

A statue glowed in the gloom. The armour resembled the other Janus statue, and the eyes were the exact same shade: an unnatural bluish green. But this was a female Janus. Her flawless face exuded a disturbing, ruthless power and her long brown hair rippled, goddess-perfect, in soft waves over her shoulders. The contoured breastplate showed off a dainty waist, and hanging from her neck, tied to a thin leather strap, was an over-sized key. She held the walking staff like a weapon, and she was eight-foot tall.

Freddy gasped, and Hugo stared.

Charlotte went into hunter mode and tracked round it. Sophie followed, holding her lead. What could she sense? 'No different face at the back. Maybe this version's a one-off?' Sophie tipped her head to see the attic above them. The interior decoration mirrored the external façade. 'What's with the food pictures?'

'Symbols of prosperity and peace,' said Hugo.

'Dovetails with Janus being worshipped as a local god,' said Freddy, 'protecting Rome.'

Local. How ironic, but a clever detail. A personal protector would be far more beloved than a generic master — or mistress — of time. Sophie studied the front of the statue. 'This reminds me of *Xena the Warrior Princess*. I'm guessing this is the beautiful woman the shopkeeper saw.' She stepped aside to let a new influx of tourists view the statue. As she did, her bare arm brushed an internal pillar and the temple interior turned dazzlingly white, even the floor.

Sunlight streamed through a wide band of clear glass bisecting the walls. The window displayed a 360-degrees view of the Forum, seen from the temple. The attic was now a plain ceiling, and the Janus statue a plank of wood, but Sophie could still smell the ceremonial incense, see and hear the tourists. She blinked. 'The builders made this,' she whispered. 'The statue, the entire building … it's an illusion.'

Charlotte was snuffling at the floor, could sense the energy barrier or whatever was generating the make-believe temple. Sophie tapped Freddy on the shoulder. 'Touch the pillar.'

Freddy warily placed his finger on it, then whirled around, his mouth open.

Did this work the same as with Janus' ship, showing the reality to non-gened individuals? Worth a try. 'Hugo.'

His intake of breath told her the answer.

Charlotte was pushing against Sophie's legs, trying to tell her something, and Sophie's heart rate sped up. The room spun, and she clutched at Hugo. 'We need to get out.'

A few streets away from the Forum, at the Villa Acilius, a tall foreign woman and her colleagues welcomed H. G. Wells into their headquarters, showering him with polite smiles. Inside their house, by means he couldn't fathom, they could understand each other in English. As instructed by Janus, he told them he was writing a textbook about ancient Rome, etc etc, and they accepted this without question, just as Janus had predicted. Academics embracing their own.

The tall woman introduced herself as Ishtar. She spoke flawless English, had beautiful dark skin but, oddly, Wells felt no stirrings of sexual attraction, and she seemed indifferent to him. One of her colleagues gave him a small cylinder that would translate his own words into Latin and allow him to understand other languages. A true treasure.

Ishtar's servants brought out the type of chair he preferred and served him a splendid roast luncheon. After the meal, he settled back in the fine leather armchair and puffed on his pipe. Villa Acilius was nothing like the luxurious Roman villa he'd expected. The interior was white and plain and, apart from his armchair, the furniture was ugly, merely functional. And the air was curiously sterile, and too warm, like in Janus' ship.

There was a frameless window that stretched around the entire wall of the reception room, but it didn't display the view outside. Instead, it played a magic lantern show that looked down from the sky at the city. The moving picture was clear and perfect. Technology he could never have imagined. And ancient Rome! What wonderful stories he could write! But Janus had been adamant. It was novels about the future that would make H. G. Wells' fortune and entice more women into bed. He felt the skin above his mouth. His lip felt strange with no moustache.

He continued puffing on his pipe, Janus' task weighing on his mind. Why did he have to kill the girl and her lovers? A line from Ovid's *Fasti* came to him about endings. *Only I have the right to turn the hinge, said Janus.* And yet H. G. Wells must inflict four endings, including on a dog. He shifted in his chair. Be strong. Changing history, stopping the Great War, saving millions, would require Janus' assistance, and the girl and her lovers were just three souls.

But somehow, they'd vanquished his hired men. The veterans of the legions had failed to dispatch them, yet still demanded payment, prattling nonsense about a ghost. He'd given them each a timepiece, taken from dead officers on that terrible battlefield in 1917. Plenty left to trade.

Wells confirmed the brooch on his awkward toga was secure and stood up to better see the Forum on the window. Janus had said the window would reveal the 'priority interests.' Green dots would identify the girl, one of her lovers, and the dog. He frowned. Numerous dots. Far more than three. Other time travellers? No matter. There was the dog with a dot, and the two dots beside it, the fair-haired girl and the man, matched Janus' description.

They would remain in the Forum for an hour and forty-six minutes, presenting the second opportunity when they'd be vulnerable. They were huddled together near a temple. Wells had seen Ishtar tap on the glass to identify buildings. He tapped on the temple and a caption appeared. *Aedes Iani.* The Temple of Janus. These people evidently had an interest in Janus. Why did Janus want to kill them? He'd said they were, 'Creatures of ill will.' An inadequate answer. There were surely many individuals, guilty of unimaginable crimes, who were far more worthy of Janus' attention.

The noise of the busy Forum was muted on the window, but the scene was still mesmerising. Shopkeepers, families, uniformed slaves, wealthy citizens in litters … all going about their business under the alert gaze of the watchmen. They put out fires, but they were also trained fighters. This might well be the second 'opportunity,' but only a fool would commit murder in front of the watchmen. He'd end up in the arena, murdered for entertainment… So, why had Janus suggested it? The question repeated in his head. Janus was two-faced, traditionally associated with duplicity. Did he believe Wells could die completing his test? Did he care? Wells touched the hilt of the dagger on the belt beneath his toga. Ishtar had wanted to confiscate it, but his reply had satisfied her, chimed with her knowledge of Rome, of brig-ands that preyed upon the weak.

Janus had listed more opportunities, and the remaining stolen watches would pay for the hire of new criminals. He wasn't a murderer.

He turned away from the window and returned to the armchair, passing the long table occupied by Ishtar's colleagues. They'd been working for hours, tapping on transparent pages that spewed out hieroglyphics, the lines of characters dancing in the air like lanterns. They were updating 'code' — whatever that was — to ensure the Festival of Janus passed off smoothly.

The unpleasant task would be over long before then.

CHAPTER 13

Sophie ran out of Janus' temple with Charlotte, and blinked, momentarily blinded by the sun blazing down on the Forum. Freddy and Hugo came out almost as fast with Jack. Sophie paused to catch her breath and gave Charlotte a reassuring pat. Slowly, her mind cleared. Get a grip. The statue was a plank of wood, and the real Janus was trapped in his ship.

'Why did you run?' said Freddy.

'I don't know. A panic attack?'

'You don't have panic attacks,' said Hugo.

'I've never liked crowded places.' And this sweltering heat could have played a part. Sophie opened her flask and drank water. 'Let's find an estate agent.'

But the dogs pulled towards a sausage stall. Freddy dug out a coin from his satchel and bought some. The next shop sold souvenirs and despite the pressing need to find a place to rent, Hugo paused. Stacked in a holder were narrow iron sticks with one pointed end. Identical writing was etched along them. He picked one up. 'A cheap stylus, the equivalent of a biro. Freddy, can you translate this?'

'A simple gift from the Temple of Janus … and my purse is empty.'

'A novelty souvenir,' said Hugo. 'I've got to have one.' He handed over a copper coin.

Statuettes with two or four heads jostled for space on the counter with tin necklaces that held dangling dice instead of gems. Every square die featured a different leering face on each of its four sides. There were also gaudy friezes the size of a greeting card. Within a gold oval frame, two youthful faces looked in opposite directions.

'These are identical to the frieze on the chapel at home,' said Hugo. 'Could be male or female.'

They'd never seen that image anywhere else. 'The church sculptor must have travelled here,' said Sophie.

'Or a similar universe,' said Freddy.

Sophie pointed at a beeswax square on a frieze. 'I wonder what that's for?'

'You write in the wax, make a vow to improve your life,' said Hugo. 'Stop drinking so much, be faithful to your spouse—'

'Like New Year resolutions?' said Sophie.

'Sort of,' said Hugo, 'but people also pledged to avenge wrongs, prayed for enemies to die, or catch horrible diseases. If they honoured their pledge, they offered the frieze up to a god. In this case, Janus.'

A familiar custom with a bizarre twist. Sophie put a coin on the counter and the stall holder wrapped the frieze in a green knitted doily. The doily was like a child's bobble hat. Sophie exhaled. Someday soon, she'd hold her baby again.

'We vow to finish Janus,' she whispered to Freddy. 'If we keep that vow, you'll scratch it in Latin on the frieze?'

'I will, though if we kill him, Janus won't be available to accept the offering.' Freddy gave her a grim smile, and Charlotte listened, her furry face solemn.

Sophie placed the frieze carefully in her satchel.

'Freddy, can you translate this?' Hugo was studying a tablet, hung on a shop wall.

'No one to sell here without a licence.'

'I thought the notice would be more memorable,' said Sophie.

'The Romans were hot on paperwork,' said Hugo. 'They had a joke that even the horses in the army had three sets of documents.'

'When we get home, you should write a history book,' said Sophie. 'Wow everyone.'

Hugo did his self-effacing shrug. 'To create the temple in the Forum without attracting attention, they must have done it overnight, in a matter of hours.'

'Maybe they can beam stuff down from space,' said Sophie, channelling *Star Trek*.

'Stay alert,' said Freddy. 'We're attracting attention, though I can't think why.' He swallowed. 'Other people are far more interesting.'

A girl with a gorgeous tan and supermodel cheekbones winked at Freddy. Her figure-hugging pale dress was literally jaw-dropping. Freddy closed his mouth and winked back. 'See what I mean?'

How is she so glamorous in this temperature? 'I'd like a café break,' said Sophie.

There were plenty to choose from. The inside of the nearest was stifling, so they opted for an outside table with a view of the Forum. An orange awning provided welcome shade.

Sophie poured the last of her flask into the dogs' travel dish. They lapped it up and wanted more. 'Freddy, can you ask for more water?'

'Will do, and we need wine.' On the café wall was a fresco

showing different coloured goblets. Beside them were Roman numerals and text.

Sophie tried to read it. 'What does per speculum mean?'

'By the glass,' said Freddy. 'With prices.'

'Let's go for the second cheapest,' said Hugo.

That choice had worked in modern London. Freddy ordered cold water, then wine, pointing at the appropriate glass.

The water and wine arrived, plus a jug of boiling water. Sophie added the hot water to chunky grey glasses evidently manufactured to handle it and took a sip. Weak mulled wine. The pepper in it irritated her throat and she coughed. 'Maybe okay in the winter, but all year round?'

'I think it's … interesting,' said Freddy. 'Look, spices to take away.' On a shelf were spice bowls and tiny, draw-string bags.

Hugo stroked the dogs who were drinking water close to his chair. 'Presumably, after the temple in the Forum was created by the builders, the locals built the other one by the crossroads?'

'I touched the statue in the crossroads temple,' said Sophie. 'It was all real.'

'The make-believe Forum temple explains the lack of archaeological evidence.' Hugo sipped his spiced wine. 'In a few centuries from now, when the builders outlaw interaction with the locals, they'll remove evidence of their interference, including the temple.'

'Taking away the building would be difficult without anyone noticing,' said Sophie.

'After the empire fell, there was chaos,' said Freddy. 'The locals would have had more pressing problems.'

'But how would the builders track down all the tourist tat, like our Janus frieze?' said Sophie.

'Perhaps pay for its return?' said Hugo. 'That would

explain the lack of it in Rome, rather than the wider empire. But they couldn't get rid of all the coins, minted with his faces or his temple.'

Freddy's attention was on the Forum. 'I'm sure that girl is watching us. Don't stare, but she's sitting near that fountain.'

The girl's skin was dark, and she had a sharp face, with a pointed chin and a strong nose. Her dress was charcoal grey with long sleeves, unusual in that most dresses and tunics here were sleeveless. She tapped her wrist as if she were nervous.

'Maybe she fancies you?' said Sophie. 'You are pretty fit.'

Freddy didn't rise to her teasing. 'She's talking to herself.'

The girl's lips were moving. Okay, that was strange. Wasn't as if she had wireless buds in her ears.

The girl jumped to her feet and hurried off across the square.

'She could have been stood up,' said Sophie. 'She doesn't seem happy.'

Hugo swore under his breath. 'If she's part of the builders' research team, she might have a hidden comms device.' The girl had disappeared into the crowd. 'We've missed our chance.'

Sophie wanted to swear too. Why hadn't she thought of that? If the girl was a builder, she was likely heading back to base. They could have gone with her. Sophie clenched her fists in frustration.

'It could be a lost opportunity, or she could just have been simple.' Freddy was consoling himself.

A passing teenager looked them up and down. 'If she was watching us, she's not alone,' said Sophie. 'It's making me uneasy.' Charlotte put her paw on the table, meaning, 'I'm also uneasy.'

'I feel out of my depth.' Hugo pushed his fringe from his eyes.

'If there's somewhere half-decent to rent,' said Sophie, 'we can hunker down and keep a low profile until the festival.'

Hugo raised his eyebrows. 'Since when have you ever kept a low profile?'

She really wanted this to be a 'let's not be noticed,' challenge. 'We shouldn't borrow trouble.'

'Amen to that.' Freddy stood up.

'First, we find a bank and exchange our sovereigns for cash.' Hugo sighed. 'If we survive this, I'm going to have to confess about the sovereigns.' He'd packed six of his father's coins.

'How many are left?' asked Freddy.

'Only two,' said Hugo. 'And I feel bad. Most of them were my grandfather's.'

They eventually found a stall selling sandals that did money changing, but when Hugo produced a gold sovereign, the stallholder gestured across the Forum and spoke too fast.

'Something about a Counting House,' said Freddy. 'He hasn't got enough coins.'

The stallholder gave them directions, Freddy caught the gist, and they hurried across the Forum.

The Counting House was on the second floor of the green shopping precinct. Flanking the entrance were two men in red tunics. They carried wooden batons and on their belts were vicious-looking knives.

Freddy said his ritual greeting. The men eyed the dogs with suspicion but reluctantly stepped aside.

A man behind a high counter spoke, and Freddy repeated the stock reply. The guy's eyes crawled from their feet to their heads, his lip curling.

On the counter were neat piles of coins. Hugo set out

sovereigns beside the coins, then stepped aside and folded his arms, his expression haughty. Freddy spoke briefly in Latin and pointed at the sovereigns and the coins.

The guy rubbed the sovereigns and held them up to the light. He fetched another man who also examined the sovereigns. He left, and soon returned with iron buckets which he lifted onto the high counter. Some buckets were filled with silver coins, others held coins made of brass. He upturned a bucket and the coins that spilled out were shiny gold.

'This is enough to buy a farm.' Freddy had memorised the currency and knew its rough value. 'The brass coins are sestertii. The silver coins are denarii. I don't know what the gold ones are called.'

The second bank employee spoke rapidly and gestured at the impressive haul. 'He says we should store them here,' said Freddy. 'Safer.'

'I'm not sure,' said Sophie. Were Roman banks secure? Were they robbed?

Hugo frowned.

'We might need cash outside of banker's hours,' said Freddy.

'If we can find a place to rent, I'd rather stash it there,' said Hugo. 'Private homes were designed to deter intruders.'

Charlotte nodded. Fortunately, the bank staff didn't notice.

They swiped the coins into their satchels. As they left, the store's heavies stared after them.

CHAPTER 14

Further on from the Counting House was a row of estate agents, all signed *Domus* and displaying the same logo: a two-sided, slanted red roof. One shopfront was twice the size of the others, so they went in there.

A man and a woman were sitting behind a counter. The wall behind them was covered with thin wooden tablets, hung up on nails. Each tablet had a house plan etched into wax. They stood up, the woman's lips moving in the hint of a sneer, but Freddy gave the standard greeting. The man repeated the words and said something else.

Freddy replied in his halting Latin before translating. 'He asked if the property is for our master. I said it was for us.' Jack was pulling on his lead, wanting to explore, but Freddy kept his lead short.

The woman removed a tablet from the wall and plonked it on the counter. The sketch was of a single room. Couldn't have taken long to draw.

Freddy shook his head and did a 'bigger' motion with his hands. The woman took down a different tablet. The house had rooms surrounding a courtyard.

Charlotte nodded.

'Ubi est?' said Hugo.

The man replied and Freddy translated. 'The property is east of here, further from the river ... with good air.'

Rummaging under the counter, the male estate agent brought out a set of thicker tablets. A leather thong tied them together, threaded inside hinge holes on the edge. The first outer page was plain. The second page had a map and dense, small text which carried on to the third page. On the final page was a recessed wax square and a groove down the centre.

Freddy studied the writing, then straightened. 'I can barely understand a word.' He spoke in slow Latin. 'I've asked if we can rent it for a week.'

The female estate agent held up six fingers, said, 'Mensis,' and made a dismissive, final gesture.

Freddy sighed. 'Minimum six months.'

The woman tapped a column of roman numerals on the third page.

'Leaves us plenty.' Freddy studied the top of the second page. 'The house is called Villa Fullia. It's on Barollo Street.' A cross on the map showed the location of the house, a few streets away from the Forum.

Hugo spoke in hesitant Latin, and the male estate agent replied.

'He says it's on a quiet road,' said Freddy.

Sophie nodded. Apparently, the noise from big carts on the main roads at night was so loud people couldn't sleep.

Freddy opened his heavy satchel and counted out coins. The woman pushed the last waxed page of the tablet towards him, and her colleague offered up a bronze stylus.

After a moment's hesitation, Freddy scratched out *MARCUS VERANIUS*. They'd invented the surname, rather than adopt a real name from classical records at home. Hugo was calling himself Lucius Veranius, assuming the role of Freddy's brother, and Sophie was Lucius' wife, Hortensia. Hortensia sounded haughty, but it meant a happy place, a garden.

The male estate agent pushed a heavy seal against the groove on the back page with a triumphant air, leaving diagonal marks, one long and two short. He touched the marks, spoke, and Freddy translated. 'We can renew the lease by courier. That's our security code.'

The woman handed over a heavy key. 'Arbor flore.'

'Tree blossom,' translated Freddy.

'Another name for the house?' said Sophie.

Freddy shrugged. 'No idea.'

Following the map on the tablet, they hurried east across the Forum.

'Look at that.' Hugo pointed off to the left. Beyond the Forum, a gold-tiled roof was glinting in the sun, taller than any other buildings. 'That's not on our maps.'

Lost to history like Juno's arch. In front of Sophie, a youth with a shaved head darted too close and she side-stepped to avoid him. He'd almost collided with Charlotte and though she seemed relaxed, Sophie cuddled her.

The youth paused to put on a cream, brimless cap, its shape resembling a jester's. A cone, with the top bent over.

'I thought ordinary Romans weren't into hats,' said Sophie, wishing she'd brought a straw one from home.

'That's a Phrygian cap,' said Hugo. 'Proves he's no longer a slave. If he was freed in an official ceremony, he's now a Roman citizen. A big deal.'

The freed slave broke into a run and swerved past a group of men who shouted and gestured. Someone threw a punch and an alarmed buzz of excitement rippled through the crowd.

Sophie didn't notice the girl in the grey dress until she was right in her face. Sophie blinked, surprised. 'Are you part of the research team?'

'Leave! It's not safe,' the girl hissed in English. 'You'll die.'

The girl thrust smooth metal objects into Sophie's palm, closed Sophie's fingers over them, and turned on her heel.

Sophie was so surprised she hardly took in the girl's words. She opened her fingers. Three metal cylinders, the size of USB sticks. Each had a keyring at one end.

When Sophie looked up, the girl was gone.

'You son of a dog!' a man shouted from the brawl.

Sophie was hearing English, not Latin, or was she hallucinating? She wiped a bead of sweat from her brow.

'Time to go,' said Hugo.

'Give me my money! I'll see you in Hades!'

Charlotte growled, showing off her splendid teeth, and created a welcome path through the agitated crowd. But as they reached the edge of the Forum, they met a line of watchmen who were advancing towards the fight. 'Clear the square!' They were brandishing swords and swinging axes.

Sophie hastily veered into a shop with Charlotte until the watchmen passed by. Hugo rushed in with Freddy dragging Jack. Louder screams and shouting erupted outside.

'A big fight?' asked the shopkeeper in English. She didn't seem to expect an answer. 'Bad for business.'

Sophie exhaled, felt dizzy. Yes, she was hallucinating. Must be heatstroke.

Hugo was by the doorway, looking out. 'We should go now.'

They rushed out of the Forum and along an unfamiliar street. They were safe, but Sophie still felt weird. 'I need to get out of the sun.'

Yards away was a cosy popina with a hanging basket of red geraniums by the door. Inside, they found a spare table, and Freddy ordered water and wine in English.

'Would you like to buy fans to keep cool?' said the waitress, gesturing at some laid out on a shelf. The fans were made from plaited leaves and tough grass and were larger than modern ones.

'Yes, please,' said Freddy.

Okay, this delusion wasn't going away. 'Freddy, are you talking in English?'

He glanced at her, bemused. 'No. You just heard me.'

Everyone in the café was speaking English with a variety of accents, ranging from lilting to guttural.

'I despair of finding a decent cook,' said a matron with arresting dark eyes.

'The Blues will win,' said a man at a different table. His voice, like the woman's, had a smooth lilting edge. 'The Reds' new trainer's useless.'

Sophie's time-travelling book had mentioned the blues and the reds. Two of the factions who competed in chariot racing. Sophie emptied the cylinders onto the table with a clatter and the speech around her changed into Latin and other languages. She lifted a cylinder and the chatter returned to English. Universal translators?

Freddy stared and Hugo took one.

'If you touch them, they translate speech into English,' said Sophie.

'What?' Hugo examined the cylinder. 'Is there a button to push?'

'No,' said Sophie. 'Just hold it.'

'It doesn't work for me,' said Hugo, 'but what a fabulous find.' He traced the outline of the cylinder with his forefinger, then picked up a second. 'They feel smooth, but I *see* keys, with handles and teeth.' Charlotte stepped closer to the table.

'Please describe them,' said Freddy, eyeing the cylinders with suspicion.

'The bases are heart-shaped, with the Janus-T in the centre, and each has different teeth combinations. Tiny versions of Janus' key.'

'What do you think they're made of?' said Sophie.

'Base metal, and cheaply finished.' Hugo set the cylinders aside. 'Where did you get them?'

'The girl Freddy thought was watching us … she gave them to me in the Forum.'

'Why on earth didn't you say something?' said Freddy.

'I didn't have time. The fight was kicking off and the next moment she was gone.' The girl was evidently practised at slipping away out of sight.

Freddy selected a cylinder — and froze. 'A Babel device but in reverse.'

'Come again?' said Hugo.

'From the bible story,' said Sophie. 'All the people in the world once spoke one language and built a splendid tower, but God destroyed the tower and created many languages, so it was more difficult to communicate.'

'Why would a god do that?' asked Hugo.

'I think it's a parable,' said Freddy. 'I'm not sure you're meant to understand them.'

The waitress bustled up and laid out glasses, a rounded wine amphora with twin handles, and a jug of hot water. Another girl put down water bowls for the dogs and Sophie smiled at her. 'Freddy, speak English to the waitress.' Would she understand him?

'Thank you,' said Freddy. The girl smiled before going on her way. He put the cylinder in his satchel, then fished it out again. 'Hmmm, it stops working if it isn't touching your skin.'

Sophie attached the keyring bit of a cylinder to Charlotte's collar and ensured the device was nestled deep into her fur. 'No need to learn more Latin.'

Charlotte hopped in delight and Jack copied her.

'I'll improve my Latin the old-fashioned way.' Hugo poured wine and water into their glasses.

At the next table, a toddler was playing near her mother's feet. The child's hair was short and wavy, like Bella's. Sophie drew up the key-rattle hanging from her neck and held it, hoping that would calm her frazzled nerves. *You'll die.* The girl hadn't seemed mischievous or malevolent, more stressed, and couldn't know she'd die here—

Freddy patted her hand. 'No one can be brave all the time.'

Hugo gave her a chin up smile. 'Or even for a day.'

'Heroes.' Sophie caught the David Bowie reference. She wasn't a hero. Right now, she felt shaky and inadequate. Shock was setting in. 'The translation keys come with a downside. The girl told me to leave, that it's not safe, that I'd die.'

Hugo and Freddy looked horrified, and Charlotte vigorously shook her head.

'Did she mean you should leave the Forum,' said Freddy, 'or go back to Juno?'

'I don't know.' Sophie picked up a cylinder and let the sound of English in the popina wash over her. Only an illusion of familiarity, of home, but it helped.

Hugo cuddled her and she leaned into him, trying to calm down.

'Was the girl trying to protect you?' said Freddy. 'Or did she sound threatening?'

The girl's tone had been earnest, urgent. 'Could have been either, but what she said was clear. I'm going to die.'

Hugo downed his wine. 'We should get to the villa as soon as possible.'

CHAPTER 15

Ten minutes after leaving the Forum, following the map on the house tablet, they left the main road. The side street was less crowded, but the midday heat was oppressive, and the stranger's warning pounded in Sophie's head in a relentless drumbeat. *You'll die.*

The gradient of the pavement became progressively steeper, then levelled out. There were no shops, just walls on both sides, painted Roman red at the bottom and white further up. At uneven intervals, there were doors of iron or wood.

An olive tree growing between the pavement stones offered some welcome shade and Sophie poured water into the dogs' travel dish. Hugo checked his printed map against the smaller one on the house tablet, and Sophie and Freddy stood in a huddle around him, shielding his printed map from view.

'That's the main road and that's this side road. The house should be here.' Hugo scanned the street. 'How do we find it?' There were no house numbers or names.

A girl carrying a heavy sack over her shoulder brushed

past them. Holding the translator cylinder in her hand, Sophie called out. 'Excuse me.' The girl turned. 'We're searching for a villa.' The girl nodded, hearing Sophie's words in Latin.

Freddy offered the girl a coin. 'The house is on Barollo Street. It's called Villa Fullia.'

The girl accepted the coin and gestured for them to follow. A few steps further on, she pointed at an iron door.

How could she possibly know this was Villa Fullia? Sophie paused. 'She could be leading us into a trap to rob us.'

The girl looked affronted.

'I think she's a slave,' said Hugo. 'Perhaps slaves memorise streets and addresses so they can deliver stuff?' He gave the girl another coin and she went on her way with the sack.

Freddy inserted the estate agent's bulky key in the lock and when it turned easily, Sophie breathed a sigh of relief. But when Freddy tried to push open the door, it wouldn't budge, barred from the inside. Charlotte barked.

Freddy took out the key. The Villa Fullia was already occupied.

Sophie took the time-turner pendant from her satchel. 'The estate agent swindled us. It's already let.' If necessary, she'd scare the occupants into leaving. She banged on the door.

Hugo grabbed his knife and so did Freddy.

'House word,' said a croaky voice from the other side of the door.

They glanced at each other in confusion.

'Some sort of password?' said Sophie. 'What the estate agent said?'

'Arbor flore,' said Freddy.

A scraping sound and the door swung open, revealing a tired-looking man in a thin tunic that flapped above his knobbly knees. Behind him, in a gloomy corridor, a teenager in a longer tunic stared at them. Black hair fell in frizzy curls about her sallow face. She registered their kitchen knives and gulped.

'Who are you?' said Sophie.

'Boy and girl.' The man eyed the dogs and backed away.

'They're slaves,' said Freddy. 'They must come with the house.'

'I should have realised.' Hugo hastily concealed his knife in his satchel, and they walked in.

Freddy lowered his blade and Hugo turned, closed the front door, and pulled across a heavy bolt. Using his key, Freddy doubly secured the door, leaving the key in the lock.

Sophie returned the pendant to her satchel and smiled at the slaves, hoping to reassure them. They'd been rented along with the property… It didn't bear thinking about.

The air was stuffy, edged with cooking smells. Daylight from up the corridor barely illuminated the passage and its green walls remained shadowed and dark. Jack snarled at the floor and Sophie glanced down at the square mosaic she was standing on. A chained-up dog baring its teeth. Not exactly a welcome mat.

'We have strange customs.' Freddy's tone was apologetic.

The slaves bowed and led the way into the villa.

Beyond the spooky corridor was a good-sized room with a square hole in the roof. Directly below the hole was a shallow pool that mirrored the shape of the opening above it. By the pool were comfy armchairs. Wood panelling lined the walls, each panel a vibrant primary colour. And it was blissfully cool.

They followed the slaves past a plinth with a miniature temple and tiny figures. There were exits off the pool room, but the slaves continued through an archway into a courtyard. Encircled by green pillars, with a tree and a fountain, the walled garden was uncannily like the courtyard illusion in Juno. But instead of stone seats there were wooden-slatted chairs, a scarlet sofa with matching cushions, and a yellow couch. Red geraniums, white lilies, and violets were growing in crimson urns. Their petals fluttered in the faint breeze, releasing soothing, sweet scents.

Sophie put the cylinder on a side table and took off her satchel. Charlotte and Jack drank from the fountain and Freddy dipped his hand into the water pouring from the cherub's mouth.

'How does this work without electricity?' Sophie splashed her face.

'The water's piped in from mountains outside the city,' said Hugo. 'Powered by head pressure created with gravity through long pipe runs.'

Of course, Hugo would know that. Sophie gave him a tender glance before picking up the cylinder and addressing the slaves. 'Is there a loo here?' According to her time-travelling book, private villas had them.

The female slave nodded, and Sophie went with her into a cramped kitchen with a battered brazier. Above the brazier was a narrow gap to the outside, but there was no mechanism for extracting cooking fumes. The smoke-blackened walls reeked unpleasantly of garlic.

Cooking pans were hung on a wall and Sophie did a double take. Some were identical to modern ones, except they were all made of iron. The round strainer could have come from her aunt's kitchen, with its sturdy handle, and a hole at the end to hang it up.

Cutlery was laid out on a narrow table against a wall. Iron knives of different sizes with bone handles, and bronze spoons. Below the table were storage pots and higher up behind it was a shelf lined with mixing bowls, plates, glasses, and amphora bottles. Presumably, the Romans didn't have storage drawers.

There was a chunky, iron tap but no sink.

Around a corner was a bench with a round hole. Beneath it was a drop and running water flowing into a drain. The slave hadn't followed her, and Sophie pulled down her knickers and sat on the bench. Hey, not fancy, but it worked.

When she returned to the courtyard, Freddy was talking with the male slave. 'There's six bedrooms and a dining room.'

Sophie told them about the loo. 'And the kitchen's … basic.' It confirmed their research. Slaves did all the cooking, so kitchens weren't fancy.

'This chap is called Drusus.' Freddy smiled at the slave who cautiously smiled back. Though Drusus' arms and legs were thin, they were muscled.

Drusus coughed, a racking, smoker's cough. But presumably caused by something other than smoking. Cigarettes had yet to be invented. When he'd recovered himself, he stood to attention and Jack sniffed at his tunic. The slave froze.

'Jack, come here.' Sophie stroked him to show he wouldn't bite, and Charlotte sat down near Sophie, keeping quiet.

'He may never lose his fear,' said Hugo.

Sophie was still clutching her cylinder. 'These dogs are family,' she said, her words coming out in Latin. 'They're, um, special.'

Charlotte did a regal nod and Drusus' mouth dropped open.

Slowly, Charlotte extended a front paw and after a moment's hesitation, Drusus reached out and held it, his gaunt face filled with wonder. 'Bran and Sceólang.'

'Your dogs from home?' said Sophie.

'No, Madam. My friend who worked with me in the baths talked about them.' For the first time, Drusus smiled. 'Bran and Sceólang are dogs of legend from long ago and distant lands.'

While Sophie translated for Hugo, Drusus cautiously embraced Charlotte and was rewarded with her resting her furry head against him. He patted Jack.

The female slave was watching Drusus and the dogs, bemused and wary.

'The girl's name is Melissa,' said Freddy.

Sophie sat on the yellow couch and set the cylinder aside, not wanting Melissa and Drusus to understand her. 'We can't let them literally slave away for nothing.'

Freddy put his cylinder on the side table. 'It's not for nothing. Drusus says household work suits him.'

'What about Melissa?' said Sophie.

Freddy avoided her eyes. 'She was bought from a brothel last year. Says she's happy here.'

Hugo shot Sophie his warning look. 'We're not here to start a slave revolt. All we can do is treat them decently and give their owners a good report on them.'

'Is that a thing? Slave reports?' Sophie asked him.

'Can't hurt.'

Drusus said something and Sophie snatched up her cylinder. 'Sorry Drusus,' she said. 'Can you repeat that?'

'When is your baggage due to arrive?'

Baggage?

Freddy had his cylinder and was only non-plussed for a second. 'We were robbed.'

Drusus gave a sympathetic nod. 'Shall we purchase appropriate clothing today? You must be eager to shed your disguises.'

Sophie's fingers tightened on the cylinder. Was the translation wrong? 'Disguises?'

'I meant no disrespect, Madam,' said Drusus. 'Such outfits are wise precautions on perilous journeys.'

Freddy's forehead creased.

'What are we disguised as?' asked Sophie, feeling uncom-fortable.

'Well-cared for slaves,' said Drusus. 'A clever deceit. Your wedding ring, though, gives you away.'

Sophie clasped her hands in her lap, covering her wedding band. Married women here wore gold rings like at home, but slaves couldn't marry.

Hugo sat down beside her and Sophie summarised Drusus' *disguised as slaves* revelation. She kept her voice low, not wanting to broadcast Hugo's poor understanding of Latin.

Freddy had recovered his composure and smiled again at the slaves. 'I am Marcus. This is Lucius and Hortensia.' He fished out silver denarii coins from his satchel. 'This should be enough for our clothes.' He spread a handful of sestertii coins on the table.

'We'll buy food as well.' Drusus scooped up some of the brass coins and selected one of the — more valuable — silver denarii.

'Melissa, could you buy fresh milk, please?' said Sophie. She'd kill for a cup of tea.

The slave took the remaining coins, and her thin, plucked eyebrows moved just a fraction. Did the Romans not drink milk?

'And honey,' said Freddy.

Drusus transferred the coins into a brown drawstring bag and Melissa went to the kitchen and returned with a long bronze container. The inside was lined with wool. She dropped her coins into it and clipped the holder around her upper arm.

'Ingenious,' said Freddy.

'Only opens when I take it off,' said Melissa. 'Cutpurses hate it.'

'Cutpurses?' said Sophie.

'Thieves,' said Melissa. She and Drusus hurried off to the gloomy corridor.

'I wonder where she acquired the bronze money carrier?' said Hugo. 'It looked expensive.'

'Cutpurses,' repeated Freddy. 'Ha! I see where the name comes from now. Urchins cutting the strings off money bags. Drusus will have to be careful.'

Sophie followed the slaves and after they left the villa, she peered down the street after them. There were four doors before theirs and there was a tree in front of the second. She needed to memorise that, or when they ventured out of here, they'd never find the house again.

When the door was closed, her shoulders relaxed. They'd found a refuge as secure as the moated manor in Shorten. Bella playing in the small drawing room... The memory filled her mind and she let out a slow breath. Rest and take stock.

She dragged across the bolt.

CHAPTER 16

Ten minutes after the slaves left the villa, Sophie came across an empty iron chest in an office. The chest had a chunky key in the lock. Along with Hugo and Freddy, she poured in most of her gold and silver coins, and they clinked as they fell. Freddy locked the chest, storing the key in his satchel.

While Freddy went over to a shelf, examined styluses, and leafed through blank pieces of parchment, Sophie sat on an upright chair at a fine desk, taking in a restful view of the courtyard through an open arch. The desk was decorated with scribes holding symbols of their profession: rolls of papyrus. The only object on the desk was a tablet entitled CENSUS. The tablet unfolded and Charlotte stood on her hind legs to scrutinise it. There were four pages of close, small writing and Charlotte shook her head. Like her mistress, she couldn't read it. The translation cylinders only worked with spoken language. 'Could this be like the census in the Bible?'

Freddy glanced over his shoulder. 'I suppose.'

Hugo opened a sideboard. 'Thick grey glasses and fancy

delicate ones.' He selected a clear glass. Etched on it were tipsy people drinking from horns. 'Alexandrian glass from Egypt.'

'You should have been a classics professor,' said Freddy, with no trace of sarcasm.

'I'd have to spend months, no years, improving my Latin.'

Sophie smiled at Hugo. 'Let's choose a bedroom.'

All the bedrooms were the same size. Not very big. But they matched the rest of the house in that they were sparsely furnished and clean. Each had a three-legged stool, a wooden storage trunk, and only one small window. The opening was square, with folding shutters instead of glass, and was so high up, it almost touched the ceiling.

Sophie examined a thin pole propped against a wall. At the top end was a hook.

'For opening and closing the shutters.' Hugo eyed the bed. 'I'm not sure we'll fit.'

She smiled. 'We will.' In modern London, though their bed was king-sized, she often fell asleep on top of him.

Sophie undid her sandals, put on her faux-leather flip-flops, and they strolled to the pool room. A trickling sound came from the kitchen, and they followed the noise.

Freddy was pouring water from the iron tap into three everyday glasses. Sophie found bowls in a cupboard for the dogs and inspected a tiny pantry. A jar of olives, flat bread wrapped in a white doily, and a hard block of cheese. Most of the cupboards were empty. Melissa and Drusus hadn't exactly been living it up.

Out in the courtyard, Sophie filled the bowls from the fountain and set them down in the generous shade cast by the tree. The branches were covered with purple bulbs. 'A fig tree, and they're ripe.' Her aunt grew figs.

Freddy folded his arms. 'There's no bath.'

'We'll have to wash in the fountain,' said Sophie. Not a

hardship. The water was cool and pristine. 'I love the steady swish of the water in the basin. It's therapeutic.'

'This house is ridiculously secure.' Hugo sat in the nearest chair. 'One door in, and out.'

Sophie nodded. 'And no windows facing the street.'

The dogs had slaked their thirst and were settling down by Hugo. Freddy lay on the scarlet sofa in the sun, stretching out like a Roman emperor.

Sophie perched on the yellow couch opposite, keeping in the shade. 'If we're dressed as slaves, no wonder the Counting House and the estate agents sneered.'

'Sneering says more about the sneeror than the sneeree,' said Freddy.

'I don't think sneeror or sneeree are words,' said Sophie. 'In English, anyway…'

Freddy shrugged. 'Reduces the kindness in the world.'

'Generally true,' said Hugo, 'but I should have taken more notice. Realised we didn't fit in.'

Sophie plumped up a cushion behind her. 'I should have realised as well.' Travelling through time, she'd had plenty of practice.

Hugo sipped his water. 'Tells about … otherness can be subtle.'

'Otherness?' said Freddy.

'A few years ago, we had a long family holiday in Italy,' said Hugo. 'In the north by Lake Como. We got into all things Italian, including fashion. When we arrived at the flight desk to go home, the guy took one look at us and said, "Londra." Despite our best efforts, our clothing, or our luggage, or the way we walked, gave us away.'

'Melissa and Drusus might help with that,' said Sophie.

Freddy sat up on the sofa. 'This lying-down malarky's hard work. If you were eating, you'd get indigestion. A pity. I quite fancied hosting a Roman dinner party.' His tone was flippant.

'We don't know anyone to invite,' said Hugo.

'Even if we did, we shouldn't,' said Sophie. 'Yes, this is the trip of a lifetime, but until the festival, we keep out of sight.' She put down her glass. 'Cooking on that brazier won't be fun.'

'Drusus and Melissa could collect ready-made meals from cafés,' said Freddy. 'Or are we being too cautious?'

'Cautious is good,' said Hugo.

He was right. This aching need to see Bella was getting worse but they should be patient, wait for the festival and the right moment to steal the walking staff.

'You worried at the first Janus temple that we were being watched,' said Hugo. 'It might have been that girl?'

'I hope I imagined it.' But she'd learned not to ignore that familiar unease and heightened awareness.

'The builders here may be tracking travellers,' said Freddy. In the mad medieval realm, a builder had remotely followed 'priority interests' as she'd called individuals with the gene, and she'd initially welcomed them into her base.

'I asked the girl if she was part of the research team, and she didn't reply, though she definitely understood me,' said Sophie. 'Right… When she first rushed up, I was in shock, so I spoke to her in English.'

'I see where you're going with this,' said Hugo.

Freddy squinted in the sun. 'I don't.'

'She replied in English, which means one of two things. She could be a native English speaker. Or, she had a cylinder. It translated my words and turned her reply into English.' They'd left the cylinders in the pool room. Not needed while they were by themselves.

'Giving us three, we can presume there's a ready supply,' said Freddy. 'Used by the research team.'

'And if the team are tracking us,' said Sophie, 'that's how she knew we needed three. For me, Charlotte, and you.' Charlotte glanced up before closing her eyes again.

Hugo patted Jack, though he was deeply asleep. 'We're naturally untrackable.'

Sophie smiled. 'A valuable power in itself.'

'In the café, people weren't only speaking Latin,' said Freddy. 'There were other tongues and the cylinder worked with all of them. Depending on the translated language, the English accent was subtly different.'

Hugo looked intrigued. 'Give me an example.'

Freddy sat back on the sofa. 'The chatter from one table made z sounds instead of s.'

'The girl's English was flawless,' said Sophie. 'I mean, she spoke like us.'

'Did she seem surprised when you mentioned the research team, or was she nonplussed?' asked Hugo.

'She didn't react at all.'

'The cylinders make life immeasurably easier.' Freddy stretched. 'A kind gift.'

'Or perhaps she gave them to establish some trust?' said Hugo. 'So, we'd heed her warning?'

'Maybe.' Sophie listened to the rhythmic splash of the fountain, and her brain whirred into action. 'My disappearing act by the river, and your sovereigns... Small things, but they could still cause a ripple effect, eventually change the timeline a lot? Interfere with their research. Would explain why she warned me off?'

'A ghost sighting and a few gold coins are trivial compared to what the research team has done here,' said Hugo. 'Invented a complex religion, built a temple, conjured up Janus every year—'

'You're right,' said Sophie. 'She may be just another traveller.' Charlotte had woken up and was leaning into Sophie's legs. *You'll die.* The girl had sounded so certain. 'Or, she's a traveller on a return visit. To this universe. To this time.'

Hugo leaned forward. 'Why do you think that?'

Sophie pushed away a stab of fear. 'Because she's watched me, or another version of me, already die?'

'We've no idea what her deal is, but this changes things.' Hugo's lips tightened. 'We should leave.'

'I'm not sure,' said Freddy.

Sophie frowned, also unsure.

'Finding a safe way back to Bella isn't worth losing you,' said Hugo to Sophie. 'Nothing is worth that.'

'The girl may have been helping us,' said Freddy. 'Once the watchmen waded into the fight, who knows how many people were killed? She might have meant we should just leave the Forum?'

Sophie nodded, hoping Freddy was right.

'The girl's words and actions are unclear and contradictory,' said Freddy, pompously. 'At this stage, we shouldn't abandon everything we've worked for.'

'If you want to die trying to find the walking staff, Freddy, I respect that,' said Hugo. 'But I won't let Sophie die.'

'That's not your decision,' said Freddy, his voice getting louder.

Sophie stood up and rubbed her brow. 'We survived Juno. This villa's safe. And we're so near to finding the staff.'

Hugo got to his feet. He put his fingers gently under her chin and she met his eyes. 'You alone can't decide this. If you die here, I likely will too. Or if I don't, I won't be swanning off home to live happily ever after.'

Sophie winced, but she was saved from replying by Charlotte growling and Jack barking.

Someone was banging on the front door.

CHAPTER 17

Sophie paused in the murky entrance at the front of the villa. More banging on the door. 'House word?'

'Arbor flore.' Drusus' voice.

Feeling foolish, Sophie drew back the bolt. With no bell, of course he'd had to hammer on the door.

The slaves were weighed down with bulging satchels and carrying tunics and belts.

Sophie went with Melissa to the bedroom to change. She took off her linen dress and folded it into the storage trunk. Melissa seemed unfazed by Sophie's big knickers and sports bra. Maybe Roman underwear wasn't that different?

Melissa gave Sophie a soft, knee-length tunic and a belt which fastened under her bust. There was a dress to wear over it. Far too hot to wear two layers but Sophie went with it. Ankle length, the dress had a fitted neckline inlaid with a band of floral embroidery. Gilt filigree edged the hem and the short sleeves. Melissa emptied her battered satchel, and gold bracelets and necklaces set with red, green, and blue gemstones bounced onto the bed.

Wow. So much bling… Sophie accepted a bracelet.

'We must dress your hair.' Melissa picked up a comb and hair pins from the bed.

Sophie sat on the stool and twenty minutes later, Melissa held up a hand-held, bronze mirror. Though the metal had a greenish hue, the reflection was surprisingly detailed. The front of Sophie's hair was plaited on top of her head, and at the back, her hair was pinned in elaborate curls. The woollen band worn behind the plaits helped to secure the pins. Sophie smiled, glad Melissa hadn't backcombed her hair, making it too thick and too high. The final touch was a long hairpin through the curls, showing off a tiny figure of a dog. That produced another smile.

She slipped off her key-rattle necklace. Taking inspiration from the statue of the female Janus, Sophie passed the chain through the small ring at the base of the cylinder and put the necklace back on. Freddy could keep his cylinder against his skin in the same way. She selected another necklace with a thin leather strap.

'If you don't mind me asking,' said Sophie, 'how did you come by the fancy coin carrier?'

Melissa stored the remaining jewellery in the chest and closed it. Sunlight shone through the high window onto the domed lid. 'A present from my last owner.'

The answer didn't ring true, but if Melissa was light-fingered, they had nothing much to steal. And the cash was locked away. They walked to the pool room.

Freddy was lounging in a chair. His tunic was a fetching pink, edged with silver, and he wore a shiny, polished belt.

'No more sneering,' said Sophie.

Freddy smiled at her. 'You look fabulous.'

'You do too, if rather decadent.' Sophie handed him the necklace. 'You can wear your cylinder on this.'

A wonderful scent of coffee was coming from the kitchen and Sophie followed it. The brazier was lit, lumps of wood glowing red under an iron stand. On it was a jug and Hugo was stirring coffee bags in boiling water. Dressed in a deep turquoise tunic with gold edging, he was like an emperor playing house.

Drusus was watching him, confused. He turned around. 'Madam, you don't cook.'

'I know,' said Sophie, 'but we want to show you how to prepare this drink.' She nodded to Melissa. 'It'll perk us all up.'

Drusus scuttled off to collect grey glasses from the sideboard in the study and only fetched three.

'We need two more,' said Sophie.

When he returned, Sophie poured coffee, added milk from a jar in the pantry, and a spoonful of honey. 'You'll probably prefer it sweetened.'

Melissa set out the drinks on a wooden tray covered with stylised grapes and carried it into the pool room. She laid it on a table, then she and Drusus stood to attention, uncertain what was expected of them.

Hugo took a glass, sniffed luxuriously, and drank. 'Nectar of the gods.'

Sophie savoured the aroma and grinned. 'Couldn't agree more.'

Jack snuffled about, but Charlotte settled by the pool. She'd tried coffee once and spat it out. The glasses for Melissa and Drusus remained untouched on the tray.

Sophie handed them their drinks. Now, they seemed terrified. Did they believe she'd slipped in poison? Sophie sipped from Melissa's glass and offered it again. Okay, the smell was fine, yet the taste wasn't right. Down to the honey, or the untreated milk?

Melissa took a hesitant sip.

'It's an acquired taste,' said Sophie.

Drusus drank slowly, as if they'd ordered him to swallow acid. Then had a coughing fit.

'You don't have to drink it,' said Freddy. 'That will be all.'

Melissa left the room holding her coffee, but Drusus returned his to the tray before disappearing off to the kitchen.

'They need time to get used to us,' said Hugo.

'We'll be gone in a few days,' said Sophie. Charlotte trailed her paw through the pool. So did Jack. 'How old do you reckon Drusus is? He doesn't seem well.'

Hugo shook his head. 'Forty something?'

'We should allocate a daily allowance for them to buy food,' said Freddy. 'I'll put money in a bowl in the kitchen.'

Sophie chewed her lip. 'I think Melissa stole the expensive coin container.'

'Let's give her the benefit of the doubt,' said Hugo.

'I wish we knew more about the girl in the Forum.' Freddy nursed his coffee.

'I'm not convinced she was a builder,' said Hugo. 'Why the cryptic warning? Why not just say hello and give the team's address?'

'Maybe there are too many travellers visiting Rome?' said Sophie. 'Tourists casually swinging by would hamper their work?'

Hugo sat straighter, his shoulders rigid. 'If she's not a builder, Janus could have sent her?'

A shudder slid down Sophie's spine. Janus could have bribed her, promised to take her to wonderful times and places, anywhere she wanted... 'No, she wouldn't have given us the cylinders. She'd have knifed us.' Another shudder. In the chaos of that fight in the Forum, no one would have noticed.

'The girl may be a red herring,' said Freddy. 'The point is, Janus can't stop us finding the walking staff directly. He has to use travellers.'

Sophie swallowed. 'Those men who attacked us by Juno's arch. Maybe they weren't there by chance?'

'They were after our money and wanted to … hurt you,' said Freddy. 'They were locals.'

'You're right.' Charlotte gave a little growl, remembering, and Sophie patted her. 'Travellers wouldn't have fallen for the ghost trick.'

'But a traveller could have hired them?' said Hugo. 'And if Janus has sent a traveller, we've no idea who they are or when they'll strike. This makes everything more dangerous.'

'Only at the festival,' said Sophie. 'Until then, we hunker down here.'

'We can't,' said Hugo.

Sophie looked at him, baffled. 'We can and we should. Half an hour ago, you agreed we should be cautious. We don't need to step outside the front door. Melissa and Drusus can go out and about and they'll hear when the festival's announced.'

'Janus knows what we do here,' said Hugo. 'What we've done and will do.'

'Oh,' said Freddy. 'I see what you mean. We must do the opposite of what is logical. Not do what we'd normally do.'

'Exactly,' said Hugo. 'Or at the festival, Janus' assassin will just choose their moment. We take the initiative. Plan C.'

Freddy's brow creased. 'Plan C?'

'Plan A is pursuing this to the bitter end, knowing it's hopeless,' said Hugo. 'B is my preferred course of action. Go home and reconsider. Plan C is an unsatisfactory compromise. We get ourselves a bodyguard.'

'The Praetorian Guard only protects the emperor,' said Freddy.

'Not the Praetorian Guard,' scoffed Hugo. 'Drusus and Melissa will know the best slave market to pick up muscle.'

'You're not serious.' The thought of buying someone made her feel sick.

'It's distasteful,' said Freddy, 'but we'd be mad not to.'

CHAPTER 18

The next day, in an open-air market off the Forum, Freddy balled his fists and averted his eyes. The young woman stood naked on a revolving wooden stand. Her hands were tied in front of her, and one foot was whitened with chalk, indicating she'd been captured outside Rome.

Sophie had refused to come, and Freddy was glad. This was too horrible. A placard hung from the slave's neck listing her skills. Freddy translated them for Hugo. 'Pleasure, cooking and cleaning.' In bigger letters was *Phrygia*. Presumably, the same country as in Homer's *Iliad*. 'She's from Turkey.'

The busy market had high brick walls on three sides. To their left was an open gate, the public entrance and exit. Ahead of them, a stage fronted the slaver's warehouse, a three-storey building with barred windows.

Around Freddy and Hugo, people were settled, waiting for better slaves to be sold, but there was movement at the edge of the crowd, people drifting to the exit and more filing in. Freddy scanned them, checking for anyone who looked shifty, a traveller intent on harming him or Hugo. But the newcomers were preoccupied with their own concerns, staring at the stage or chatting with their friends.

On the stage, the fat man in a red tunic spread his hands wide. 'Soft and pliant.' He pulled on the slave's hair, forcing her chin up. 'Starts at 500 denarii.'

'What's that in sestertii again?' Hugo asked Freddy.

'A denarius coin is roughly four times the value of a sestertius. So, 2,000 sestertii.'

A man beside Freddy raised his arm and yelled, '550.'

'600,' shouted a woman from the back of the crowd.

They'd been here for hours. All the slaves were sold naked, individually or in groups: elderly people, blind men, and unfortunates with scars and limps. According to Drusus, this market specialised in security slaves, but cheaper ones were auctioned first. And all the while, potential buyers gossiped and laughed and waved fans.

The chap next to Freddy burped. He stank of garlic and was drinking wine from a bottle. A hawker, wending her way through the crowd, caught Freddy's eye. He shook his head at her. No doubt the watered-down wine and cheese wraps were tasty, but this place soured the appetite.

'I can't watch this much longer,' said Hugo.

The slaver on the stage waved his arms. 'Don't be shy. She's untouched, with good teeth.'

Some of the crowd jeered, not believing the sales patter, but Freddy was seized with a sudden urge to buy her. There was enough coin in his satchel to outbid everyone. He could save her from ill treatment—

'Yours, Madam.' The slaver brought down his hand. '600 denarii.' Freddy swore under his breath.

A lady slaver, dressed in bright orange, strode down the stage and untied the ropes on the girl's wrists. The woman slipped a pale tunic over the girl's head, twisted her arms through the short sleeves, and tugged the garment down to cover her upper legs. Then the slave was bound again.

The buyer stepped up to collect her purchase. Wearing an ankle-length silk shawl that floated over her dress, the plump matron looked like a ship in full sail. Beside her, a tall man seized their prize, and they marched away together.

Freddy set his mouth in a frustrated line. He should have acted sooner.

A child of around three was pushed onto the stage. Pale-skinned with red hair, his face was slick with sweat, and he stared, his eyes blank. Something was tattooed on his brow and his placard said *Caledonia*. Freddy trawled his mind. Roman campaigns in Britain… The boy was from Scotland.

No one bid, and the trader lowered the price.

Dear God. That could have been Bella. Freddy gestured, but Hugo grasped his wrist and pulled his arm down.

'We can't adopt him,' hissed Hugo. 'If we're still alive after the festival, we'll be leaving straight afterwards!'

'100,' yelled a skinny man. The slaver's hand dropped. 'Yours.'

Freddy threw Hugo off and glared at him, regret souring his throat. 'Sophie would have bought him.'

'Good that she's not here then,' said Hugo.

The lady slaver put a tunic on the child. His buyer grabbed the end of the rope that bound the boy's wrists and dragged him along, his purchase trailing a few feet behind him. The child was shaking, making a token effort to resist.

Freddy's stomach churned. He glanced down at the auction tablet he'd collected on the way in, listing all the slaves' details. He barely understood a word. A shame the cylinder didn't work for writing. Surely, security slaves would be sold soon? He peered at the last biography. The most expensive slave with the most skills. A minimum bid price of 1400 denarii, he was from Greece, described as

Medicus. Freddy knew from history lessons at school that many Greek doctors had been slaves, but this brought it home.

The jowly slaver clapped. 'These are worth waiting for.'

Two slaves were dragged out and tied to separate stands. The man and woman couldn't have been more different from the terrified child. They'd probably been listed after the boy to emphasise their proud demeanour — and hike up their price. Their placards said *Germania* with skills Freddy couldn't translate. The man had an un-Roman short beard and unfeasible muscles. The woman had long dark hair and strong eyebrows, and her stare was haughty and defiant. Unashamed of her nakedness.

'Barbarian soldier and wife,' shouted the slaver. 'Excellent for close protection. You'll never be robbed returning home from a dinner party.'

Freddy translated for Hugo, who nodded.

'Just the soldier,' yelled a youth. '800.'

The trader's face hardened. 'Only for sale as a pair, minimum 1000.'

'1050,' shouted an elderly man.

'The woman's a fighter too,' said the slaver. 'Ex gladiator.'

This seemed unlikely, but Freddy translated the claim.

'1080,' yelled a young woman.

Both slaves were grimacing, murder in their eyes, and Freddy frowned. 'We shouldn't buy them. They'll kill us.'

'The trader's making the slaves put on a show,' said Hugo. 'No one would bid if they posed a threat to their owners.'

'Very well.' Freddy raised his arm. '1200.' The trader brought down his hand.

CHAPTER 19

$\mathcal{I}$nside the Villa Fullia, Drusus hauled aside the bolt and swung open the front door.

Hugo came in with a huge bear of a man. The guy was as tall as Hugo, but his shoulders and legs bulged with muscles under a flimsy tunic. Behind them was Freddy with a dark-haired woman who looked around with wild eyes.

Drusus bolted the door and as they all emerged into the pool room, Sophie shook her head. 'What happened to the "one bodyguard" plan?'

'The couple were a job lot,' said Freddy.

Jack barked and Charlotte stared, curious. Drusus and Melissa cut the ropes binding the slaves' wrists, and Sophie gestured to the newcomers to sit down.

The huge guy obeyed but the woman hesitated, finally choosing a seat as far from him as possible. Unlikely they were a couple. Her long hair reached her waist and there was a scar on her knee that slashed down to her ankle.

'Melissa, can you make tea for everyone please?' said Sophie. Melissa had rustled up tea at breakfast time with no bother but appeared surprised. That seemed to be her permanent expression.

Drusus brought in more chairs from the courtyard.

'How did you persuade Mr Muscles to play nice once you'd bought him?' whispered Sophie to Hugo. Even with his hands tied, the slave could easily have got away.

'He came quietly,' said Hugo. 'I'm guessing escaped slaves get horribly punished and it's not worth the risk.'

Drusus hurried into the kitchen to assist Melissa and there was an uncomfortable silence. Hugo and Freddy shifted in their chairs and Sophie frowned. What did you say to people you'd just bought in a market?

Melissa handed Mr Muscles a glass of tea and backed off as if he had an infectious disease. The dark-haired woman had calmed down. She accepted her tea and sipped, unfazed by the unfamiliar drink.

Freddy cleared his throat. 'We only require that you protect us outside the villa.' This was the tone he used with the junior servants in Shorten.

The woman didn't respond. Mr Muscles said a word that wasn't Latin.

This needed a slow lead-in, not orders. 'Please tell us how you came to be slaves,' said Sophie. Her words were changed by the cylinder into a language that wasn't Latin, and they felt strange on her tongue.

Mr Muscles looked up. 'Captured in battle.' His speech was deep and guttural. 'It's the Roman way.'

'He's not speaking Latin,' said Hugo.

'He's German.' Freddy folded his arms. 'Treating slaves decently is *our* way.'

'What's your name?' asked Sophie.

'Tarchon.'

'I'm Hortensia.' Sophie turned to the woman. 'Can I ask your name?'

'Aelia.' The word spoken in Latin was smooth and lyrical.

'We should obviously treat them well,' said Hugo, 'but not so well that it draws attention to us.' Neither the old nor the new slaves could understand his words in English.

Sophie decided to treat this like a job interview. 'Aelia, can you tell us something about yourself?'

Aelia raised her chin. 'I'm not a slave. I'm a Roman citizen.'

'I don't understand,' said Freddy.

'I fought in the arena for my freedom. After that, I trained other women to gain theirs.'

Sophie nodded politely, but she'd misunderstood. Female gladiators? She repeated what Aelia had said to Hugo.

'At home, women definitely fought as novelty acts,' said Hugo, 'and there's some evidence they fought for real.'

'Barbaric,' said Freddy.

'Why is women killing for entertainment worse than men doing it?' said Sophie.

'I don't know,' said Freddy. 'It just is.'

Aelia was following their conversation, seemed surprised.

'Please tell us more,' said Sophie.

'Three weeks ago, on my way home from the baths, I was kidnapped by a street gang and sold again into slavery.' Aelia paused. 'I shall be avenged.'

The set of her jaw suggested she meant it. Sophie translated.

'We can't keep her,' said Hugo. 'Her manumission paper will be in the House of Freedom.'

'What's that?' said Sophie.

'Proof that a slave has been freed,' said Hugo.

Sophie repeated this to Aelia.

'My lover's ex-mistress wanted him back, so she paid a gang leader to kill me. If I return to the gladiator school, he'll finish the job.'

Sophie stared at her. Aelia's matter-of-fact tone made her account sound horribly plausible. Was contract killing common here?

Freddy addressed Tarchon. 'If you protect us until after Janus' festival and then guard Aelia, we'll free you.'

For the first time, Tarchon made eye contact. 'A fair bargain.' He drank his tea. 'I understood some of Aelia's story.'

Melissa shot a shy glance at Sophie. 'I can teach Tarchon Latin. I speak his tongue.'

'Do you?' said Sophie. She'd assumed girls in brothels were uneducated. What did she know?

Melissa gestured for Tarchon to follow her, and they walked out to the courtyard. Aelia went too, and Drusus collected up the tea glasses.

'Melissa's decided Tarchon won't bite,' said Hugo. 'Quick turnaround.'

Sophie summarised the final bit of the conversation and Hugo sighed.

'I'll work harder on my Latin,' he said. 'It's not fun needing constant translations.'

Sophie drummed her fingers on the arm of her chair. 'We should free Melissa and Drusus.'

'Whoever owns this villa owns them, and they can only be freed by their owner,' said Freddy. 'But...'

'But what?' Sophie sat up straighter.

Freddy clasped his hands under his chin. 'We could make an offer for Drusus and Melissa through the estate agent.'

'Not exactly an abolition campaign,' said Sophie. 'Yet better than nothing.'

'And with the promise of freedom,' said Hugo, 'they'll stay loyal.'

Sophie gave him a cynical look.

'Madam, do you mean it?' Drusus was collecting the last glasses.

'Sorry,' said Sophie, 'mean what?'

'You intend to free me and Melissa?'

'Yes.' Sophie smiled at him.

'Can I ask why?' said Drusus.

'Because we can,' said Freddy.

Drusus covered his mouth to cough. Intense and harsh, the cough shuddered through him. 'Excuse me.' He rushed off to the kitchen, presumably to fetch a drink of water.

Sophie stared after him, concerned.

'We should have stayed at the market till the end,' said Freddy. 'Bought the doctor.'

They ate lunch late and it was mid-afternoon when Drusus served up the meal in the villa's airy dining room. Despite his skimpy tunic, he displayed the same air of gravitas as the butler did in Shorten Manor: Freddy's childhood home and where Bella was.

Freddy squeezed Sophie's hand. 'We'll be with her again,' he said.

'How did you know I was thinking about Bella?' said Sophie.

'Your expression,' said Freddy. 'Half sad, half determined.'

'You have the same expression when you're thinking about Clarissa,' said Sophie.

Freddy bit his lip.

'I'm looking forward to lunch.' Hugo was trying to distract them.

Sophie dragged herself into the here and now. Well, to 95 AD. The dining room had no table. Chairs were arranged around a low, three-legged bench, with smaller benches at the side. Melissa had laid out the plates and bowls she'd washed up after breakfast. All the crockery was a dark, glazed orange. The plates were plain, while the bowls had outlines of leaves, animals, or abstract patterns.

The meal was goat stew and flat bread, with figs from the courtyard tree for dessert. Sophie fed the dogs stew, and ate the bread and figs.

Melissa and Drusus had been clearly uncomfortable eating breakfast with their owners, so Freddy had suggested the slaves eat their meals in the courtyard. After initial confusion — they'd expected to eat in the kitchen — Melissa and Drusus adjourned outside with the new slaves.

After lunch, out in the courtyard, Melissa patched her tunic, still wearing it.

Presumably, she only had one. 'We'll buy you more clothes,' said Sophie.

Melissa kept her eyes cast down. 'Thank you, Madam.'

'And clothes for Drusus,' said Sophie.

Drusus acknowledged her words with a brief nod. 'You might consider acquiring uniforms and weapons for Tarchon and Aelia, to deter thieves and fraudsters.'

'Absolutely,' said Freddy.

Drusus and Melissa left to go shopping. When they returned, they were sweaty and dusty and laden down with purchases. They disappeared into the kitchen to wash.

'When they've completed their ablutions, I'll freshen up,' said Aelia.

'There's not enough space in there to swing a cat,' said Sophie.

Aelia frowned. 'Swing a cat?'

'It's just an expression,' said Sophie. 'You should use the fountain.'

Aelia strode off to the courtyard and splashed her face

and legs with water. After that, she stripped off and washed her whole body.

'She doesn't seem at all embarrassed,' said Sophie to Hugo in the pool room. She would have been mortified if she'd been naked in front of strangers.

Hugo dragged his gaze from the courtyard. 'She's nothing to be embarrassed about.'

Sophie pretended to punch him on the arm. Freddy turned away from the courtyard, his cheeks pink.

'Seriously though, her lack of modesty probably helped her cope with the slave market,' said Hugo.

He hadn't shared how slaves were sold and Sophie didn't want to know.

After Tarchon cleaned himself up, he and Aelia put on their new gear. Tarchon looked a bit like a watchman, except his armour was more expensive, his cloak was of finer cloth, and his belt held four knives. His aura of menace was further enhanced by his beard.

'Whoever Janus has sent, they'll be no match for Tarchon,' said Freddy.

The knives were terrifyingly sharp, and Sophie winced, imagining Tarchon wielding them. 'I thought it was illegal for slaves or any private citizen to carry weapons within the city?'

'Evidently not,' said Hugo. 'That's different from our ancient Rome.'

Aelia wore a polished breast plate over a short linen tunic. Metal encased her upper arms, and she was also sporting an alarming knife collection on her belt. Like the statue of the female Janus, the body armour was contoured to show off Aelia's shapely figure. Only some of her hair was tied off her face, most of it tumbling attractively over her shoulders.

More desirable than deadly.

CHAPTER 20

The estate agents in the Forum were surprised to see them.

Tarchon and Aelia remained in the precinct, flanking the shop entrance. They cut quite a dash in their uniforms.

Sophie was wearing too many layers of clothing: a tunic, a dress and over that, a pink shawl called a palla. The ankle-length garment was secured at the shoulder by a brooch. Melissa had turned out to be the Roman equivalent of a lady's maid, and had insisted that, as a respectable married woman, Sophie couldn't go out without covering her hair. But despite the brooch, the silk material was impractical, threatening to fall off at any moment. Sophie hitched it up, glad they'd left the dogs in the villa, enjoying the fountain and the shade.

'Isn't the villa satisfactory?' said the guy behind the counter.

'Perfectly,' said Freddy. 'We'd like to buy the slaves.'

The female estate agent opened a thin tablet. Her hair was tied up by a similar woollen band to Sophie's, but her head wasn't covered. Hugo thought the full-on shawl was a 'look how rich I am' thing.

'From your experience,' said Freddy, 'what would be a sensible price?'

The woman read off her tablet. 'Ex-whore, plus labour slave with stoking cough … 500 denarii for both. We take five per cent commission.'

'Please proceed,' said Freddy.

'What's a stoking cough?' Sophie asked her.

'Too long working in the baths.'

Sophie nodded, though none the wiser.

'We'll submit the offer and send you word.' The woman made a note in the tablet with a bronze stylus.

Down in the Forum, they retraced their steps out of the square and towards the villa.

'Let's check out the gigantic building with the gold roof,' said Hugo. 'It could be Janus' third temple.'

'Isn't that a myth?' Freddy shielded his eyes to see it a few blocks away.

'I'm curious,' said Sophie.

They crossed the busy road with ease. One look at their bodyguards and people got out of the way. They rounded a corner, came into the Forum of Domitian, and Tarchon gave a low whistle.

The tallest building in the city was a temple on a colossal scale. The green and gold structure straddled two bridges that arched over a sunken river. At the top of the building, gilded tiles sparkled as if made of diamonds.

'The third temple,' said Freddy. 'Goodness.'

Sophie sniffed. The air was scented with sulphur and something nasty…

'I think the river's a sewage drain,' said Hugo.

The temple was the regular Roman design, with steps and pillars and a triangular frieze below the roof. Except it was ten storeys high.

They moved closer. Not far from the temple steps was a long, elevated altar and burning on it was a sheet of flame, undulating like the surface of a lake. Wafts of pungent sulphur masked the smell from the drain.

They joined a snaking queue into the temple, Tarchon in front of them and Aelia behind. Excited tourists clutched city guides on red-framed tablets and locals, mostly families, chatted in low voices, their toddlers gazing up at the temple. Freddy's gaze flicked from the children to Sophie, and she squeezed his hand. Their baby, so far away, was an aching void inside her, a horrible, hollow yearning. She had no doubt it was the same for him.

Eventually, they reached the majestic columns and the shadowed space before the entrance. As with the crossroads temple, there was also a locked door, with a narrow, rectangular gap.

Could this be another builders' illusion? As Sophie and Freddy went through the main door, they touched the door-jamb with their fingertips. Despite half expecting it, Sophie gasped. The queue was shuffling around a twenty-foot plank, propped up on a stand. Like in the temple in the Forum, this interior was pristine white except for a wrap-around window, and the reveal of the temple's true nature hadn't interrupted the tourists' murmuring or the familiar incense-smell of pine and citrus.

What was different were the creepy stones. Circling the edge of the room in even intervals, they were grey, twelve feet tall, and half a foot wide. Identical and vaguely human-shaped, their surfaces were smooth and blank.

Freddy was gripping her arm, so tightly it hurt. And Hugo needed to see this. She said his name.

Hugo registered the stones and swallowed. 'The view's different too.'

In the Forum temple, the window on all sides had showed the area surrounding it, as you'd expect. This band of glass, though, was a video feed, an aerial view of Rome, not from the top floor of the temple but far higher up, from a satellite. The defensive wall, robust and impressive, was a protective arm, encircling the city and the Tiber was blue and misleadingly clean. Barges and smaller boats were tiny toys. On the western bank, there were only a few buildings, but the other side had docks with warehouses and cranes, and further to the east there were theatres and the Colosseum. There were tenement blocks and town houses, and parks with trees and lakes, and narrow, haphazard streets crammed in between. The city's inhabitants were ants scurrying across the squares and along roads, and tiny chariots were speeding on a racetrack.

'I wish we had our phones,' said Hugo, 'so we could capture this forever.'

Sophie watched it, trying to fix the view in her memory, but without warning, the panic she'd experienced in the Forum temple was back. Her brain was trying to tell her something, but what? She focused on breathing slowly. In, out.

The view disappeared, replaced by a solid green wall: the illusion of the temple. Feeling calmer, Sophie tilted her head to see the make-believe attic. Predictable pictures of food and the yellow flower but too distant to show any detail. The temple walls were green up to two storeys. Above that, they were gold.

Freddy touched the wall, and the view and the builders' temple returned. Must be on a timer.

They watched the panorama until it reverted to being a wall, and turned around, once again in the impressive illusion of a temple.

The plank of wood was now an elderly Janus in a grey traveller's cloak. His glowing statue had four faces: two male and two female. One of the male faces was fashioned to reflect African heritage, with high cheekbones and dark skin. The others were Caucasian. Janus' right hand rested on the head of his walking staff, the other offered up an over-sized key like a gift.

The creepy blank stones were all marble figures, some wearing heavy, green robes. Others were housewives, shopkeepers, artisans, and soldiers, looking towards Janus with awed expressions.

At the rear of the temple, people waited in line to give offerings, supervised by a handsome man with black skin and dyed blond hair. Donated plaques and statuettes were displayed on a long counter, on an emerald cloth.

'We should search the genuine building,' said Sophie. 'Maybe there's a room where the research team store equipment, including the walking staff?' She addressed Tarchon and Aelia. 'We're looking for an artefact. If we go through an invisible door, don't be alarmed. It's part of the mystery of Janus.'

Aelia and Tarchon looked sceptical but accompanied them.

Sophie patted a statue of a woman in a green robe. She turned to stone as the real building appeared.

'Perhaps there's a cellar?' In response to Freddy's question, the outline of a wide door appeared at the rear of the room, just after the line of stones.

Hugo gave a low whistle.

They hurried over to it and Sophie pulled on a horizontal

steel handle. The door opened easily, swinging into the temple.

Tarchon and Aelia jumped back as if they'd been burned by fire. Sophie hadn't said their names, but they could see the door. The builders' illusion didn't cover it.

'Witchcraft!' said Tarchon in German.

'No witchcraft or witches,' said Sophie. 'Just a cellar.'

'The doorway is blocked by the temple wall,' whispered Aelia to Tarchon, who nodded.

'Aelia, Tarchon,' said Freddy.

The slaves saw the cellar and gawped.

'Stay here,' said Sophie. 'We won't be long.'

White steps without a rail descended sharply for ten feet into a hall. The space was empty, harshly lit, and cooled by silent air-conditioning. The aroma of incense was absent, the air sterile.

'Why build a basement with temperature control, but not store anything?' Hugo walked forward. 'Ow!'

'Are you okay?' said Sophie.

'I've stubbed my toe.' Hugo felt around in front of his legs. 'A metal box.' He straightened. 'There's an extra barrier, preventing us from seeing it.'

'Or opening it.' Sophie walked cautiously forward and met a much bigger object.

CHAPTER 21

In the cellar of Janus' temple, it took Sophie ten minutes to explore all of the huge invisible object with her fingertips. 'It's some sort of stone, and on one side, there's carved letters—'

Shouting in Latin and German came from the doorway to the temple, and someone screamed.

Aelia rolled down the cellar stairs, holding her arms tight around her body, hitting every step until she reached the bottom.

At the top of the stairs, a man in a toga walked through the doorway. 'Goodbye.' He stepped back and the cellar door shut with a thud behind him.

Hugo paled. 'That was H.G. Wells.'

Was it? The guy had been young, in his twenties, and clean-shaven. The outline of the door was still there. Sophie ran up the stairs, turned the handle and pushed as hard as she could. The door didn't move. Which made no sense. There'd been no keyhole, no key on the temple side. And definitely no bolt.

'Open the door,' said Sophie, with authority, hoping the

cellar had a voice-activated mechanism for trigging an emergency exit. Nothing happened.

Hugo and Freddy ran at it together, but it still wouldn't budge.

Panic rose in Sophie's throat, and she forced herself to try and think. No use. Her brain had frozen.

'Sons of dogs.' Aelia struggled to sit up and rubbed her shoulder. 'They rushed us out of nowhere. I killed one, Tarchon killed more, but there were too many.'

'Too many?' asked Sophie. She'd only seen Wells.

'They were hired muscle,' said Aelia. 'Fought like hell. Tarchon's dead.' Her eyes flicked across the cellar. 'Does anyone know we're here?'

Freddy sat down heavily on the stairs. 'No.'

'The big stone's too heavy to use as a battering ram,' said Sophie. 'Even all of us couldn't pick it up.'

'The metal storage box,' said Hugo.

They carried it together and struggled up the stairs with the invisible load. Balancing it on the top step to rest for a moment, they then lifted the box and repeatedly bashed it against the door. They couldn't make the slightest scratch. The door was made of something that couldn't be damaged, and it wouldn't budge.

'Something very heavy is blocking it from the other side,' said Hugo.

Cold horror twisted Sophie's stomach and her breathing sped up. Of all the ways she'd imagined a traveller killing them, trapping them under a temple hadn't figured. And H. G. Wells? He was an author, not an assassin. Rational thought dissolved, drowned by despair. 'Help!' she screamed as loud as she could. 'Help!'

Silence.

Freddy kicked the invisible box down the stairs, and it thumped, its contents cracking and rattling.

No sound in response came from the temple above them.

Hugo met Sophie's eyes. 'The cellar must be sound-proofed. The builders wouldn't have wanted work down here to disturb the sacred space upstairs.'

Sophie hurried down the stairs and found the box. 'Still sealed shut.'

'They would have installed a backup system for opening the door,' said Freddy. 'We've just got to find it.'

Sophie looked wildly around. 'There might be a lever, a fuse cupboard, or a sign that can help us.'

But there was nothing.

'We should feel the walls,' said Hugo.

They systematically searched, sweeping with their palms for hidden objects. There were no levers or sockets or raised surfaces of any kind.

Finally, they all sat on the floor. The despair inside Sophie had turned into helplessness, a debilitating ache. 'Does anything survive of the third temple into the 21st century?' She had to ask, though she knew the answer.

Hugo put his head in his hands. 'Not even an offering. The huge stone with the carved letters could be the black stone, moved here for safe keeping with other relics. If it is, in a few centuries, when the builders outlaw interaction with the locals, they'll bury it under the Forum.' He let out a desolate breath.' Then, they'll reverse however they built this temple. Reduce the cellar, and us, to atoms.'

Freddy's face contorted. 'I can't bear it. After *everything*.'

Silent tears were running down Aelia's cheeks.

'I'm really sorry we involved you,' said Sophie.

'There are worse deaths.'

Sophie hugged Hugo. 'Your instinct was right. We shouldn't have come to Rome.'

Hugo stroked her hair. 'Your stubbornness is part of your charm.'

Sophie lost it and cried into his chest. Those panic attacks had been a warning to stay away from the builders' temples. A psychic gift, bestowed by this universe? Whatever it had been, she should have listened.

Her stubbornness had killed them all.

~

They'd left their analogue wrist watches in modern London and, with no windows in the cellar, they couldn't know if it was night or day. Rationing would just prolong the inevitable, so they shared the water from their flasks with Aelia. And they talked freely. She wouldn't live to share their secrets.

Sitting against a wall, Freddy drew up his knees. 'H. G. Wells hired the thugs by Juno's Arch.'

From what Sophie had read, Wells was a gentle soul. 'Why did Janus send him?' Her voice echoed in the cellar.

'I'm guessing that wasn't our Wells or the Wells from the Shorten universe,' said Hugo. 'Janus will have chosen the version most likely to kill us.' Parallel universes often contained the same people.

'Janus planted thoughts in my mind, made me forget I wanted to return to Bella and Clarissa,' said Freddy. 'That wore off after I left the ship. Janus can't make Wells commit crimes.'

Hugo shifted his sitting position on the hard floor, trying to get more comfortable. 'Janus doesn't need to directly force him to do anything. Wells wants to visit more parallel worlds, find inspiration for successful novels that will bring him unimaginable wealth and fame.'

'And for such a prize, that version of him was prepared to do Janus' bidding,' said Sophie, 'including murder.'

'When you speak of Janus,' said Aelia, 'do you mean the god? That is who hunts you?'

'He sent the man who trapped us here,' said Freddy, his voice flat.

Aelia listened as they explained about the builders, about the walking staff, and about Bella. Maybe she believed them. She looked at her sandals. 'Character is destiny.'

Sophie glanced at her, impressed. 'You've studied philosophy.'

Aelia shook her head. 'Everyone knows the wisdom of Heraclitus.'

Sophie didn't.

'An ancient Greek philosopher,' said Hugo. 'I know the name but nothing else.'

'I studied him in school,' said Freddy. 'But words can't help us. Only a miracle could do that.'

Believing in miracles wouldn't change their fate. *Character is destiny.* Sophie's character had led her to this moment, yet not completely. 'Sometimes bad stuff happens, however determined or clever you are.'

'I underestimated Calpurnia,' said Aelia, her tone bitter.

'The woman who betrayed you?' said Freddy.

'Yes.' Aelia hugged her knees. 'She concealed her jealousy well, but I should have been wary. With the Lanista's attention comes money and influence, and corruption.'

'Who's the Lanista?' said Sophie.

'The manager of the gladiator school, Octavius.' Aelia's eyes hardened. 'Soon after I arrived, he took a liking to me, then got serious, talked about divorcing Julia, his wife. Calpurnia was furious.'

'Did you have feelings for him?' said Freddy.

'Enough. Marriage would have brought security, though I'd have been saddled with his brats.'

'Wouldn't his wife have got custody of the children?' said Sophie.

'With divorce, wives lose their children.'

Hugo frowned, frustrated he couldn't understand, and Sophie summarised.

'Calpurnia warned me off, saying I'd regret it, and I laughed at her. She wouldn't last a minute in a fight, works in the office.' Aelia rocked to and fro. 'I told Octavius I'd marry him, and the next day a gang dragged me into an alley, chained me up, and shoved me inside a sack. I thought they meant to drown me in the Tiber. Turned out, that's what Calpurnia had paid them to do, but I gave the leader what he wanted, and he dumped me in the slave market. I was locked up for weeks until Tarchon arrived, and they paired us up for a better price.' Aelia snorted. 'Female bodyguards are less valuable than men.'

'Where did she hire a gang from?' Freddy asked her.

'I don't know what district they control. Calpurnia's brother's one of them.'

Street gangs like in London or New York. 'Surely Octavius and the other staff must have gone looking for you?' said Sophie.

Aelia wiped her eyes. 'I hope they did, but people disappear all the time. Never seen again.'

Three days after their drinking water ran out, Sophie said her goodbyes. She lay between Freddy and Hugo, her head on Hugo's chest. The girl's warning in the Forum would soon come to pass. It hurt to speak or to swallow or move. Dehydration had taken its toll.

But Sophie was calm. 'Goodbye Bella,' she whispered, and despite knowing it was pointless, she willed her daughter to have a happy life. Her mind moved to Charlotte. When enough time had passed that she knew they were lost, she'd return home with Jack, seek out Elliot and Lorna. Be safe and loved…

She was half-dreaming, half-hallucinating. A Roman coin tumbled in the air in slow motion and dropped onto a polished mahogany table. The coin quivered and clanged as it fell. Both sides showed two youthful faces, looking in opposite directions.

The side facing up shimmered into different faces: Sophie's late parents. She wanted to be with them.

Not long now.

CHAPTER 22

'In broad daylight, and in a temple... The gangs are getting worse.'

Tarchon understood more Latin than he could speak, but the words didn't make sense.

'Oi! More water here.' Something clanked, followed by a swishing noise.

Tarchon's eyes were stuck shut, sticky with blood. Pain overcame him and he struggled to remember his training. Identify the worst injury. Concentrate. Hip. The burning stabbing there exploded, and he gasped.

'Hey, this one's alive.'

Cold water drenched his face, and Tarchon gasped again, this time in shock. But he could open his eyes. Looking down at him were two bucket men, the Roman firefighters.

Cloying incense invaded Tarchon's throat and he had a coughing fit. When he'd recovered himself, the watchmen helped him sit up. He screamed as his hip yanked, but he succeeded in standing, nearly fainting with the effort.

'Come on, mate.'

The watchmen guided him out of the temple, and he somehow made it down the steps without falling. They dragged him past the foul-smelling altar, across the crowded square, the people and sounds around him fading.

A souvenir shop … customers … a matron behind the counter speaking fast, gesticulating.

He was lying on his back. The world was almost black and Tarchon steadied his breathing. Stay conscious. Keep with the light.

Something hot and terrible burned into his hip, and he welcomed the dark.

'Hello, gorgeous. How are you feeling?'

The matron wiped Tarchon's brow with a cloth. He sat up, his hand going to his hip. Bandaged and the wound closed. It ached and was itchy. It was healing. 'You have skill,' he managed in Latin.

'My owner was a freed doctor. I watched and I learned. I'm Silvina.'

'Thank you, Silvina.' He was in a storeroom lined with statuettes, and friezes stacked neatly on a table. Dust mites danced in the stuffy air and an emerald curtain fluttered in a doorway. Beyond it, people were talking. The chink of coin. 'Where am I?'

'Not far from Janus' tall temple.' She put a cup to his lips. 'Drink.'

The water was tepid but wonderful. 'What did you burn me with?'

'Burn you?'

He gestured at his injury.

Silvina limped across the storeroom using a crooked

walking stick. She took down a dark bottle from a shelf and removed the stopper. 'Stops infection. Very rare, from far away in the north.'

Tarchon sniffed it and gagged with the stench. He'd tasted this once. Never again. It sent men mad.

'I used this too.' Silvina prised off a lid from a small tin on the table, revealing a thick white paste. 'Your friend delivered it.'

'Aelia?'

'I don't know her name. Had a sharp face.'

Didn't sound like Aelia. Tarchon closed his eyes. His owners must be dead, and so was his chance of freedom.

How had those men taken him by surprise? They hadn't entered the temple through the entrance or the exit. He'd known he was in trouble when the first man had produced a gladius, the two-edged sword used by the legions. Superior to any dagger you could openly buy.

The patrician who'd hired the thugs had spoken the same hissing language as his late owners. He'd failed in his duty to protect them. They'd been decent.

A fresh pang of regret. This time, for their loss.

Three days later, Tarchon left Silvina's care and queued to enter the tall temple of Janus. If his wound wasn't punched or kicked, he'd recover. The fire water and the mysterious paste had done its job.

He'd given Silvina his red cloak as payment. He wouldn't part with his armour. Whatever agenda the hissing foreigner was pursuing, it might include finishing off survivors. But Mannus had told him to return to the temple cellar and Tarchon knew better than to ignore his god.

To the right of the temple entrance, was the door with the gap above the keyhole. That could lead to a self-contained room, or it might be a way into the main building? If the latter, that would explain how the thugs had surprised him. He pushed at the door, but it was locked.

Tarchon walked through the regular entrance and asked the stout attendant in hesitant Latin about the locked door.

'You may see but not touch.' The attendant strode towards a statue of a soldier. Behind it was a half-height door painted the same green as the wall and signed in gilt letters, *Privatus*. The attendant selected a key from his belt, unlocked the door, and opened it with a flourish.

Tarchon stooped to investigate. A gloomy room with an emerald and gold altar and unlit candles. He straightened.

'A special place of worship.' The attendant locked the door and smirked. 'Requires at least 300 denarii.'

This attendant hadn't been here three days ago. The thugs must have bribed another wretch to keep the door unlocked.

Tarchon's thoughts turned to Mannus' command and the cellar. Might his owners be down there? Was it possible they were still alive? He strode past Janus' statue.

Before, the cellar door had opened at the rear of the temple, after the line of statues, but now there was an extra statue, right where the door had been. Compared to the majestic perfection of the others, this new one came up short. The paint on the blacksmith had been bodged, the brown of the undershirt leaking over onto the paler arm, and the legs lacked the subtle outline of muscle and bone.

The back of the statue had a short metal truss wedged against the wall, keeping the statue in position. Common-place for cheap effigies to stop them falling. Unnecessary with marble statues. Tarchon glanced to his left. No supports on the others.

The attendant was beside him. 'This is a recent donation. An anonymous benefactor.'

'When was it given?' asked Tarchon.

'I came on duty the day after the thieves desecrated the temple. It was there by then.'

It required a fair bit of effort to erect a statue. Tarchon rubbed his beard.

A tourist called to the attendant for advice on an offering and the man scurried away. Tarchon gripped the support. It was jammed in place against the statue. He managed with a huge effort to inch the statue forward. As he did, the support clanged onto the floor. The marble statue was unaffected and didn't move.

Tarchon brushed his hand across the wall and found the outline of the door. He felt for a handle and pulled the door open, but only saw the green wall.

Was he going insane? No, there'd been steps descending into a cellar. He was sure—

'Tarchon.' A woman's voice, so cracked and faint, he hardly heard it.

He could see the white steps! He made his way down them, blinking in the bright light. The cellar was lit up as if by the sun. By the great Mannus! The bodies of his owners and Aelia were huddled together. What evil was this?

His mistress stirred. 'Tarchon.' Another faint croak.

She was alive, though barely. He ran forward, scooped her into his arms, and ran with her up the stairs.

'Water,' she rasped. 'The others need water.'

Tarchon laid her gently on the floor. The attendant scooted towards them, his fat lips pursed as if this woman were a stray dog.

'Fetch water for this lady, now!' said Tarchon, hoping his Latin was clear. 'Go get help!' He pointed at the cellar.

The attendant shook his head and rushed off. The man couldn't see the cellar. Tarchon frowned. So why could he?

No matter. Save them. He scrambled down the cellar stairs, gathered up Aelia, and dashed back up, two treads at a time.

The men were heavier. He dragged them.

CHAPTER 23

The litter swayed, a bouncing, jarring rhythm. It jerked to a stop, then set off again.

In the stifling heat, Sophie drifted in and out of consciousness. She remembered — or thought she remembered — Tarchon rescuing her, his breastplate banging against her as he ran up the cellar stairs.

Sophie scrunched the edge of a sheet she was lying on, the material soft inside her palm. Beyond thin orange curtains, shapes ebbed and flowed. People and animals and carts. A hawker shouted and smells drifted into the litter: spice, cooking meat, flowery perfume.

If she was dead, she wouldn't still be here in ancient Rome, would she?

Relief... But the next moment that was less important than the pain in her stomach and her throat. She curled up in the litter, tried to think about Bella, but the memory of Hugo and Freddy slumped on that hard, white floor, too weak to move, was more sharp, more real.

The litter stopped, bumped on the ground, and a curtain

was pulled aside. Sophie stared at Tarchon. Okay, this was real.

He stepped forward to carry her, but she shook her head. 'Thank you,' she whispered. 'But I can walk.'

She stood on the pavement on shaky legs. Other litters were waiting in a line. Three of them. She swayed and Tarchon steadied her. Hugo and Freddy must be alive, and Aelia. Joy flooded through her.

Melissa guided Sophie into the villa and the bedroom. Sophie lay on the familiar bed. Charlotte came in and rested her muzzle on her mistress' legs. Jack was in the hall, barking.

'I'm okay,' said Sophie to Charlotte. 'I'll tell you all about it later.'

'We were worried,' said Melissa, presuming Sophie had been speaking to her.

'I just need water,' said Sophie. 'And bread.'

As Melissa hurried off, Hugo staggered in and fell onto the bed.

Two days after their escape from the third temple's cellar, everyone was in the villa's courtyard enjoying the shade, a breeze, and the cooling sound of the fountain. The slaves sipped hot spicy wine, Jack drank water, and Sophie, Hugo, and Freddy enjoyed the tea they'd brought from home. Charlotte lapped up the Earl Grey blend and though the slaves surely thought it odd, they didn't comment.

'Tarchon, you did well using the food money to pay the litter company,' said Freddy.

'We believed you'd been killed,' said Sophie.

'My god, Mannus, sent a sharp-faced girl with a healing mixture.'

Sophie rubbed her temples. The girl from the Forum? But if she was monitoring Tarchon, aiding him, why hadn't she rescued them as soon as Wells blocked the door?

'The concealed cellar was truly a marvel,' said Tarchon.

'Built by a civilisation more advanced than Roman engineers,' said Freddy.

Aelia had shared their tale of the builders, Janus, and his walking staff. Who knew if the other slaves believed it?

Melissa had scratched Latin letters onto a tablet and Tarchon was copying them onto another. Charlotte sat beside them, watching his efforts.

'Your dog is clever,' said Melissa. 'I swear that sometimes she understands you.'

'She only understands the tone of my voice,' lied Sophie.

'Janus' assassin and his thugs lay in wait, concealed in a private shrine.' Tarchon rubbed his injured hip. 'Its entrance door outside had an odd gap over the keyhole.'

'Most temples have them,' said Melissa. 'So, when they're closed, you can leave offerings.'

'Your grasp of German is impressive,' Freddy said to her. Tarchon had spoken rapidly in his native tongue.

'My previous owner was a freed German slave. Sadistic son of a…' Melissa gave Tarchon an embarrassed glance. 'When you first got here, I assumed you'd be like him.'

'And yet you still taught me Latin?' said Tarchon. 'You have a generous soul.'

Melissa flushed.

'Did your owner really give you the bronze coin container?' Sophie sipped her tea.

'No,' said Melissa. 'His most prized possession, so I stole it. A revenge of sorts.'

'Understandable,' said Hugo, in English. 'Who knows what she suffered in the brothel?'

'Your secret's safe with us,' said Sophie.

The breeze picked up, blew a pale rag across the court-yard, and Melissa jumped to her feet and retrieved it. 'Apologies. I thought I'd tidied the bedding away.'

Drusus looked sheepish. So did Aelia and Tarchon.

Bedding?

'I think they've been sleeping out here because the kitchen's so small.' Hugo's knowledge of spoken Latin was improving.

This culture would take a lifetime to understand. 'Everyone, please choose an unused bedroom,' said Sophie. 'For yourself, or to share, if you'd rather.'

Incredulity flashed over Aelia's face and Drusus studied his sandals, but all four slaves trooped into the house.

'I'm surprised more slaves don't rebel,' said Sophie.

'Compared to those who work in the mines or on farms, many house slaves have relatively decent lives,' said Hugo.

'And a realistic prospect of freedom,' said Freddy. 'Compassionate owners put aside savings to help their slaves once they're freed.'

'I can't get my head around it.' Sophie sighed, and half lying on her mistress' lap, Charlotte fidgeted, restless. 'Our plan to act out of character didn't work.' Understatement. 'Wells knew the date and the time we'd visit the third temple.'

Hugo nodded. 'Janus probably gave him our complete itinerary while we're here.'

'Wells will assume we're dead,' said Sophie. 'He'll have gone back to Janus, might be home in the 19th century by now.'

Hugo bit his lip. 'This isn't over. Janus will know we've survived, so Wells will too.'

'Janus might not,' said Freddy. 'With an infinite number of parallel universes similar to this one, he may have to make an educated guess as to which one this is, giving us wriggle room.'

Sophie frowned. 'Infinite numbers of universes?'

'In the mathematical sense,' said Freddy. 'A state of endlessness or having no time, space, or other quantity limits.'

Clear as mud. But Sophie smiled at him.

'At the moment, we're prey, and Wells is the hunter,' said Freddy. 'We need to turn that on its head. If we have wriggle room, continually changing what we would logically do may just defeat the odds.'

'What would a sensible person do?' said Hugo.

'Presume Wells is still here,' said Sophie, 'that he has the current address of the builders' base from Janus. Wells could be staying there?' She looked down at Charlotte. 'We should hunker down until the festival.' Charlotte blinked in agreement.

'What would a reckless, foolish person do?' said Freddy.

Sophie shot him a sardonic glance. 'Such a person would wander around Rome carrying a sign, saying, "I'm here. Attack me." But that would be crazy.'

'Dodging fate may be impossible,' said Hugo. 'Even if Janus knows only some of what we do in this universe, haven't we already made our choices?' He exhaled. 'As in Death's appointment in Samarra.'

Freddy made a face. 'That old tale.'

Sophie said, 'Quick summary?'

'A slave goes to the marketplace in Baghdad and meets Death there,' said Hugo. 'Terrified, he persuades his master to let him flee many miles away to Samarra. The next day, his master visits the marketplace, sees Death, and asks her why she frightened his slave.'

'She?' said Sophie.

'Not sure why Death is a she,' said Freddy.

'Anyway,' said Hugo, 'Death says, I didn't expect to see

him here in Baghdad. You see, I have an appointment with him tonight, in Samarra.'

Sophie's skin prickled with goosebumps. 'How can we know if we're acting out of character? We might be doing exactly what different versions of us have done … who knows how many times before?'

Tarchon and Aelia returned and sat on upright chairs in the shade. Tarchon had a board game from the study, and he opened it on the desk between them. Jack, asleep under the table, didn't stir. The hinged wooden tablet was criss-crossed with squares. Tarchon rolled an oblong die. It made a faint tap-tapping noise and landed half on the central square. Aelia frowned in concentration and rolled hers. The player who landed cleanly on the most squares won the game.

'It seems to me,' said Freddy, 'doing what we shouldn't … means we should leave the house. We have our guards.'

'Lure him out,' said Hugo.

'We'd be bait?' said Sophie. Charlotte lifted her head. 'Too risky. Even with Aelia and Tarchon, we'd be heavily outnumbered by Wells' thugs.'

Aelia looked up from the board game. 'Forgive me for interrupting, but at least five of his men are no more.'

'I killed three,' said Tarchon.

Which meant Aelia must have killed two. Sophie gulped, saw her with new eyes.

'You should take additional precautions.' Aelia took the die.

'Go on,' said Freddy.

'Men exaggerate their battle skills to gain employment with security agencies. The respectable agencies are expensive, but their people are vetted.'

'Were the thugs from an agency?' said Hugo, in careful Latin.

'The better sort.' Aelia rolled the die.

Tarchon lifted his hands in surrender and got stiffly to his feet. 'Hiring experienced agency guards on a permanent basis could expose you to a greater danger.'

'From what?' said Freddy.

'The Speculatores.'

'Gamblers?' said Sophie.

'The emperor's spies.' Tarchon shifted his weight from one foot to another, testing his sore hip. 'Domitian fears betrayal, as he should. Unexplained foreigners with coin and conspicuous muscle would attract attention, end up dead.'

'Aren't you … conspicuous muscle?' said Sophie.

Tarchon shrugged. 'Aelia's presence suggests that we're a fashionable escort for dinner party guests. Nothing more.' His eyes flicked to Aelia, a gesture of apology.

He received a resigned smile in return.

'Everyone's speaking very fast,' said Hugo to Sophie.

'I'll summarise in a bit.'

'What do you know about the emperor's spies?' Freddy asked Tarchon.

'After we were captured and brought to Rome, I was given a choice and so was my brother. To be sold as a slave or spy for the emperor. My brother made the wrong decision.'

'Why did you choose slavery?' said Sophie.

'I'd have chosen death rather than serve my tribe's enemy.' Tarchon hesitated. 'The senator my brother watched had his own spies and they murdered him.'

They'd faced challenges here, but nothing like that. From the bottom to the top of this city were layers of violence and cruelty—

'Attracting any attention of that kind would mean death or worse,' said Tarchon.

'Worse?' said Freddy.

'Torture with claws and pincers.' Tarchon's face turned hard. 'Better to mete out our own justice. We won't be taken by surprise again.'

Sophie relayed the gist of the conversation to Hugo, and something clicked in her mind. Freddy was right. To defeat Wells, they needed to abandon logic, make choices that were more unpredictable, verging on crazy. But at the same time, they could choose with care. 'We should go somewhere public, where he can't catch us by surprise.'

'The Colosseum,' said Freddy.

Sophie grimaced. 'Too gory.'

'What's the Colosseum?' said Aelia.

Sophie stared at her. Hadn't she fought there?

'At this date, it's called the Flavian Amphitheatre,' said Hugo.

Aelia recognised the name and nodded. 'A location that would favour your enemy. We'd be split up.'

'Why would we be split up?' said Sophie.

'Slaves and women are relegated to the highest stands,' said Aelia. 'Men have prized seats at the ringside, to smell the blood.'

Yuk.

Charlotte left Sophie's lap and pawed at Aelia's arm.

Aelia watched her, part-curious, part-annoyed. 'Domestic animals aren't allowed in the amphitheatre, in case they find a way through the nets into the arena.'

'I find myself fond of your dogs.' Tarchon sounded surprised.

'Dogs are the best,' said Sophie. 'Aelia, did you ever have a dog?'

'No, but I had a friend who loved her dog like a child. When he died, she was distraught, insisted on putting an obol in his mouth for Charon.'

'My cylinder's playing up,' said Sophie. 'Obol?'

'A low value coin,' said Freddy.

Sophie repeated the conversation for Hugo. 'I should know,' she said, 'but who is Charon?'

'A god and a ferryman,' said Hugo. 'He carries souls across the river Styx to the underworld. The coin placed in the mouth of the dead person pays for safe passage. Otherwise, their soul's condemned to wander the riverbank, haunting those they leave behind.'

'I remember.' The warm breeze rustled Sophie's hair, tugging a tendril free from the woollen band. 'It always struck me as rotten that the poor get a rough deal even after they've died.'

'What about the chariot racing?' Freddy's face was animated. 'Are spectators segregated there?'

'No,' said Aelia. 'Illegal gambling funds the Circus Maximus. Entry is free, though extra payment gets you better seats, regardless of whether you're a citizen, a slave or a woman.'

Hugo understood and seemed intrigued. 'I think that's different from our Rome.'

'We could go this afternoon?' said Freddy.

Aelia stood up. 'May I give an offering to the Lares for our safe return?'

The household shrine in the pool room.

'Can't do any harm,' said Sophie.

The bronze figures within the miniature shrine in the pool room were clad in short, girdled tunics, standing in a dancing pose. The taller character held a drinking horn aloft, the other clutched a shallow dish.

Melissa poured olive oil into a small, sunken square. Drusus had lit a taper from the brazier in the kitchen and he transferred the flickering fire to a woollen wick in the square.

In turn, they burned pieces of bread and when wine was added to the oil, the flame flared.

Jack watched, but Charlotte looked away. Distrustful of gods, even benevolent ones.

CHAPTER 24

Sophie heard spectators cheering themselves hoarse long before they reached the Circus Maximus. 'Have we missed the start?' she asked as they hurried down the road.

Aelia rested her fingers on the handle of one of her knives. 'The chariots race until dusk.'

They rounded a corner. The Circus Maximus was up ahead. It dwarfed the streets around it. The building that fronted the racetrack had countless arches on the exterior of every floor, resembling the Colosseum. But it was bigger, with a red-roofed tower built over the entrance.

Freddy paid for seats in the shade. 'Faction?' said the man in the entrance booth.

'Blue,' said Freddy.

'You sound very certain,' said Sophie.

Freddy shrugged. 'I like the colour.'

There was no delay for bag searches, and they walked into a wide, high corridor lined with shops. There were jewellery stores, launderettes, betting shops, and cafés, and places selling tunics in the six charioteer colours: blue, green, white, red, purple, and gold.

'I thought there were only four factions?' Sophie said to Hugo.

'The current emperor introduced the Purples and Golds. They'll be disbanded after his death.'

Hugo's capacity to remember detail never ceased to amaze her. She stopped by a store with commemorative cups and picked up a glass goblet. The front was adorned by a proudly prancing horse, holding a tree branch in its mouth.

The next shop sold good-quality brass figurines. Each had a distinctive face, presumably representing a real charioteer. Sophie peered at the paintwork, admiring the details, including creases in the tunic. 'What an incredible shopping mall.'

'It goes right around the Circus.' Aelia gestured at a doorway. 'The latrines are nice here too. The new aqueduct supplies running water.'

There was no gender picture over the doorway. 'Separate loos for men and women?' asked Sophie.

Aelia gave her a puzzled glance. 'No.'

They followed Aelia up a flight of stairs. When Sophie reached the top, she looked out at the huge stadium, her mouth slack with wonder. Three tiers of stands bordered the oval-shaped track, except for the far end where six bright banners hung from the roof of a warehouse. In a courtyard in front of it, horses, chariots, and men of the rival factions were preparing to race.

The arena was buzzing with energy, fed by the living, breathing beast that was the crowd. The air was thick with excited chatter, punctuated by the shouts of vendors hawking their wares: honey cakes, roasted nuts, and spiced wine. The scents mingled with an earthier smell of sweat.

'Wow,' said Hugo.

Tarchon took in the view, also seeing this for the first time, his new red cloak flapping in the breeze. In each stand, spectators wore tunics in their faction's colour, so from a distance, the stands resembled distinct, agitated flags.

'How many people can fit in here?' said Freddy.

'190,000,' said Aelia.

In the middle of the track, acting as a barrier, was a watercourse that was open in some places and bridged in others. Decorating the bridges were temples and statues of various deities. There were also fountains and cages.

Sophie pointed. 'What's the deal with the cages?'

'Shelters for the faction's support teams,' said Aelia, 'when they evacuate wounded charioteers.'

Hugo gestured across the stadium to a triple arch on its own tier. 'I'm guessing when he attends, that's where the emperor sits.'

Sophie shielded her eyes from the sun to better see it. So distant, she couldn't make out the decorations on the façade.

Their allocated place was halfway up the stands under an awning. Like all the ones shading spectators, it was a neutral orange colour. Tarchon settled himself on the long stone seat. Aelia sat at the other end. Seated in between with Hugo and Freddy, Sophie checked for Wells. No sign of him.

A woman in front of Sophie had a dog on her lap. A pang of guilt. She'd persuaded Charlotte to stay with Jack at the villa in case the worst happened. Charlotte would be safe, would find her way back to Juno, taking Jack with her. Luring out Wells was a high-stakes gamble. The worst might happen.

She pulled aside the shawl covering her hair and wiped her brow. The silk was thin but made her feel hotter. She hitched it up where it was falling off her shoulders.

A girl in a skimpy pale tunic — and no annoying shawl — strolled along the aisle between the seats, a horizontal tray secured with a strap about her neck. Sophie did a double take. The girl was selling burgers, though the patties of minced meat were nestled between slices of flat bread, not a seeded bun.

Freddy bought some and handed them out to everybody except Sophie.

'As good as a modern one,' said Hugo, between mouthfuls.

'What's in it apart from meat?' Sophie asked him.

'Pepper, a bit of wine and I think pine nuts … all bound together with the brown fishy sauce.'

Aelia and Tarchon were alert, watching nearby spectators, and reassured, Sophie turned towards the track. Waiting behind gates were six chariots, each attached to four restless horses. The charioteers wore white tunics with a broad stripe in the centre, depicting their faction. The white faction's stripe was outlined in grey, or it would have been invisible. The horses' reins were tied around the charioteer's waists, and each man carried a curved knife to cut himself free if he crashed. They were all wearing round, white helmets.

The crowd in Sophie's stand was chanting, 'Blue, blue.'

'This is awesome!' said Hugo, his eyes shining. 'What a spectacle!'

'There'll be shipwrecks,' said Aelia, her attention on the spectators.

'There aren't any ships,' said Freddy.

'Shipwreck's slang for crashes,' said Aelia.

A lad walked along the aisle and stopped near Aelia. 'Good odds on the Blues.' The slave had a tray of coins and papyrus strips.

Freddy leaned over. 'No, thank you. We haven't studied the odds.'

The lad shrugged and paused at the next row where there was keen interest.

'Spoilsport.' The corners of Hugo's lips lifted in a wry smile.

In the next row down, the woman with the dog was waving a frieze. It looked like the souvenir they'd bought in the Forum, vowing to defeat Janus, except the woman's frieze had an image of Neptune. The god was in the sea, astride a horse, and holding a trident.

The woman had probably cursed whatever faction was most likely to beat the Blues.

The chanting was growing louder. Adults hoisted children onto their shoulders. What would Bella have made of this spectacle? Taken it in her stride like these toddlers? Probably.

A trumpet blared, silencing the stands, and all eyes turned to the racetrack. Behind the wooden starting gates, each man stood by his chariot, taut with anticipation. The four horses in each team were pawing the ground and snorting, eager to be off.

But the gates remained closed, and a procession came out. Men in orange robes marched beside the central barrier and bowed to a statue. The image on it was the same as on the woman's frieze.

'Why do they pay their respects to Neptune?' said Freddy. 'And why is the god of the sea riding a horse?'

Aelia briefly glanced away from the spectators to the track. 'Neptunus Equester. Gives divine blessing for a safe and thrilling race.'

'So, he's the god of horse racing and the sea,' said Sophie. 'Is that why, when there are crashes, they're called shipwrecks?'

Aelia kept her eyes on the crowd. 'Perhaps.'

The procession left the track, and the spectators erupted in cheers and applause. They waved coloured ribbons, impatient for the race to begin. The charioteers mounted their two-wheeled chariots and gripped the reins already tied around their bodies.

Beside the starting line was a raised platform and standing on it was a man in a toga.

'Who is that?' Sophie pointed.

Aelia's eyes didn't move from the crowd. 'He's sponsored the race, gives the signal to start.'

The sponsor dropped a white handkerchief. The gates flew open with a crash and the horses leaped forward, their powerful legs pounding the dirt, kicking up clouds of dust. A deafening roar erupted from the spectators, a wave of sound that followed the racers as they hurtled along, jostling for position, chariot wheels separated by inches. As they thundered past, lumps of mud flew from the horses' hooves.

The spectators were stamping in unison, waving betting slips and yelling, their words lost in the din. The horses' mouths were foaming, but the charioteers were whipping them on. Sophie winced and looked away. An almighty bang made her look back. The reds chariot in second place had collided with a horse and was careering into the barrier in a tangle of metal and flesh. Chariots behind them swerved, but it was too late. Men and horses screamed.

The woman with the dog cried out and sobbed into a handkerchief. 'Celeritas,' she repeated.

Freddy grimaced at the pile-up, then glanced at the woman. 'Isn't she a Blues supporter? That chariot's not involved.'

'Celeritas is a famous horse,' said Aelia. 'He won't survive the crash.'

Sophie sat down, cutting off her view of the track, and tried not to vomit. She should have stayed in the villa.

CHAPTER 25

*L*ong minutes ticked by and despite the grisly crash
on the Circus Maximus track, the surviving chariots and horses kept racing. The spectators'
stamping became a base rhythm, keeping time with the
chanting, and in Sophie's stand, the shout of 'Blue' was
working up into a frenzy. Around her, children were chanting, as excited as the adults. She shifted in her seat. The
violence of the crash had been bad enough. Were children
also taken to the Colosseum to watch gruesome fights and
executions? Didn't bear thinking about. Her thoughts flipped
to Bella, and she closed her eyes.

Hugo put his hand on her shoulder. 'One lap to go—'

A different commotion broke out behind them. Spectators were shouting and standing on the seats, but they
weren't cheering. Some were screaming. They sounded terrified. Sophie jumped to her feet. More spectators yelled and
gesticulated. This wasn't happening in other stands. What
was going on?

Freddy stood on their seat and hauled Sophie up beside
him. 'They're saying there are snakes,' he said.

Hugo jumped up as well.

Snakes? How could there be snakes up here?

Aelia was slashing with two daggers at something on the floor. A snake?

'Run along the seat,' shouted Tarchon. 'Flee!'

Sophie hurried over to the other aisle away from Aelia, but when she jumped down, Tarchon grabbed her and threw her over his shoulder. He sprinted towards the bottom of the stand and Sophie clung to him, too shocked to protest. Hugo and Freddy were running too.

Tarchon dropped Sophie on her feet, drew two daggers from his belt, and sprinted back up the aisle.

Freddy and Hugo were by the barrier that fronted the stand. Sophie ran, holding her shawl so it didn't fall off, and reached them. Here, lower down, people's attention was on the remaining chariots still racing. Throughout the stadium, the crowd's roar reached a crescendo, a chaotic symphony of voices. The winner crossed the line, his chariot barely holding together, the horses frothing and exhausted, and the air filled with the sound of victory — cheers and the triumphant blare of trumpets.

But Hugo and Freddy were oblivious, their backs to the track, staring at something.

'What is it?' she gasped.

'Defend yourself!' yelled Freddy, waving his kitchen knife.

Sophie turned around and froze. A snake was slithering fast down the steps. Yellow, with dark lines, its triangular head was rearing up. She fumbled in her satchel.

The snake lunged. Hugo swung his knife at it and swung again. The head came off, the forked tongue hanging out, and its body twitched, still slithering. Sophie stifled a scream.

Hugo stared at his red blade and slowly put it away. Freddy returned his knife to his satchel.

Sophie exhaled, a slow, shuddering breath. The creature

must have been terrified by all the noise. How on earth did it get here unnoticed, hundreds of feet from the ground? She was unhurt… Fear gripped her. 'Were you bitten?'

Hugo shook his head. So did Freddy. She slid her knife into its sheath and dropped it into her satchel.

With the race over, spectators who hadn't noticed the snake were stretching their legs, chatting and smiling. Sophie climbed up towards their row with Hugo and Freddy but before they reached it, Tarchon and Aelia approached them.

Tarchon was holding a skinny teenager in a wrestling clench. 'By some miracle, no one was bitten except for this wretch.' His prisoner was writhing, scraping at his leg.

'Is there any treatment?' said Sophie.

'He might last a few days, though he'll be in agony.' Aelia was holding an empty satchel. 'He released the vipers.'

Sophie shuddered.

'How many snakes were there?' said Hugo, in halting Latin.

'Two.' Aelia kicked the remains of a snake closer to a seat, out of the way. 'Thanks to you, the other one didn't get far.'

Tarchon tightened his hold on the boy. 'He says a foreigner paid him 50 sestertii to release them. He can't use the payment now.' Tarchon gave coins to Freddy.

'We should take him with us,' said Sophie.

Confusion crossed Aelia's face. 'He's an assassin.'

'We should buy opium,' said Freddy. The boy's face was contorted with pain.

'What's opium?' said Aelia.

Hugo grimaced. 'It's either not been discovered or the poppies don't grow here.'

For all its similarities, this wasn't their Rome. 'What painkillers are available?' asked Sophie.

Aelia's eyes were on the boy. 'None that can help him.'

'Wells will be waiting somewhere to check we're dead,'

said Freddy. 'Aelia, what's the last exit you would choose to leave the stadium? No … the second last.'

'Roundabout route via the passage used for horses.' Aelia led the way up the stand.

With the snakes dealt with, most spectators had returned to their seats. Sophie stepped past a slave who was handing out more betting slips. People were already gambling on the next race.

Aelia disappeared down steep steps, different from the staircase leading to the shops, and they followed. Tarchon strode behind Sophie, carrying their would-be assassin.

At the end of the stairs was a sunken corridor. A few paces further on, at a junction of passages, slaves were pulling an injured horse along with ropes. The horse was grunting and whinnying. Aelia darted across the junction and further down a corridor.

They emerged into a sandy marshalling yard, the ground littered with straw. Slaves dressed in white tunics and a green stripe were busy tying horses to chariots. None of them looked up.

'Like a Formula One pit stop.' Hugo wiped sweat from his forehead.

'You did good with the snake.' Sophie's words came out as a whimper. Shock was setting in.

'I was lucky,' said Hugo. 'It moved so fast.'

The boy was whimpering, pleading for his mother, and Aelia took him from Tarchon. She dragged the boy along, his feet leaving a trail through scattered straw.

Tarchon rubbed his hip. 'Thank you. Apologies.'

'You need to heal,' said Aelia.

They came to another yard, went through a tall arch, and emerged onto a side road at the rear of the stadium. Beyond a grille-covered drain was a building site.

Using a patch of grass, Hugo cleaned snake blood off his

knife. His hand was shaking. 'Janus knew where we were in the stand, so Wells knew. Freddy, what are the chances there were other places we'd have chosen to sit, and Janus made a lucky guess?'

'Almost nil.' He grimaced. 'This is my fault. I should have chosen a different faction, a colour I dislike. We'd have been in a different stand.'

'Second guessing every single decision is hard,' said Sophie, dearly glad they'd left the dogs behind. Charlotte would have taken on the snakes, been bitten for sure.

Aelia was marching with the squirming boy to the building site. She gestured at a pile of rubble in a cart. 'The brickies will return early tomorrow and find him. I'll dispatch him quickly.'

Sophie made to stop Aelia, but Hugo pulled her back. 'Kinder to finish him now,' he said.

'I know he'd have killed us.' Sophie welled up. 'He was likely desperate for money.' She rummaged in her bag.

Freddy nodded. 'A victim of Wells, and Janus.'

'Aelia, wait!' Sophie offered a coin.

Aelia accepted it and looked up.

Sophie held her gaze. 'For the ferryman.'

In the street behind the Circus Maximus, Sophie concentrated on putting one foot in front of the other, trying not to picture the dead lad they'd left on the building site.

The road widened into a courtyard. Young boys were sitting on the ground cross-legged in the shade, scratching on tablets with styluses. A man with an impressive grey beard was reciting, 'Avoid that wicked temptress, laziness.'

'Peculiar coincidence,' said Freddy. 'I was given those lines at school. Had to write them out a hundred times.'

'What for?' said Hugo.

'Being late for chapel. I've hated Horace ever since.' Freddy folded his arms. 'I much prefer Ovid. *Fortune and love favour the brave.*'

'I wish my wise thoughts could last two millennia,' said Hugo.

'They should do.' Sophie gave him a fond glance.

By the teacher was a sign and Freddy translated it. 'Top Greek School.' Beside the name was a drawing of a hairy naked man. He was cradling a sheaf of corn and showing off an oversized penis.

Sophie swore under her breath. 'On a sign for a school…'

'The symbol brings good luck and wards off evil spirits.' Hugo took in her pained expression. 'We think we're so relaxed and modern, but we're prudish.' He shot her his suggestive half-smile. 'At least in public.'

Sophie rolled her eyes.

They walked on, Aelia slightly ahead. Tarchon stayed at the rear, holding his hip. They reached the end of the square, turned onto a main thoroughfare, and passed a jewellery shop.

The wares on display were at least a distraction from the dead boy. 'Just don't buy me a phallic necklace,' said Sophie to Hugo. 'Or a phallic … anything.'

'That hadn't occurred to me, but now you mention it—'

Freddy pulled up short. 'In the café across the road, that looks like Wells. He hasn't spotted us.'

They all moved into a shadow cast by an awning at the front of a shop. From there, they could watch the man without being seen. 'That is the assassin from the temple,' said Aelia. 'His toga is secured by a brooch.'

'Doesn't mean it's him,' said Freddy. 'Aren't all togas kept on with brooches?'

'Draped correctly, togas don't need them,' said Aelia. 'The wool is prickly, so the folds keep together. Some men cheat by using a brooch but keep it hidden. He is ignorant of this.'

'He's watching the stadium's main entrance, checking if we come out,' said Sophie. 'And he's alone.'

Hugo found his knife in his satchel. 'Aelia mustn't be a part of this. Nor should Tarchon.'

'Wells doesn't know them,' said Sophie. 'And they're less … squeamish than us.'

'We bought them to deter Wells, not to … do our dirty

work,' said Hugo. 'Tarchon's a slave and, unless she can prove otherwise, so is Aelia. If they're caught, their punishment would be horrific.'

Freddy nodded. 'Aelia, please return to the villa. Tarchon, you go too.'

Tarchon squared his shoulders. 'I have sworn to protect you and so I will.'

Aelia raised her chin. 'As will I.'

'Please respect our wishes.' Freddy's tone was adamant.

'If we fail in this, please take the dogs to the Arch of Juno,' said Sophie. 'As we explained in the temple cellar, this is the only way they can return home.'

Both slaves frowned. They hadn't believed them about the ship and didn't understand their concern for the dogs.

'Respect our wishes,' repeated Freddy.

'Very well.' Aelia turned and marched away.

Tarchon scowled but followed her.

'Wells has the address of the builders' base,' said Freddy. 'And he might know where the walking staff is kept?'

'He's not going to give us directions,' said Hugo, 'and we can't … persuade him in such a crowded place. Killing him without alerting the watchmen will be hard enough.'

Freddy's mouth compressed in a grim line. 'Hugo, we must do this together.'

'Janus will have given Wells our descriptions,' said Sophie. 'He'll recognise you before you reach him. You'll lose any advantage of surprise.'

'I could use the pendant,' said Freddy. 'Take it off at the last minute.'

Sophie shook her head. 'A ghost in a café? That would start a riot.' She sighed. 'I need to do it.' She took the kitchen knife from her satchel, removed the sheath, and secreted the blade in the folds of her shawl. She tugged down the shawl covering her hair, so it covered most of her face. Finally, a use for the wretched thing.

Hugo and Freddy glanced at each other, conflicted.

'Space out behind me. If I do the "rich lady walk" he won't realise it's me until the final second.' Deep breath.

'Don't hesitate.' Hugo's voice cracked. 'Or you're dead.'

'Got it.' To see Bella, she had to do this. Pretend it's a play, that it isn't real.

Sophie moved confidently down the street. Wells' attention remained on the Circus Maximus. The scent of grilled meat and sweet wine drifted over her as she glided between the café tables. When she was right beside him, he looked up. She stabbed the knife as hard as she could into his chest through his thick toga, and he cried out. But only the blade tip had gone in. She'd hit a rib.

She hauled the knife out to try again, the pale toga staining red, and Wells grabbed her hand and for a long moment, they wrestled. His eyes, an unusual cobalt blue, bore into hers, horrified and surprised. But he was stronger.

Hugo strode up. 'Salve.'

Wells' face jerked up. He released Sophie's hand and drew a dagger from his belt, hidden under his toga. The weapon was twice the size of their knives.

Sophie stepped back and before Wells could attack, Freddy stabbed him, the blade sinking up to the hilt. Wells didn't cry out, just stared down at his chest. Freddy pulled out the knife.

Wells stared at Freddy and coughed, bringing up blood. Still gripping his dagger, he was fighting for breath.

The three of them were blocking Wells from view, and the customers and staff had seen nothing amiss. 'We should go now,' said Freddy.

Sophie's shawl had slid off her hair and she shoved it back up. 'He's not dead.'

'He will be soon,' said Freddy.

Hugo frowned. 'How do you know?'

'From hunting.' Freddy had grown up culling animals on the Shorten estate.

Sophie met his gaze and saw disgust at what they'd done, and the same disgust slid over her like slime. But she secreted her knife in the shawl and with her heart pounding, she left the café, Freddy and Hugo keeping close.

She'd expected a hue and cry, but none came. Stumbling along the sunny, busy street, Wells' anguished eyes filled her mind, and she felt sick. She'd assumed Janus' assassin would be ruthless and evil, but when she'd wrestled with him, he'd seemed … ordinary.

Hugo held her arm, guiding her left into another road, then another. The Colosseum loomed up on their right, dominating this low-lying part of Rome. Finally, they hurried under a two-storey aqueduct. 'Are you okay?' Sophie asked him.

'Not really.'

Freddy's expression darkened. 'I didn't appreciate the price we'd pay for seeing Bella and Clarissa again.'

Sophie nodded. Not a price in money, a bargain struck and forgotten. They'd killed in cold blood, and the price, the memory, would eat away at them.

They cut down a narrow street, tenements on both sides obscuring the sun.

CHAPTER 27

*A*while after leaving the main road, they were in another gloomy street lined with tenements. Hugo paused and studied his map. 'We're too far east. This is Subura.'

Sophie remembered the name from her time-travelling book. Two women in shabby tunics with hard faces hurried past them. Neither were wearing silk shawls. Sophie pulled hers off, rolled it into a ball with the knife inside, and ventured down an alley. A few feet in, she stumbled on pottery shards, broken sandals, and blotchy bedsheets. Further on was more rubbish, piled between raised stepping-stones. The stench was vile.

Sliding the knife from the shawl, Sophie wiped it on the nearest bedsheet, before slipping the blade into its sheath and into her satchel. The pink shawl was smeared red, and she shoved it under a rotting mattress. 'I can't get Wells out of my mind.'

'I know.' Freddy cleaned his knife. 'But if he'd had his way, we'd have starved to death or died in agony from snakebites.'

They stumbled out of the stinking alley. 'We shouldn't retrace our steps,' said Sophie.

Hugo checked his map. 'Half a mile to a safer district.'

But the next street was even narrower, gloomy, and with no raised pavement. A child waddled out of a run-down shop and emptied a foul-smelling pot into a drain.

'Seeing beyond the flats for a landmark is impossible,' said Hugo. 'Feels like we're just getting more lost—'

The sound of chanting cut him off.

'Maybe we've gone in a circle, towards the Colosseum?' said Sophie.

'The sound's too close,' said Freddy. 'It's coming from up ahead.'

Sophie could make out the words. 'Death to Aquila.' And there was different chanting from behind them. 'Death to Plinius.'

'Gangs.' Hugo paled. 'We're in the middle of a turf war. We need to get off the street.'

'There.' Freddy pointed to a deserted popina.

They ran in, but there was no rear exit and nowhere to hide. They dashed out again.

The chanting was louder, and people on the upper floors of the flats were on their balconies, peering down. 'The staircase into this tenement shouldn't be far.' Sophie hoped it wasn't.

The outside stairs were barred by a tall gate. Solid wood, it wouldn't budge. Freddy shouted over the chanting. 'Please let us in!' He banged on the gate.

The residents on the balconies jeered.

Sophie glanced back. Gang members were on the road, armed with axes, pikes, and swords. They advanced as one, stamping their feet. At the opposite end of the street was another armed gang. There was no escape route. In a moment, they'd be cut to pieces.

She could survive if she used the pendant, but it would only work for her, or for Freddy. She yelled as loud as she could against the chanting. 'Let us in! We have money!'

Hugo dragged his gaze from the gangs, his eyes desperate.

'A lot of money,' shouted Freddy.

At an invisible signal, both gangs rushed towards each other, yelling war cries.

'1,000 denarii,' yelled Freddy.

A key turned in the lock and the gate to the tenement opened. The three of them sprinted in and the gate shut with a clunk. A pace away, the gangs met in a roar of savagery that shook the door.

A man looked at Sophie with a one-tooth grin and they followed him up the staircase. From the street came shouts and screams and a jarring clang of steel.

'How many coins have we got to pay him off?' whispered Sophie.

'A few coppers,' said Freddy.

Hugo grimaced. 'Same.'

They entered a single room on the first floor that smelled of damp and stale spice. 'Thank you for opening the door,' said Sophie.

'My pleasure, little one.' The guy frowned at Hugo and Freddy. 'Smart getup for local pimps.' He chuckled to himself.

'We're happy to exchange our clothes for yours,' said Freddy, his voice steady.

'All of 'em?'

'Just the tunics,' said Freddy. 'They're worth a substantial sum.'

'I don't doubt it, but I want the woman.' His eyes glinted with lust.

Hugo and Freddy scrabbled in their satchels for their knives.

'I've a better idea.' Fishing out the pendant, Sophie addressed their host. 'You can't have sex with me. You see, I'm dead. I'm a ghost.' She slipped on the pendant, and everything was sepia.

The man almost fell over and he scrambled away from where she'd been, mouthing and gesticulating.

Sophie ran to his balcony. She hauled off the pendant and the smell of alcohol and blood invaded her nostrils. Clashing metal assaulted her ears. The road was a seething mass of men in skimpy, belted tunics, fighting at close quarters. Some were hacking with swords and daggers, others were stabbing with spears or swinging iron-studded cudgels. Directly under the balcony, a man with a shaved head swung a club and connected with a sickening thud on another fighter's face. His opponent crumpled. The victor dodged a heavy metal chain and spun to parry a knife with his own. The blades met, sparks flying.

As an accidental time-traveller, Sophie had seen — and inflicted — violence, but this was a new level of gruesome. She took a step back.

A family on the balcony opposite had moved out chairs to experience in comfort the tang of blood and sweat, the grunts of exertion, and the screams of fallen fighters. A young woman swigged from a glass and called, 'Death to Plinius.' In response, a man from the street threw an amphora bottle, and it smashed on the wall, narrowly missing her balcony.

Sophie retreated into the flat.

The resident was cowering, staring at Freddy and Hugo. 'I'll do anything.' The guy jumped when he saw Sophie. 'Don't hurt me.'

'Is there a rear exit?' Freddy asked him.

'No.'

'Once the way's clear,' said Hugo, 'if he can show us the

quickest route to the Forum, we can find our way to the villa.'

Freddy addressed the guy in a solemn, sonorous voice. 'Guide us home tomorrow and you will come to no harm.'

The street fight carried on into the night but despite the noise, their host dozed. When the road outside finally went quiet, his snoring meant no one else could sleep. His unwelcome guests sat on hard chairs around a tiny, battered table and waited for dawn.

Freddy sighed.

'You're thinking about Wells.' Sophie's shame and disgust had grown, weighing her down. If — no, when — they were reunited with their daughter, could they share what they'd done? Or would Bella be sickened, revolted? This could create a gulf between them, one too deep to heal.

'Janus will send another version of Wells,' said Hugo.

Freddy tensed. 'I can't kill him again.'

The thought made Sophie wither inside. 'Count me out.'

'Then we must abandon the search for the walking staff and return to Juno,' said Hugo. 'Because the next Wells is coming.'

CHAPTER 28

An hour after dawn the next morning, half a mile from the dangerous district of Subura, another version of H. G. Wells settled in the armchair in the Villa Acilius. He scratched his lip. Where his moustache had been, the skin was itchy.

When he'd arrived in this curious house, hidden away in ancient Rome, the exotically beautiful woman and her colleagues had welcomed him *back*. He'd considered correcting them, saying this was his first visit to the city, and to this residence, but Janus had been clear. Don't be over-friendly with Ishtar and her team. Don't question them. Keep your own counsel.

The man they'd mistaken him for shared his taste in food and so forth, down to his preferred tobacco. Had the other man travelled with Janus? Why hadn't Janus mentioned him? If this chap was still in Rome, Bertie could enlist his help. Not that he required assistance, except from Janus. Alone amongst humanity, he'd been befriended by a god. Proof he was special.

It had been wonderful to travel from the 19th century to

the early 20th, but he had no wish to write novels about the Great War, to dwell on such a terrible event. Visiting ancient Rome held much more appeal — save for Janus' test. Designed to prove Bertie's loyalty or his ability? Perhaps both.

For Janus, killing travellers who irked him might be trivial, but for Bertie, completing this task was daunting and, frankly, disgusting. Yet between them, they could stop the Great War, and Bertie would prove himself worthy.

Janus had insisted that Bertie end these people personally, so Bertie had bought an impressive dagger. But using his basic command of Latin, he'd also procured help. Deserters from the legions, drinking in a rundown bar, had readily entered his service, enticed by the expensive pocket watches he'd stolen from those dead officers in the trenches. Even here, centuries in the past, Bertie inwardly winced, remembering that battlefield. Though he'd see no credit for it, he'd act on Janus' suggestions, work tirelessly to prevent the carnage: lobby parliament, write letters to *The Times*, all the while not revealing his knowledge of the future or how he'd acquired it.

Ishtar glanced at him as she strode over to supervise the men and women gathering 'data,' as she referred to it. Bertie had no idea what data was, only that Ishtar needed it for the upcoming festival. Janus had told him not to concern himself with the festival, that this task would be finished by then.

Bertie smiled at Ishtar. She'd presumably slept her way into this role, or why would she be in charge? Soon, there'd be countless gorgeous women to satisfy him, and his travels with Janus would inspire novels that would make his fortune.

Across the room, one of the team closed his metal book and looked up. 'I've lost my enabler. It must have fallen off yesterday.'

Ishtar tutted and gave the man something from a drawer. She addressed Bertie. 'Did you find the device useful?'

Bertie nodded politely. 'I'm afraid mine has gone missing too.' He accepted the tiny cylinder she offered and dropped it in his pocket. Best not to ask its purpose. Wouldn't do to appear dim-witted.

He got to his feet to better view the magic lantern film on the long window that encircled the building. The whole of Rome seen from the sky! And there were the green dots Janus had talked about. But there were far more than three.

Two dots were in a street in the tenement district. The girl and her lovers. What on earth were the priority interests doing there?

He turned his attention to the area north of the Forum and found the place that Janus had called the 'opportunity.' A large pleasure garden, enclosed within a winding colonnade. In the centre of the garden was a substantial building. Bertie touched it on the window and a label displayed a name. *Thermae Titi.*

The Baths of Titus.

Following Janus' instructions, Bertie adjusted the brooch on his toga to ensure it was concealed under the garment's folds. In a few hours, the relevant green dots would appear at the entrance of the baths, showing the girl, one of her lovers, but not the dog. The girl would be inside for less than fifteen minutes, but her lovers would stay for half the day. The girl and the dog were supposedly part of Janus' test but were obviously of lesser importance. Dogs had limited intelligence, like women.

This would soon be over.

CHAPTER 29

Freddy paced back and forth in the courtyard of the Villa Fullia. They'd returned from the tenement district an hour ago, utterly exhausted, but he was too wired to sleep. Sophie couldn't sleep either. Faced with trudging off to Juno empty-handed or murdering another Wells, they were locked in a state of anxiety and indecision.

Hugo had managed to fall asleep on the yellow couch and Jack was dozing beside him. Charlotte, though, was wide awake and alert. They'd glossed over stabbing Wells and the terrifying street fight, but Charlotte hadn't been fooled. Her ears pricked up and she barked.

Banging came from the front door. It had a distinct pattern. One bang, then two in quick succession.

Freddy stopped pacing. 'The courier's code. That's what those marks are, on our house tablet.'

Sophie frowned. 'You've lost me.'

Freddy disappeared into the study and returned with the tablet. 'See.' On the groove on the back page, left by the estate agent's seal, were diagonal lines, one long and two short.

'Reminds me of Morse code, except this combination is unique, known only to us, the estate agent, and the courier.'

Sophie touched the marks. Yes, not random. Careful and precise.

Drusus hurried into the courtyard carrying a tablet. On the front was the estate agent's red-roof logo.

'Would you mind reading it?' Sophie asked Drusus.

'Nothing less than 700 for both slaves is acceptable.' He cleared his throat. 'A negotiating ploy. Offer less?'

Talking with Drusus about buying *him* turned her stomach, but Sophie said, 'Offer 600.'

Drusus scribbled a reply. 'I sincerely hope the sale goes through.'

Sophie nodded, unsure what to say.

He walked off to give the tablet to the waiting courier.

'I'd like to free all four slaves before we leave Rome,' said Freddy. 'A good deed to offset an evil one.'

'I don't think you can equate the two things.' Sophie stroked Charlotte. 'Should we go, or should we stay? I wish you could help us decide.' Charlotte shook her head, as undecided as her mistress. Sophie pictured herself in Juno, dejected, defeated. She might land safely in a Shorten universe and discover her daughter wasn't there. That would be even harder than … ending a second Wells.

Hugo woke up with a yawn. He blinked at them. 'I'm sorry. I know we need to decide, but I couldn't keep my eyes open.'

'We're still wrestling with the problem,' said Freddy.

Hugo stared at the gushing fountain. 'I'd love a proper shower.'

'We should visit the public baths,' said Sophie. 'Venturing out to another public place so soon after the chariot racing has to be illogical. Not predictable.'

A crease appeared between Hugo's brows. 'I thought—'

'So, you've decided?' said Freddy, his gaze on Sophie.

'Yes. We've come too far.'

Hugo rubbed his eyes. 'There'd be no shame in turning back.'

'Shame will follow us whatever we do,' said Freddy. 'Very well. We stay and continue the quest.'

Sophie managed a bitter smile. 'I suppose this is a quest, just not an honourable one.'

'Can any quest succeed in a wholly moral way?' said Freddy.

Hugo wiggled his shoulders. 'I'm so knackered I can't think.'

'The traditional "Let's go kill a dragon" quests are only symbolic, but I always hated the premise,' said Sophie. 'In most of them, the dragon's peacefully sleeping in a cave, not flying around, hunting down the knight in shining armour.'

Freddy strode over to the fountain and splashed water on his face. 'The quest idea's bucked me up.'

Sophie rested her hand on Hugo's shoulder. They were the knights and Wells was the dragon.

The slaves came into the courtyard. Melissa was carrying a tea tray and Drusus had honey cakes.

After breakfast, Sophie felt stronger. 'Which are the best baths?' she asked Drusus.

'The Baths of Titus. I'll accompany you.'

'As will we,' said Aelia, glancing at Tarchon. 'You did well, dispatching your enemy in the café,' she said.

'You watched?' said Freddy, horrified.

'We were ordered to adjourn here but you didn't specify when,' said Tarchon, his gravelly voice quieter than usual.

Freddy nodded. 'No harm done.'

'You need to know that although the man who pursued us is dead,' said Sophie, 'he has, um, a brother who will seek revenge.' Trying to explain infinite versions of Wells — and them — had been too complicated in the temple cellar and was still too complicated.

'We'll be ready,' said Tarchon.

'I don't suppose dogs are allowed in the baths?' said Sophie. The bewildered looks from the slaves told her the answer.

'We won't need Melissa there,' said Freddy.

Melissa stroked Jack. She was comfortable with the dogs now, would happily mind them.

Charlotte studied her paws. She'd wanted to see the baths.

On the main road to the baths, a funeral cortege was making its slow journey south. The mourners' high, harsh wailing gave Sophie goosebumps. Small carts were pulled over to the side and pedestrians bowed their heads.

At the front of the procession were torchbearers, the flames from their batons flickering yellow in the sunshine. Then came men playing flutes, blowing slow, solemn notes. Behind the musicians were women in black shawls, moaning and lamenting.

Sophie checked that her shawl was covering her hair. Melissa had bought it that morning. The emerald material was thicker and heavier than the previous one, and she wiped her brow with it as the cortege passed by.

Men in black tunics and incongruously bright red caps carried the open bier, gripping long handles at the rear and the front.

A couple beside Freddy made a weird, squishy sound, like they were slurping soup.

Sophie glanced at Hugo, her face questioning.

'No idea.'

The bier had high sides so Sophie couldn't see the corpse. But she could smell him or her. Even ten slaves waving their incense torches couldn't mask it. Sophie held her breath.

The lengthy procession of mourners was heading towards the city boundary and the city of the dead.

'All those tombs and sepulchres on the Appian Way would be quite a sight,' said Hugo, half to himself.

'No wish to visit.' Sophie grimaced. 'Too morbid.'

The deceased's family shuffled past in shabby, dark clothes. Stubble marred the men's chins and the women's hair was undressed and messy.

Unbidden, the memory of her aunt holding her hand at a very different funeral filled Sophie's mind. Her parents were far in the future, yet to be born, yet to die. She forced herself back to the present, to this moment, standing on a pavement in ancient Rome, but the memory of the recent past was too raw. The temple cellar, the snakes, killing Wells, not to mention the street fight… It had all knocked her sideways.

'Sophie?' Hugo touched her arm.

'I'm fine.' Get a grip.

At the end of the cortege were doleful men and women wearing cream liberty caps, freed by their dead owner's Will.

'They must be secretly happy,' whispered Sophie. 'And relieved.'

'I never cease to be surprised how people adapt, act a part to survive,' said Hugo.

Freddy looked at his sandals. 'I don't want to die here.'

'The over-the-top funeral is entirely optional,' said Sophie, trying to lighten the mood. 'Anyway, the girl in the Forum didn't say *you* would die.'

Freddy frowned. 'I shall do my utmost to keep you safe.'

She squeezed his hand.

After the procession had passed, they followed streets that climbed and dipped, criss-crossing one of Rome's famous seven hills. When they finally reached a park surrounding the baths, Sophie was glad to pause. The grass was lush and green, nourished by underground pipes that also fed ornamental fountains.

'I didn't realise the Romans had lawns,' said Hugo.

'Pliny the Younger had a splendid garden.' Freddy's Edwardian classical education was proving a treasure trove of obscure facts.

Despite the summer heat, families were out strolling and, in a fenced off area, women in red bikinis were playing an energetic ball game. During her research, Sophie had come across a similar scene online, from an ancient mosaic in a villa in Sicily. She hadn't believed women wore bikinis. Now she did. And the bikinis were like her underwear. She'd fit in fine at the baths.

Drusus was having a coughing fit, and Sophie sat on the grass, so he'd feel comfortable taking a rest. Hugo and Freddy got the hint and sat down too.

When Drusus had recovered himself, they followed Aelia through the baths' impressive entrance pillars and into the foyer. The double-height room was a study in pale marble, in contrast to the reception counter that was decorated with blue waves and silver fishes. As they approached, slaves behind the counter stood to attention.

A notice on the wall showed the entrance fee: one quadran for men, two for women. Freddy selected the correct copper coins.

'Why do we have to pay double?' Sophie asked Aelia.

'Women primp, want more fuss.'

Sophie went with Aelia into a changing room. Lockers lined the wall and there was a curtained-off toilet. Women and girls were sitting on benches, gossiping and eating snacks. Some had brought their sewing.

Remembering the mixed loo in the Circus Maximus, Sophie asked, 'Why is this women-only?'

'Poets rail against skimpy clothing and immorality,' said Aelia. 'I think that's why.'

Logical. Sophie smiled to herself. In Shorten, she'd fantasised about Hugo in his boxers…

An attendant acknowledged Aelia, who nodded back. Alarming armour was evidently commonplace. An older woman came in with four slaves who undressed her. The lady waddled out of the changing room without a stitch on.

Sophie frowned. Surely, wandering around stark naked risked more temptation than wearing 'skimpy clothing?' Yes, this resembled a modern changing room, but she was missing something. She undressed to her undies, kept on the translator necklace and Bella's key-rattle, and folded her tunic, dress, and shawl.

'I shall guard your clothes,' said Aelia.

The far door led to a gymnasium where naked men were lifting heavy stones. Others were sprinting on a circular track. Sophie fixed her eyes on Aelia.

The main bathhouse was in a spacious hall, and Sophie paused on the threshold. Men, women, and children were swimming and larking about in a large rectangular pool. There were wide, crescent-shaped steps at both ends. In a smaller pool, where the water churned like a hot tub, three women were talking, hardly pausing for breath. Directly above both pools, the ceiling was open to the outside.

Around the edge of the room were columns depicting Neptune with his trident, curling waves, and orange sea dragons, and between the columns were tall red pots planted with pink geraniums and green ferns. Beside the main pool, naked people sat on couches or on chairs near low tables. Personal slaves and those serving food were clothed: a few in security gear, others just wearing loin cloths, and some dressed in thin, almost transparent, tunics.

Happy chatter mingled with splashing and enticing aromas from customers' hot snacks. Sophie systematically scanned the hall for the new Wells and drew a relieved breath. Nowhere to be seen.

Tarchon was standing with his back to a pillar. In front of him, Drusus was folding cream towels onto a stand. Hugo and Freddy were lounging on wicker chairs, towels across their laps. Freddy was wearing his translator necklace. He leaned forward and selected salted peas from a table.

Sophie sat down opposite them. Aelia, holding Sophie's clothes, remained standing.

'We've paid extra for better white wine but it's not cold.' Hugo slid a glass across the table towards her.

'The bathhouse at Shorten was smaller but must have been similar,' said Freddy.

A Roman bathhouse... Yes, mentioned in *A History of Shorten*. Sophie sipped the wine, wishing she could take out the spice.

'And we have the answer to an issue that's polarised historians for decades.' Hugo gestured at the pool.

'Which is?' Sophie asked him.

'Were the baths clean, or were they filthy and a breeding ground for bacteria and disease?'

'Surely, if bathers got sick, nobody would come?' said Sophie.

'According to the attendants,' said Freddy, 'fresh water is pumped in from underground, and old water pumped out through the sewers.'

'Cool,' said Sophie.

'In a hundred years from now, they'll build even more splendid baths,' said Hugo. 'Complexes of 30 acres, accommodating 3,000 people. As well as pools, there'll be concert halls, dentists, theatres, libraries, and art galleries.'

'Might be worth coming back for,' said Freddy.

Hugo warmed to his theme. 'Hairdressers, nail bars, rooms for playing dice and discussing poetry, and of course, brothels.'

They'd seen a brothel on the way here. The frescoes in the windows had left little to the imagination.

'It seems unimaginable that Rome will fall,' said Freddy.

Excited whooping diverted Sophie's attention to the pool. Children were learning to swim, supervised by doting mothers. One day, she'd teach Bella to swim. A familiar melancholy swept over her, and she couldn't shrug it off. The happy babble was sapping her energy and she craved the undemanding calm of the Villa Fullia.

A man with a paunch walked past, glanced at her, and wiggled his oversized eyebrows. The Roman equivalent of a leer? She looked at her lap. Yes, she needed solitude and me-time.

'Sophie, you can keep on your necklaces in the pool,' said Hugo.

She glanced up. Many swimmers were wearing jewellery. Showing off, or to keep their valuables safe? But that was all they were wearing. 'You could have warned me that clothes aren't allowed.'

'I didn't know until five minutes ago.' Hugo pointed at his boxers, folded with Freddy's on top of the towels.

'We're the same as everybody else.' Freddy stood up, handed his towel and cylinder necklace to Drusus, and gave her a reassuring smile.

Hugo also got to his feet and put aside his towel, showing off his impressive abs — and everything else.

In private, Sophie would have admired him, but this was too public.

'There's nothing of you we haven't seen before,' said Freddy, his face deadpan.

'He's right.' Hugo was trying not to laugh.

'One. More. Word,' said Sophie, 'and you won't be seeing any more of me for a good long while.'

'You're too inhibited,' said Hugo, stretching to show he wasn't.

'I'm just not in the mood.' Sophie sighed. 'I'm sorry, I'm going to the villa.'

'What about the Caldarium?' said Freddy.

'Too cold.'

'No,' said Hugo. 'Apparently, it's as hot as a sauna.'

Unconvinced, Sophie took her clothes from Aelia and dressed.

Freddy looked conflicted. 'Seems a shame for us all to leave?'

'Go with her, Tarchon,' said Hugo, his eyes serious. 'Aelia, please stay.'

Sophie turned to retrace her steps, but she was stopped by an attendant. 'No exit there.' He pointed to a door on the far side of the pool.

Sophie followed Tarchon out, her faux leather sandals slipping on the wet floor. The next room was so filled with steam that the pool and the customers were barely visible, and neither was Tarchon. She hurried to catch up with him.

They passed through into another room and cold air hit Sophie like a slap. The pool had white slivers on the surface, rippling out from the swimmers. 'Ice?'

'Aelia said they bring it from mountains called the Alps,' said Tarchon.

Incredible. Why didn't it melt on the way?

Beyond a foyer with arches leading to more changing rooms, was a gift shop. Teenage girls were queueing at the counter, clutching tiny glass bottles with loopy, brass handles. 'His sweat is divine,' said one.

Her friend opened the stopper on her own bottle and sniffed. 'Nah, Blandus is better.'

Tarchon headed for a door helpfully signed Exitus.

'Did I misunderstand?' Sophie asked him, as they came out into the gardens. 'Those girls were buying *sweat*?'

'From gladiators,' said Tarchon. 'Adds to their already considerable income.'

'How much do they earn?'

'A hundred times more than the best lawyer.'

Sophie raised an eyebrow. The equivalent of modern footballers.

'Women add the sweat to their rejuvenating skin packs.'

'Do female gladiators sell their sweat?'

'I've no idea.' Tarchon's face creased into a rare smile. 'We should ask Aelia.'

An hour after Sophie and Tarchon left the Baths of Titus, Freddy eased himself out of the pool in the caldarium. 'Gosh, that's almost too hot.'

He could just see Aelia's distinctive shape with the curve of her chest armour through the steam and he spotted Hugo lying face-down on a couch. Drusus had rubbed oil into Hugo's back and was scraping it off with a curved, bronze tool.

Freddy's satchel was on a stand. He took the cylinder necklace out and put it on. He hadn't wanted to test how robust it was by swimming in it, but it should be all right in this steam.

Drusus coughed.

'Is the steam making your cough worse?' asked Freddy.

'Up here, the steam's clean. Might do it good.' Drusus pointed at a raised bed of heated coals. 'Would you prefer it warmer? I can fetch more hot water?'

'No, thank you.' Freddy flattened out a towel on a couch and lay on it. 'You said you'd worked at the baths. Did you work at this one?'

'I did.'

'I wish Sophie had stayed,' said Hugo. 'She'd have enjoyed this.'

Freddy's thoughts flitted to Bella, picturing her splashing and giggling in the pool, but a moment later, he was distracted by another customer's conversation.

'The date has been chosen for the Festival of Janus. Two days from now.' The woman on the nearby couch was talking to her slave, a slip of a girl who was meticulously plucking hairs from her mistress' legs. 'I was right about the date.'

The girl nodded. 'A run of days that aren't unlucky.' She straightened, putting the tweezers aside. 'All done.'

Her mistress climbed off the couch and strolled from the room with the slave.

'I only caught the word Janus,' said Hugo.

Freddy repeated what he'd heard.

'Two days… I thought we'd have longer to prepare. I don't feel ready.'

'I don't either,' said Freddy.

Clinking came from somewhere in the steam. Hugo turned over and sat up, and Drusus stepped away from the couch.

The clink was familiar, though Freddy couldn't place it. Metal… Perhaps Aelia's armour?

Clink.

A shadowy shape loomed out of the steam. The man had broad shoulders, weathered skin, and muscular arms. His brown hair was cut short and around his neck was a faded, battered amulet that sat oddly with his polished leather jerkin. His eyes were hard and his expression set.

Someone's bodyguard? Or a thug hired by the next Wells?

Freddy rolled as fast as he could off the couch, grabbing his towel. The man thrust with a dagger and the blade wedged in a cushion with a twang. 'Hugo, look out!' Freddy scrambled backwards, hoping the steam would hide him, and almost fell over Hugo who was squatting on the floor, rifling through his satchel for his knife.

Freddy kept his balance and tied the towel about his waist. In the steam were two, faint shapes. One was Aelia. She was squaring up against a bald man who towered over her. 'Flee,' she shouted.

The harsh sound of metal against metal rang out, and every chivalrous instinct told Freddy to protect her. Where was his satchel with the knife?

Drusus was crouched beside Hugo, Freddy's satchel slung across his chest, and Freddy crawled over to them, his heart pounding in his ears. If Aelia and that man were visible in the steam, so were they.

'There's a thug guarding the two exits,' whispered Drusus. 'Come with me.'

Freddy and Hugo followed Drusus past a pillar. Drusus deftly moved aside a screen that had appeared to be part of the wall, revealing a half-height gap. On the floor, flanking the doorway, were buckets of steaming water.

Behind Freddy came new noises of scraping steel, and he hesitated. He wouldn't escape like a coward while Aelia fought and died. He ran back past the screen. 'Aelia! Follow my voice! That's an order.'

Hugo had turned around too. Naked, he crawled forward, keeping his body low against the floor tiles. Freddy's attacker stepped through the steam and Hugo thrust his blade into the man's leg. But the thug hardly flinched and slashed down with a heavy knife, missing Hugo's head by a whisker.

Drusus rushed over with a bucket. 'Scald them,' he hissed.

Why hadn't he thought of that? Freddy sprinted to the half-height opening and, with an effort, lifted a bucket by its wooden handle. The water sloshed, heat coming off it in waves. Hugo was beside him, panting.

A scream. Freddy's stomach clenched. Aelia.

They charged into the steam together.

Drusus had thrown his water. A thug was on his knees, his hands over his face. The scream had come from him. Aelia was still sparring with the other man.

'Aelia, step clear,' shouted Freddy.

Her attacker glanced at them. Aelia dived sideways, and they threw the water. The result was immediate and graphic. The thug let out an agonised cry, covering his ruined face. His blade hit the hard tiles.

'I'll finish them,' said Aelia. The woman was unflappable.

She was as good as her word, and Freddy winced. Hugo seemed rooted to the spot.

'Flee,' said Aelia. 'There are more.'

'No,' said Freddy. 'We go together.'

Aelia gave him a curt nod.

Drusus was waiting by the half-height doorway. Bent double, they all ventured through. With any luck, their attackers wouldn't see where they'd gone.

'The assailants must have entered by this route,' whispered Drusus, 'so as not to be seen. The others will follow.'

Freddy inwardly cursed. His bare foot slipped on the narrow step, and he almost fell headlong down steep stairs. There was no rail.

The limited light from the steam room faded, and Freddy felt his way down. At the bottom was a level corridor. In the low brick ceiling were cracks, slivers of daylight, so he could see what was ahead. Billowing grey smoke, an eerie orange glow. And it was beastly hot.

Behind them came the noise of heavy boots. Drusus sprinted into the smoke and so did Freddy, in front of Hugo and Aelia.

Sweat was dripping down Freddy's face and the cylinder lying against his chest was damp with it. 'This is horrible.'

'We'll be out soon,' muttered Hugo. But there was no sign of an exit, and it hurt to breathe.

They ran into an underground scene from hell. Naked slaves were tending a line of braziers set into a wall. Red coals were evil eyes, staring through the stoves' iron railings. Other slaves were carrying logs or dragging planks of wood on sheets. Metal pipes covered the ceiling. On a wall off to the right, in sconces, were long flaming torches. The stench of burning coal tasted rancid in Freddy's mouth and he gagged.

Drusus dodged past a slave and dashed on into another corridor. Everyone sprinted after him.

The new passage was as dark and smoke-filled as the brazier room, and Drusus slowed. How had he kept this pace until now?

The beat of running boots was louder, catching them up. Freddy took Drusus' arm, forcing him to go faster. But when they came into another room filled with slaves and braziers, so did two thugs.

Aelia whirled around, her knife in her hand. Hugo selected a fiery torch from a wall and held it up as a shield.

'Good idea.' Freddy grabbed a torch.

'You'll die here,' Aelia told the men, flourishing her blade.

A man in a toga strode regally between the thugs and gave Aelia an admiring smile. This Wells had longer hair, covering his ears, but his face was the same.

'He's too confident,' said Hugo in English. 'He might not know what happened to the previous version of him?'

Wells frowned. 'What do you mean?'

Act while he's distracted. Freddy stepped forward with his fiery shield.

'You think you're special, that Janus chose you.' Hugo brandished his torch. 'But you're just one version of many. We killed the last H. G. Wells and we're going to kill you.'

Confusion showed in Wells' eyes, and in the same instant, Aelia threw a small dagger with her left hand. The blade met Wells' neck, embedded itself in his throat, and he slid to his knees. He clutched at the knife, making a horrible gurgling sound.

Thank goodness for Aelia. But Freddy tightened his grip on the torch, eyeing the thugs. This wasn't over.

Aelia addressed the thugs. 'Leave, with no dishonour to your legion. Don't cross us again or we'll tell the Vigiles that you murdered the son of a senator.' She said 'senator' with a flourish.

She pulled her knife from Wells' neck. 'The word of equestrians...' She gestured at Freddy and Hugo. '...against army deserters.' She gave the men a hard stare. 'We have a deal?'

CHAPTER 31

The day after Aelia vanquished the second Wells at the baths, Sophie fetched a bottle of expensive Falerian white wine from the study. Melissa had bought it in a market that opened only once a month.

Sophie poured out a thimbleful and placed it on the Lares shrine. The Lares weren't real, but the ritual was comforting. They were all safe in the villa and Wells was dead … twice.

She walked into the courtyard. Everyone was there. Charlotte was dozing in the shade next to Jack. Sophie sat down on the red sofa beside Hugo.

'How long did you work under the baths?' Freddy asked Drusus.

'Ten years. A third of my life.'

From Hugo and Freddy's description of the brazier rooms, many slaves surely didn't last that long? As it was, Drusus couldn't shake off its poisonous legacy, the stoking cough. 'I never thought about how the bath water was heated,' said Sophie.

'If I were emperor, I'd make customers tour the underground passages,' said Freddy. 'A condition of enjoying the baths.'

Sophie chewed her lip. She deeply regretted leaving them at the baths. But it was done now.

'What did you say to the brother that made him hesitate?' Aelia asked Hugo. 'Gave me the chance with the knife?'

Freddy answered for him. 'That his master had lied to him and didn't care if he lived or died.' He shuddered. 'We were fortunate the thugs accepted your bargain.'

'You don't wear equestrian rings,' said Aelia, 'but you dress in their style.'

'I prefer being the middling sort,' said Freddy. 'Not plebs struggling to survive and not the other extreme, patricians too close to the emperor, jostling for power.'

'Those men will keep our bargain,' said Aelia.

'How did you know they were army deserters?' said Freddy.

'From the tattoos on their wrists and reminders of past glories clanking on their belts.'

Sophie sat up straighter. Sounded like the men by Juno's arch. 'You've come up against them before?'

'Not them,' said Aelia. 'Others from the same stable.'

Sophie started on a quick summary, but Hugo said, 'I caught the gist.'

'I fear there are more brothers,' said Freddy.

Tarchon frowned. 'How many?'

'Perhaps only one,' said Hugo in Latin.

'Why?' Sophie asked him.

'The research team should be at the festival tomorrow, with the walking staff,' said Hugo. 'Hopefully, in plain sight.'

Sophie nodded. Their chance to take the staff, defeating the last version of Wells—

The dogs barked and ran into the house. A courier was at

the front door. The pattern of banging matched the estate agent's code.

Drusus stood up stiffly and plodded into the house. When he came out with a tablet, he was grinning so much it creased up his whole face. '*Your offer for the slaves is accepted. Pay now,*' he read. 'And there's a falsified certificate of health.' He was still smiling.

Freddy took the tablet and squinted, trying to read the dense text. 'Girl. No record of running away.'

'That's a lie too,' said Melissa.

Drusus held up a leather drawstring bag. His hands were shaking. 'The courier waits outside for your reply and payment.'

They all went into the study. Freddy took a stylus pen from the shelf and on the tablet, scratched his assumed name. *MARCUS VERANIUS.* Then he opened the iron chest and counted out the cash.

Drusus went back through the house to give the tablet and payment to the courier and returned with a spring in his step.

'Time to increase happiness and cement loyalty,' said Hugo.

'We can free everyone in our Wills,' said Sophie, remembering the ex-slaves in the funeral procession.

'Better to go before a magistrate,' said Freddy. 'When we leave Rome, with no proof we're dead, our Wills might not work.'

'There's an easier way.' Drusus opened the census tablet on the desk. 'You're legally required to list the members of the household and submit this before September. To free us, you put a cross in the "freed section" by our names.'

Charlotte stood on her hind legs and stared at the tablet.

'My written Latin leaves a lot to be desired,' said Freddy. 'Drusus, you need to do it.'

Drusus sat down and filled out the wax boxes.

'Aelia doesn't need freeing, but please include her just in case,' said Freddy.

Drusus nodded. 'Already done.'

'I'll go with you to deliver it,' said Melissa. 'The House of Freedom isn't far.'

'Where is it?' said Hugo, in Latin.

'Near the Forum,' said Melissa.

'What's the process after that?' asked Freddy.

'After we lodge the tablet, our names are copied in ink onto papyrus and stored for posterity.' Melissa wiped her eyes. 'I can't believe this is happening.'

Sophie was welling up too.

'We have business at the Festival of Janus,' said Freddy. 'After that, one way or another, we're leaving Rome.'

Understanding every word, Charlotte leaned against Sophie's legs. They'd cross in Juno — or they'd be crossing the river Styx.

Drusus and Melissa left, taking the census tablet, and when they returned, Freddy opened more bottles of Falerian wine.

Sophie raised a glass. 'To freedom.'

The next morning, the ex-slaves didn't wake up for breakfast. Getting drunk on watered down alcohol was a challenge, but they'd managed it.

In the courtyard, Jack was playing a fetch-game with Freddy, retrieving a rag soldier Melissa had made. Charlotte, though, was pacing, worrying about the festival. She only stopped when Hugo brought out breakfast.

The dogs demolished flat bread and sausages, as did Hugo and Freddy, though the sausages were burnt. The brazier in the kitchen had a steep learning curve. Sophie tucked into a honey wrap.

After breakfast, Freddy read aloud from a flyer that Drusus had picked up in the Forum. The papyrus had the familiar Janus logo. '*Day One of the Festival of Janus,*' he translated. '*The procession begins at the Pons Fabricius bridge. Bring wine and food and song.* There's a list of cafés, souvenir stalls... *The celebrations end at dusk near the Theatre of Marcellus at the temple.*' Freddy paused. 'That's the crossroads temple.' '*Join the free feast, after the sacrifice of the ram.*'

Sophie grimaced. She wouldn't stay for the sacrifice, even if that was predictable behaviour for her.

'Nothing about Janus going walkabout?' said Hugo. His voice sounded anxious over the soothing sound of the fountain.

Freddy shook his head. 'The builders must be summoning him tomorrow, or on the final day of the festival.'

'So, the walking staff will still be in their headquarters,' said Sophie.

'They'll be remotely monitoring the procession,' said Hugo, 'but they might have people mingling with the crowd to ensure the celebrations pass off smoothly. If we can spot them, introduce ourselves as travellers, they might share the address of their base?'

Freddy frowned. 'They've run this festival for so long. They'll surely be adept at blending in?'

And there was another problem. 'Say they give us the address, we shouldn't just swing by, assume they'll be friendly,' said Sophie. The builder in the medieval realm had seemed welcoming, but fearing they'd change the timeline and ruin years of research, she'd turned on them. They'd barely escaped with their lives.

'We can only hope that trying to kill us in Georgia was a one-off,' said Hugo.

Freddy tapped his fingers on the arm of the couch. 'What if the next Wells is there?'

'We take him on,' said Sophie. 'He might not know about the pendant, and it'll be three against one.' Charlotte harrumphed. 'Sorry, four against one.' She glanced over at Jack. 'Maybe five.'

'I wonder how many versions of Wells there are?' said Freddy. 'Presumably, there are some universes where there isn't one. And there must be universes where we don't exist.' He blinked. 'Where Bella and Clarissa don't exist.'

Sophie rubbed her eyes. 'We can't know, can we?'

'Why hasn't Janus sent all the versions of Wells after us together?' said Hugo. 'We'd stand no chance.'

'I've been giving some thought to that,' said Freddy. 'If we look at the issue on the basis of linear time, the number of parallel universes may be continually increasing, splintering off, created by each additional decision that individuals make in an infinite number of universes.'

Charlotte seemed worried, or was she baffled? She wasn't alone. 'Difficult to picture,' said Sophie.

'As universes increase exponentially,' said Freddy, 'Janus has to keep abreast of more detail, increasing the possibility he'll overlook something important.'

Sophie stared at her lap. She'd tried to understand the latest multiverse theories at home but *Quantum Physics For Dummies* had defeated her.

'Janus didn't anticipate Wells' reaction, which gave Aelia the chance to throw her knife,' said Freddy. 'If he had, he would have told the second Wells that the first assassin he'd sent had died. Knowing that would have changed Wells' response to Hugo's taunt and may have affected Aelia's throw. She could have just injured him or missed him.'

'Okay…' said Sophie.

'The different ways that events play out must be complex

even for Janus' software,' said Freddy, 'and I believe it will become more so with the passage of time.'

'But time isn't linear,' said Hugo.

Sophie knew this. Well, she knew the theory, despite struggling to wrap her head around it.

'Time not being linear makes this more complicated and Janus has to account for everything, all at once,' said Freddy. 'Sending one version has consequences to be tracked and adjusted for. Sending two, let alone more, would make adjustments far more difficult.'

'Adjustments to what?' said Sophie.

'He's interfering with time.' Freddy exhaled. 'Other versions of us are searching for the walking staff in different universes. If his adjustments aren't done, or done wrong, with unpredictable ramifications for countless timelines, all of that may be impossible to unravel.'

Hugo nodded. 'Changing one thing allows you to track the consequences and adjust for it. Making more than one change, you can't tell what has caused what, and you have a confused mess.'

'Which is why he can't tell every version of Wells every possible relevant fact,' said Freddy. 'Even if Wells could take it in.'

Melissa came into the courtyard, walking with her head down and her shoulders slumped. Despite her hangover, she should have been ecstatic at being free.

'What's wrong?' said Sophie.

Melissa sat on a wooden-slatted chair. 'I've no family, no home. I'll end up back in a brothel.'

'We've paid the rent for six months,' said Freddy. 'You can live here until you find your feet.'

Sophie carried the dirty breakfast dishes into the house and reflected on unforeseen consequences — in just one universe. It hadn't occurred to her that escaping unpaid servitude wouldn't bring unalloyed joy.

Tarchon and Aelia were in the pool room, sitting close and whispering. Initially so wary of each other, now they were joined at the hip. They stood up when they saw her.

'We've been discussing what we'll do,' said Aelia.

'You can do anything you want,' said Sophie, embarrassed she'd disturbed them.

'Indeed,' said Tarchon. 'Even get married?'

Aelia grinned, and Sophie was saved from replying by Freddy and Hugo coming in from the courtyard.

'Time to set off for the festival,' said Freddy, his voice brisk.

Sophie went to the kitchen, poured water into a mixing bowl, and hastily washed the breakfast dishes, using a squidgy sponge, and 'house sand' from a jar.

When she returned to the pool room, Jack was running around Freddy's legs, sensing an outing. 'We may leave Rome today, so we're taking the dogs.'

Charlotte was sitting by the pool, staring at the water, and Sophie hugged her. She worried about taking Charlotte into harm's way, but she worried more about Jack. Too gentle to defend himself.

'You won't go alone,' said Tarchon.

Aelia raised her chin. 'We fight with you.'

CHAPTER 32

By mid-morning, the streets leading to the Pons Fabricius bridge were jam-packed with pop-up shops for the festival. There was no sign of Wells number three, but Sophie was wired, alert to her surroundings. Trinket stalls jostled for space with crowded bars selling freshly cooked snacks, and wine with Janus' logo on the bottles. The two young faces were everywhere.

But the revellers' favourite drink was slushy ice.

'Far too hot for mulled wine.' Freddy spooned orange-slush into his mouth.

Hugo, Tarchon and Aelia opted for pomegranate and Sophie chose honey for herself and the dogs. She put down the slush bowls and Charlotte and Jack lapped it up.

A herd of goats came over the bridge, bleating as they weaved between the stalls. The smell of their droppings mingled with the scent of grilled pork, and Sophie covered her nose with her shawl.

Somewhere further up the street were Drusus and Melissa. Freddy had told them there might be trouble and to keep their distance.

The dogs strained on their leads towards a counter covered in a cloth. Running the stall was the man who'd sold them breakfast on their first day.

'Health and great joy,' said Hugo in Latin.

'Offal?' The shopkeeper peeled away the cloth.

The dogs' noses were wiggling in ecstasy and Freddy bought them two wraps.

'Before proceeding south, we should check for the brother from the bridge,' said Tarchon. 'From there, we'll have a clear view.'

Tarchon strode forward, revellers parting in front of him. Aelia was causing another sort of stir. Men stared, admiring her figure or her uniform or both.

At the entrance to the bridge was a statue. The top of it was four Janus heads, looking in different directions. Two were female, their long hair tied up with bands like Sophie's. The others were male, short-haired and clean-shaven. One female face and one male face were a light flesh-colour, the others darker. The column below them was green and decorated with gilded figures: musicians blowing trumpets, tumbling acrobats, and toned athletes.

They all followed Tarchon and stood at the highest spot where the bridge spanned the river. Sophie leaned on a rail and systematically scanned the busy streets. 'He's not here.'

'But the sooner we find the research team, the better,' said Hugo.

They walked back off the bridge and joined the crowd moving south on the eastern bank.

Standing on a wooden box on the pavement was a man with grey hair and a straggly beard, surrounded by a gaggle of excited children and interested adults. He spread his hands in a theatrical, expansive gesture. 'Have your coin ready,' he shouted. 'You'll hear a tale of wonder. Who protects Rome?'

A ragged chorus answered him. 'Janus.'

'Janus protects us from the living but not from the dead.' A dramatic pause. 'The most esteemed of men have been haunted by unfortunate souls, slain and unavenged.'

'Pliny's haunted house,' called a woman.

'A terrifying spectre in chains…' The bard told the tale with relish, emboldened by oohs and gasps from his audience.

'I can understand some of it,' said Hugo. 'A ghost story?'

'A man was murdered and buried under a house, and he only stopped haunting people when he was found and lawfully buried,' said Freddy.

They moved further down the street and Sophie perused a fancy jewellery stall. Its white awning had an image of a mysterious figure in a scarlet, hooded robe. Startling blue eyes stared out of her wrinkled face. The stallholder finished serving a customer and stared at Sophie, her gaze as intense as the hooded figure. Sophie glanced down at the counter, pretending to examine a necklace.

'For you and yours.' The stallholder picked up a silver brooch and held it out. On it were swirly gold lines joined at the centre, stretching out four ways like Janus' heads.

Sophie put down the necklace. 'The brooch is pretty. I haven't seen that symbol of Janus before.'

The woman shook her head. 'This is more powerful than any god.'

Charlotte set her front paws on the counter, her expression solemn, but Sophie almost laughed. Talk about over-egging a product to get a sale.

'Be careful,' whispered Aelia to Sophie. 'She's a Sibyl.'

'Four souls,' said the stallholder, 'forever bound by love.'

The woman's voice was inside Sophie's head, surging up like the sea curling into a wave. The midday heat was rippling the air through the stall and the seller seemed to be flowing towards the brooch she was holding.

Sophie pulled her flask from her satchel and took a good swig of water.

The stallholder was still holding the brooch. Sophie accepted it and flipped it over. On the back was carved *AETERNUM*.

'Eternally,' translated Freddy.

'A lovely souvenir.' Hugo rummaged in his bag for coins.

The woman closed Sophie's fingers, firmly against the brooch.

'No price,' said the stallholder. 'A gift freely given.'

'Are you sure?' Freddy asked her. 'It looks valuable.'

'Only to you and yours.'

'Thank you.' Sophie pinned it on her shawl.

The woman greeted another customer, and Sophie moved on. As she walked, Sophie asked Aelia, 'What's a Sibyl?'

'A seer. They tell your future for coin.'

'But she refused payment,' said Freddy.

'Many shops do giveaways. They hope you'll return and buy.' Aelia turned, doing another check for Wells.

Sophie traced the surface of the brooch. Each of the lines could represent her and Charlotte, and Hugo and Freddy. Weren't they bound by love? Or they wouldn't be here. She remembered Freddy's quote from Ovid. *Fortune and love favour the brave*. When Bella was older, she should have this.

Twenty minutes later, they reached the crossroads, and the procession flowed around the theatre and the vegetable market, spreading into the square in front of Janus' temple.

The green and gold columns, the emerald façade, the farming symbols of plenty, and the yellow flower, impressed her anew. This had been built with the blood and sweat of Romans, labouring over concrete and stone and marble, and painted in loving detail. Not conjured up by the builders under cover of darkness.

The flame on the altar was being tended by a slave dressed in a fine green tunic, and people were queueing to donate food and wine.

The steps of the temple were less busy, so Sophie headed in that direction. A youth who was sitting on them looked up. His plain tunic was bright yellow with long sleeves. She paused. It was blisteringly hot, and the only other person she'd seen wearing full-length sleeves here had been the girl in the Forum. Could this guy be connected to her?

As she approached him, there was a faint electronic bleep, then two more. Coming from something in his satchel? He gave her a friendly nod, as if he knew her.

Sophie smiled at him. 'Hello.'

Tarchon stepped between her and the youth. 'He may be armed,' he said.

The guy leapt up, his tunic clinging to his body in the heat. Sophie glimpsed the outline of a translation cylinder and a knife at his waist. But he made no attempt to grab his blade. It was smaller than their kitchen knives.

'Can I help you?' He said in English. His accent was slightly mechanical, though the rest of him seemed human.

'His legs are hairy,' said Hugo.

The youth frowned.

'So?' said Sophie. 'You and Freddy have hairy legs.'

'Not having plucked legs is unusual here,' said Freddy.

'Right. That gave me away.' The youth sat down again.

'You're one of the research team?' said Sophie, needing to be sure.

The youth nodded. 'I hope you enjoy the festival.'

'What were those bleeps?' said Freddy.

'The system recognised you as travellers.' The youth

tapped his wrist under his sleeve and the material fell back, revealing a gold bracelet with inlaid jewels of green and red.

Sophie recognised the distinctive design. Each gem was a different shape: oval, square, oblong, and round. In medieval Georgia, the woman who'd shot her with an arrow had worn a bracelet identical to that. And her wolf had worn a matching collar. The jewellery had blocked the rare gene, preventing them from being tracked by the builders. But this guy was a builder, so his device might do the opposite? She smiled at him. 'Your colleagues can track you with the bracelet, keep you safe?'

'You know about security bands?' said the youth, surprised.

'I came across them a while ago,' said Sophie. 'What else does yours do?'

Now he looked wary. 'It's standard issue, with several functions.'

Freddy cleared his throat. 'Is there a girl in your team who wears a grey tunic?'

'You mean, in the field?'

'Er, yes.'

'We wear yellow. Easy to spot if we get separated.'

Sophie bit her lip. If that girl wasn't in the research team, who was she?

The youth stroked Charlotte and Jack who were nuzzling at his legs. 'This is your first visit?'

'Yes,' said Hugo. 'Rome's … wonderful.'

Sophie sat down beside the youth. 'Does the whole team attend the festival?'

'On the last day.'

'How many of you are stationed here?' asked Freddy.

'Six.'

Encouraged by the guy's ready answers, Sophie took the

map from her satchel. 'Could you show us the location of your headquarters, please?'

'I'm sorry, we don't do tourist visits.'

Hugo's guess about time-travelling tourists had been correct. They did visit Rome. Who were they? Where did they come from?

'We're historians, with a particular interest in Janus.' Hugo's lie had a ring of truth.

The youth tapped a spot north of the Forum. 'Villa Acilius, on Tiburtina Street.'

Same house name, but different road. Sophie found the pencil in her satchel and marked the place with a cross.

They thanked him and hurried across the square, buoyed up.

Checking her map, Sophie turned down a side street. The youth had been cagey about the bracelet's functions, but otherwise helpful. If the team at their base were as friendly as him and there were loads of walking staffs, maybe they could simply ask for one?

CHAPTER 33

Tiburtina Street appeared no different from any other residential road. But for the cross on Sophie's map, there would have been little chance of finding the builders' base. Charlotte, though, once she was close enough, could sense or hear the barrier that concealed it. She cocked her head. A few paces further on, Charlotte trotted across the road, and inspected the far pavement. The barrier was close.

Sophie dashed after her. In the medieval realm, individuals with the gene had passed through the builders' barrier unharmed. But this was a different universe and time. In front of a smooth iron door, Charlotte's head disappeared, so did her body and tail, and Sophie hastily followed.

An intense tingling sensation prickled her skin like tiny needles. Familiar, disorientating, and for a split-second, painful. Ouch.

They were on a driveway, leading to a single storey building with sharp angular corners, opaque glass walls, and a flat roof. The oppressive heat of the Roman summer was absent. A cool breeze ruffled Sophie's hair but the air smelled sterile, like the inside of the builders' cellar.

Charlotte seemed okay but Sophie hugged her before they stepped back through the barrier.

Tarchon and Aelia were staring, open-mouthed.

'All is well,' said Sophie. 'It's just an invisible fence.' She addressed Hugo and Freddy. 'The same barrier.'

'Tarchon and Aelia shouldn't see the prep for the festival,' said Hugo, in English. 'We don't want to get off on the wrong foot.'

Freddy shortened Jack's lead. 'Absolutely.'

Janus was a creature of algorithms, designed for academic study, but the success of the festival rested on the locals believing in an all-powerful god. Tarchon and Aelia would compromise that and given their past form, the builders would either kill them or ensure they never left.

'Please stand guard outside.' Sophie shot the ex-slaves a reassuring glance, and they nodded.

'I didn't get a bad vibe from the guy in the team,' said Hugo, 'but best to be prepared.' He rummaged in his satchel for his knife.

Freddy found his, and Sophie pulled out the pendant. To ensure Hugo passed through, she held his hand and said his name. She held her breath, met the needles-sensation, and they reached the other side.

Hugo shivered. 'Hurrrrr. I'd forgotten how unnerving that is.'

Freddy appeared with the dogs, Jack writhing as if he'd been in a puddle.

Up ahead, a door slid open, and a woman with fabulous cheekbones strode out. On her feet were flip-flops and she wore a yellow, sleeveless tunic.

'Hello.' Sophie's greeting came out in English.

'Please come in.' The woman's voice had a mechanistic edge. The guy from the research team had sounded the same.

They trooped inside and the front door slid closed behind them.

A false window stretched around the spacious reception room in a seamless band, showing the crossroads temple from above. The crowd in the square was moving and the flame on the altar flickered. Live footage from a satellite. A few revellers had small green dots by their heads.

The reception room was empty except for metal, upright chairs, a long desk, and a dark red armchair with cream antimacassars on the back and arms. The protective squares of fabric had been commonplace in Shorten, named after a brand of hair oil, popular in the 19th century. The fussiness of the armchair contrasted oddly with the other furniture.

Hugo was frowning, also eyeing the chair.

Freddy introduced them, and the woman's lips lifted in a polite smile.

'I am Ishtar.'

'Like the Mesopotamian goddess?' asked Hugo.

Ishtar glanced at him, surprised he'd spoken out of turn. But Hugo took it on the chin, used to pet status.

'I inspired her,' said Ishtar. 'What brings you to Rome?'

'We're here to see the festival,' said Sophie.

A girl in a black tunic came in. Her dark hair and eyes suggested she was a local. Once recruited, the servants and their descendants could never leave the base.

'Would you like a beverage?' said Ishtar.

'English breakfast tea would be very welcome,' said Freddy.

'Charlotte prefers Earl Grey.' Sophie patted Jack. 'He's fine with water.'

'Please make yourself comfortable.' Ishtar gestured at the office chairs.

Charlotte promptly sat on one, Jack stayed on the floor, and everyone else sat down.

'I'd lend you enablers,' said Ishtar, 'but I see you have them.'

'Enablers?' said Freddy.

'The translation devices.'

'Your large temple over the canal is very impressive,' said Hugo, 'including the cellar.' He was choosing his words carefully. Something here was worrying him.

Ishtar raised a thin eyebrow. 'The cellar's used for storage.'

'Forgive me if this is impolite,' said Freddy, 'but what's stored there?'

'Rare, pre-Roman artefacts. We moved them when we built the temple. The most fragile items are packed in boxes.'

Sophie winced. Who knew what precious things had taken a bashing when Freddy had kicked the box downstairs?

'There was a large block of stone with writing on it,' said Hugo.

Ishtar nodded. 'A priest's grimoire. Details an unpleasant ritual that was conducted every twenty years. A king sacrificed to ensure a plentiful harvest. There's also a curse to deter anyone but the priest from touching it.'

Sophie relived tracing the hieroglyphics with her fingers. 'What kind of curse?'

'A litany of ill will,' said Ishtar, 'but nothing unpleasant befell those who excavated it.'

'When was the temple built?' asked Freddy, keen to move on from curses.

'Many decades ago.'

The servant returned with a china teapot, a matching milk jug, a sugar bowl, and cups on a tray. The crockery featured a rustic Victorian scene and garish gold lids and handles.

'Mr Wells requested these drinking vessels,' said Ishtar. 'You may be acquainted with him.'

Hugo exchanged a glance with Sophie.

Right. The Victorian armchair was for Wells. 'I've heard of him.' Sophie kept her tone mildly interested.

'We hope we're not intruding at what must be your busiest time,' said Freddy.

'We welcome historians.' Ishtar gave them a tight smile. 'I hope the festival lives up to your expectations.'

'We're very much looking forward to seeing Janus,' lied Sophie.

'Unfortunately, the device that facilitates his appearance was recently sent away to be upgraded and a little moisture got in. Hopefully, it will be repaired soon.' Ishtar sighed. 'Fireworks, however impressive, can't convey the expected gravitas.'

'Is it being repaired here?' Freddy's enquiry conveyed just the right amount of academic interest.

'No. That process is integral to our ship, so my team must make the necessary adjustments in situ.'

Sophie glanced down, hiding her disappointment. Many centuries from now, when Janus became sentient, the builders' ship would become his. Was the ship in Rome? If so, where? But those questions wouldn't gel with being an historian, primarily interested in the festival and ancient Roman culture. She risked a trivial observation, probably common knowledge. 'The ship camouflages itself, to blend into its surroundings.'

'Indeed.' Ishtar seemed unfazed.

'You only have one summoning device?' asked Freddy.

A slight crease marred Ishtar's brow. 'This has never happened before.'

Could Wells have sabotaged it? 'When did you discover the moisture problem?' said Sophie, her voice matter of fact.

'Two weeks ago.'

They'd been in Rome eleven days. The first Wells had arrived before them, had enough time to hire his thugs, but if the walking staff had been upgraded elsewhere, then secured in the ship... Wells couldn't have sabotaged it.

'The device should be ready for the field test tomorrow.' Ishtar's lips thinned.

'Field test?' said Hugo.

'Exposure to direct sunlight, from midday until three, in the gardens of Augustus. The result determines how we proceed. On the last day, Janus must appear three hours before sunset or not at all. The master of time can't be late.'

'Do you summon him in the same location every year?' asked Freddy.

'We do. We vary elements of the display, but the traditional location on the riverbank engenders trust, and for us it's convenient. We move the ship into Juno's arch.'

That figured. The walking staff had to be near the builders' ship to summon Janus out. In the same way that they'd needed to be in the students' union, near the landing site there, when they'd called Juno. If they survived this, they'd need to be in or near the arch to call her again.

'The arch is the only location in Rome where ships can land?' said Sophie.

'Quite so,' said Ishtar. 'Incoming vessels access our database, record what dates to avoid.'

That tied in with what Juno had told them. *Juno's automated systems communicate with their air traffic databases.* And the future builders' ship, controlled by Janus, must interact with Ishtar's database too, before spewing out the next version of H. G. Wells.

'Is Mr Wells staying with you?' said Sophie. If Wells number three was here, they couldn't stay overnight in this base. He'd knife them in their sleep.

'He is.' Ishtar waved at the false window. The view of the crossroads temple zoomed higher, showing the whole city, then swooped down onto the Forum and a man in a toga. By his head was a green dot. It was Wells, standing in front of a clothes store in the promenade.

'He's out shopping,' said Ishtar.

Sophie looked at her lap to hide her surprise. The new Wells browsing souvenirs… Well, he had form. At some point, one walking staff ended up in his home in the 19th century. But hopefully this walking staff, in this universe, would be going home with them.

'Are the other green dots tourists?' said Freddy.

'I imagine so.'

Sophie searched the green dots, hoping to see the girl in the grey tunic, but she wasn't there. Outside the Forum, dots inside private houses were just dots. You couldn't see inside to identify the person.

'Does your system show travellers who've run into trouble, even died?' said Hugo, likely thinking of the first two versions of Wells.

'Rome has been overrun by tourists for centuries. Many must have fallen prey to disease or accidents. Their dots would blot out the footage.'

'So, there's no way to identify deceased tourists?' said Hugo.

'After a week's inactivity, our system flags their last recorded location and, if practical, their remains are recovered.'

So, if they'd died in the temple cellar, their bodies would have been found.

Ishtar tutted. 'Your ship should have briefed you on emergencies and deaths. Ships send reports to the registered next of kin and the retrieval department.'

'What does the retrieval department do?' asked Freddy.

Ishtar shot him her polite smile. 'It's responsible for retrieving deceased individuals and repatriating them.'

Juno hadn't mentioned procedures for emergencies. This was more evidence that her systems were outdated. But more to the point, Juno couldn't send a message to the retrieval department, let alone their families.

Freddy stood up, his face shuttered. 'Thank you for the tea. We should be going.'

Sophie felt queasy. If they died here, no one would ever know.

Bella would never know.

CHAPTER 34

*L*ate that evening in the Villa Acilius, Ishtar and her team retired, leaving George Wells alone in the reception room. He sat in the comfortable armchair and sipped brandy from a fine glass. The alcohol had been produced by a machine, apparently out of nothing. Wondrous.

Ishtar had a treasure trove of marvels. She'd asked him if he'd enjoyed the 'enabler's' benefits. When he'd hesitated, she'd looked annoyed, given him the clever cylinder, and insisted he return it before he left the city. But he'd keep it. It had proved invaluable in the Forum, buying the workman's tunic, and would greatly assist him when he visited the distant future, far beyond his home in the 19th century. Hopefully, the other destinations would be more pleasant than 1917. At least now he knew to avoid the Great War. He'd emigrate to America.

Two men had already failed Janus' test in ancient Rome. Janus had claimed they were lesser versions of George Wells! The men must look similar to him but lack his skill and determination. Yes, his experience of ending someone's life was limited to a drunken brawl and bribing witnesses. Not easy on a schoolmaster's income. But a less resourceful man would have hanged.

Before he'd stumbled through the pub door in Derbyshire and encountered Janus, he'd never considered writing for a living. Janus' promises of immortality, of endless beautiful women and men, could be as fanciful as the nonsense about different versions of George Wells. Yet returning without killing the travellers for Janus would stymie any further time travel, along with the unique opportunity to source priceless inspiration for novels. He pictured returning to the 19th century, living the life of a genteel, successful author. Never again would he have to toil away in that tiresome school, teaching unappreciative brats...

George swallowed the last of the brandy and wiped his mouth, regretting shaving off his beard. Without it, he felt uneasy, not himself. He stood up and went over to the window. The magic lantern show never stopped, even at night. Most of the green dots were inside private villas, unable to be viewed and identified. Other time travellers? Tourists?

He tapped on the Colosseum. A label appeared. *Amphitheatrum Flavium.* He touched a random house on a nearby street, but nothing happened. Only important sites were labelled.

Seen from high above, the water of the Tiber glinted in the moonlight, dark and mysterious. The festival would reach its climax by the riverbank in two days. Janus had told him the creature that would be conjured up was just an animated golem, but given Ishtar's technology, it would be memorable. He'd stay for that.

He adjusted the brooch on his toga, hidden from sight as Janus had instructed him, and concentrated on the matter in hand. The workmen's clothes he'd bought in the Forum would ensure he could act without suspicion, and those pocket watches he'd stolen in 1917 had more than paid for the bodyguards, and their silence.

Tomorrow, a crane would drop its load, demolish a building, and kill everyone in it. And George Wells would return to Janus with more trophies: a trinket from the dead girl, locks of her dead lovers' hair, and for good measure, a dead dog's collar.

CHAPTER 35

*E*arly the next morning in the Villa Fullia, the ex-slaves were still asleep, and Sophie was washing up breakfast dishes. Birdsong and splashing from the courtyard fountain couldn't be heard from the kitchen, and the only sounds were the dogs' paws padding on the floor tiles and Jack's wagging tail. Sophie wiped her eyes. Hugo was getting better at not burning sausages, but any cooking on the brazier produced eye-watering smoke.

'*Day Two. Music and poetry in the Forum of Domitian.*' Freddy was showing off, translating as he read. '*Then feast and make merry in the Gardens of Augustus.* That's where the builders are testing the walking staff.'

'We shouldn't venture out today.' Hugo dried a plate. 'We should let the third Wells stew. Might mess with his head. And if he starts second-guessing, he'll be more stressed, more prone to making mistakes.' Charlotte blinked her agreement. 'An easier opponent tomorrow.'

'Doing nothing would certainly be illogical,' said Freddy. 'We'd be missing our first opportunity to take the staff. Perhaps our only one.'

'We'd be acting in a counter, *counter*-intuitive way,' said Hugo. 'Unexpectedly unpredictable.'

Sophie rinsed the final plate. 'You're overthinking it.' They were so close to getting the walking staff, to seeing Bella. 'If we can deal with Wells this morning, we'll have a clear run to grab the staff.'

'You make it sound as if ending him is a formality,' said Hugo. 'Surely, the more times we have to confront him, the greater the risk?'

'We've survived so far,' said Sophie.

'With help,' said Hugo. 'Doesn't mean we will the next time.'

'The level of risk hasn't changed,' said Freddy, 'but the stakes have. If we succeed today, we might be back in Juno this afternoon.'

Hugo frowned.

It was a fifteen-minute walk from the Villa Fullia to the colossal third temple of Janus. The sun blazed down on the streets leading to the Forum of Domitian, its rays dancing on the garish canopies of festival stalls. The aroma of wine and snacks scented the air as revellers drank from amphora bottles and tucked into skewers of beef, pork wraps, boiled eggs and grapes, and plums wrapped in vine leaves.

Sophie and Charlotte followed Tarchon, skirting around stalls with Janus figurines and friezes. Hugo was behind them with Freddy, who had Jack on a short lead. Aelia brought up the rear.

In the Forum of Domitian, they stayed at the edge of the square. Sophie didn't look at the temple, kept her eyes on the crowd. After almost dying in the cellar, she had no wish to go anywhere near the building, let alone go inside. Fortunately, the festival event was happening in the square. A stage had been erected and the audience was hushed, listening to a man in a pink tunic. His gold necklace with flashing gems was as dramatic as the cascade of bracelets that jangled on his wrists.

'A magnificent welcome to the second day of the festival.' The presenter made a sweeping gesture, encompassing the crowd. 'By tradition, the emperor cannot be here, but we salute his generosity!'

Sophie only vaguely took in the presenter's words. She stood on tiptoes to check for Wells, but Aelia and Tarchon, standing protectively in front of her, restricted her view.

'First up, the Fearless Five!'

Acrobats curled, human balls, tumbling from each side of the stage, narrowly avoiding each other. They leapt and did the splits. The smallest climbed up the others who had locked arms as a human pyramid, and the child posed like a classical statue.

Furious clapping echoed across the square, with whistles, appreciative yells, and calls of, 'Show us different tricks!'

Hugo and Freddy were watching the crowd, and Sophie stopped trying to, wishing she were taller.

After the acrobats, there were musicians playing flutes and trumpets and drums. Jack began to howl along with the tune and Charlotte determinedly nuzzled him, persuaded him to stop. Following the music, a succession of earnest men made up poems on the spot, based on the presenter's suggestions: Athena born through her father's forehead, a boastful weaver of cloth who was turned into a spider, Zeus punishing Prometheus for giving humans fire…

'I've lost track of the poetry,' said Hugo.

'Most of it's painful,' said Sophie. 'But the winner will get a plaque and 1,000 sestertii from the emperor.'

'Some of the rhyming's impressive.' Freddy tipped his flask and shook the last drops of water into this mouth.

'We should leave before the end,' said Aelia. 'We don't want to be crushed in the stampede to the feast.'

'Is a stampede likely?' said Sophie.

'People have perished before.' Aelia's tone suggested it was commonplace.

Tarchon cleared a path through the square and they took advantage of the space in his wake.

'I'm parched,' said Freddy.

When they reached the Forum, they headed to the nearest café. There was still scaffolding on the temple opposite, and from the roof came the sound of banging and shouted orders.

'The renovation was supposed to be finished by now,' said Aelia.

Most of the façade was up, displaying flattering images of Julius Caesar and admiring minions. On an adjacent building, a bulky crane was swinging a stone slab towards the frieze, the slab attached by a double rope. As the slab was lowered, giant wheels on the crane turned. Men in loin cloths were within the wheels, moving them by determinedly plodding, like slow-motion hamsters in a cage.

On the highest floor of the temple, leaning precariously from a window, was a man also holding a rope tied to the slab.

More workmen were climbing on top of the crane and lunging forward, as if cutting something. Other men were yelling and jumping from the temple roof onto the other building, scrambling towards the crane.

Sophie walked into the welcome shade of the café's awning. The sign on the popina said SALVIUS, meaning hospitality. There was a free table outside, but Freddy opened the door. 'It's too noisy out here.'

Inside, the food served was depicted on the walls: grains and pulses, pork, cheese and olives, and honey cakes. A young woman moved gracefully between the tables, setting down bottles and glasses. Another woman with a lined face was balancing trays laden with cakes and bowls of eggs in brown sauce. The smell of the wine sweetened the tangy fishy smell coming from the sauce. The older woman's voice rang out above the chatter of her customers, calling for bread, and a teenager dashed through a swing door to fetch some.

Sophie followed Freddy to a table, and half turned to Charlotte and Hugo.

'The honey cakes smell so fresh,' she said. 'Yummy—'

A tremendous bang reverberated around them, deafening and deep, and Sophie's ears popped. She reached out to Hugo and Charlotte, but they weren't there.

Then there was nothing. Oblivion.

It was snowing in the café.

Lying on her back, Sophie watched the white slivers floating down. Oddly shaped snow. Peaceful though.

The silence she associated with snow snapped off. Instead, there was screaming. Sophie sat up. She was covered with pieces of plaster and smashed crockery and glass. Someone pulled her to her feet.

Tarchon's forehead was split with a nasty gash and blood was dripping into his eyes. 'Are you injured?'

'No, but you are.'

He wiped his face with his fingers. 'Just a cut.'

Customers and waitresses were clutching at each other. Outside, a trumpet sounded.

Charlotte's fur was white from broken plaster, and she

jumped up at Sophie. So did Jack, and Sophie sagged with relief. Freddy was sitting on the floor. He was staring at nothing but looked okay. Where was Hugo? Sophie desperately cast about but couldn't see him. Finally, she spotted a sliver of deep turquoise material under a pile of debris. Hugo's tunic. She and Tarchon tore at the rubble, throwing it aside.

Hugo was grey with dust. He blinked but didn't move. Charlotte licked his face and he groaned. Sophie frantically checked him for injuries. There was no blood she could see. 'Hugo, Hugo!'

'I'm okay.' His voice was a croak.

'What's hurting?' she asked him.

'Something knocked me down.'

Sophie pulled Hugo to his feet, and he put his hand to his head, dazed.

Freddy stood up, pulling plaster from his hair. 'What happened?'

'The crane dropped its load,' said Aelia.

Sophie stared at the entrance. The door was hanging off its hinges. All those people sitting outside... She steeled herself and went through the gap. The slab had crashed onto the awning, killing everyone directly underneath. Those with minor injuries were standing about in shock. Others required immediate first aid.

'The Vigiles will be here soon.' Aelia tore a strip off her scarlet cloak.

'The watchmen are medics?' asked Sophie.

Aelia wrapped her makeshift bandage around a woman's arm. 'They do whatever's needed.'

Freddy and Hugo helped to sort the dead from the living, and Sophie used her knife to cut off the bottom of her sturdy shawl to assist Aelia. Charlotte sniffed at a tangle of industrial-sized rope and gave a single bark. She pushed one clear with her paw and Sophie gulped. The end had been cut.

Tarchon grabbed Sophie's arm. 'We must leave.' He pointed at the rope. 'If another Wells brother did this, he'll soon be here to finish the job.'

'Let him,' said Sophie. 'We'll finish *him*.'

'He couldn't have done this alone,' said Aelia. 'Retreat to survive.'

'Agreed.' Hugo tapped dust off his tunic.

They hurried back into the café, through the kitchen, and out onto a narrow side road.

'Isn't this predictable, leaving like this?' Freddy checked the street.

'The way's clear,' said Hugo.

Sophie caught Hugo's arm as they made their way along the street, eyes darting left and right. Her anger and bravado had dissolved, and she was consumed by fear.

CHAPTER 36

An hour after fleeing from the wrecked café, Hugo was sitting in the pool room in the Villa Fullia. He tapped his fingers on the arm of the chair. 'Janus told Wells when we'd go to the popina but he didn't anticipate we'd sit inside.'

Charlotte stopped making patterns in the water with her paw.

Escaping in one piece hadn't lessened Sophie's fear and something more insidious was gathering strength. Hopeless-ness, a sense that seeing Bella again was a doomed fantasy. Every time they inched closer to the walking staff, they got knocked back. Yes, Janus didn't know everything they did, but he knew where they went each day, knew they'd retreated here. A shiver slid down her spine and she stood up from the armchair. 'Janus must have told Wells about this villa, given him the address.'

Freddy folded his arms. 'He'll see our dots on the builders' window, but as we're in a private house, he can't be sure the dots are us.'

'And this road is very long,' said Hugo. 'Hopefully, there'll be time-travelling tourists renting other villas. And with no street or house names displayed on the road, tracking down our property won't be straightforward.'

'Unless he asks a passing slave for directions.' Sophie sighed. "He doesn't need to do that. He just waits until we leave the villa and checks it's us on the builders' window. He's identified the house.'

Freddy got to his feet. 'I should put on the pendant when we step outside. I might not show up?'

Sophie shook her head. 'Even if we take turns, we'd have to wear it for hours. Not a good idea.' Juno had confirmed that using the pendant for too long would trap the wearer in the near past. Unable to interact, to eat or drink, they'd soon suffer a lonely death.

'If we stick together, and we should,' said Hugo, 'just you being invisible wouldn't help.'

'We shouldn't panic,' said Freddy. 'Even if he has identified our dots, he's no way of checking our location outside the headquarters. He'd have to draw a sketch of where our house is, and the surrounding streets. He could easily make a mistake.'

'No harm in tightening up security protocols.' Hugo ruffled Charlotte's head. 'Let's do that now.'

Out in the courtyard, Tarchon was rolling a dice, playing the board game with Drusus, while Jack dozed at their feet. Aelia was doing one-arm press-ups. Melissa was sitting on the ground, armed with a collection of nuts, waiting for Aelia to join her in a game. On the grass was a chalk triangle divided into sections. Taking it in turns, the winner was the first person to roll five nuts neatly into a section. As the nuts rolled quicker than the board game's oblong dice, winning required a deal of skill.

Hugo sat on the yellow couch.

'Listen everyone.' Sophie sat beside him. 'When we first

arrived, we had to say the house word for Drusus to let us in. You recognise our voices, so we haven't used it since. But from now on, you must never open the front door unless we say, "Arbor flore," and never unbar the door to anyone else.'

'Your enemies know of this house?' Melissa glanced up, alarmed.

'I fear so,' said Freddy.

Hugo bit his lip. 'We should pass on the feast, even though the walking staff will be there. That would be really unpredictable, given our recent past decisions.'

Freddy repeated Hugo's words so everybody could understand.

Tarchon frowned. 'You're trying to avoid your fate by tricking a god that knows all.'

Sophie hugged herself. Put like that, it did sound insane.

'If you find the magic walking staff and slay Janus, he would no longer watch over Rome,' said Drusus. 'That would be a calamity.'

'It's difficult to explain,' said Freddy, 'but he'll still appear at his festival and protect Rome for hundreds of years.'

Drusus looked relieved.

'The Janus feast is held in an open park,' said Aelia. 'If a brother is there, we can seek him out and end him.'

Charlotte was listening, seemed undecided.

'Each time we confront Wells, it's a terrible risk,' said Hugo kissing Sophie on the brow. 'I can't forget what that girl told you. That you're going to die.'

Sophie shuddered. 'Maybe I die whatever we do?'

'We haven't seen the girl since the Forum,' said Freddy.

'I don't care,' said Hugo. 'We should play it safe.'

'I agree with Aelia. Taking the initiative usually pays off,' said Sophie. Frustration, and hurt, showed on Hugo's face but she set her mouth. She wouldn't be ruled by fear.

Twenty minutes later, out on the pavement, Sophie adjusted the strap of her satchel across her chest. She pulled her shawl over her hair. The hem had been ragged, hacked off to make bandages in the café, but Melissa had turned it up, making an invisible repair.

As she walked, Sophie waved her fan. Charlotte trotted ahead of her, staying in the shade where she could, Jack beside her. Tarchon was striding at the front of their group, Freddy behind him. Aelia was at the rear as usual.

Hugo took Sophie's hand. 'I hate it when we argue,' he said. 'It's just, I'm knackered—'

'Arm yourselves.' Tarchon snagged a dagger off his belt.

A group of men in shabby tunics had rounded the corner, three abreast. The straps of their sandals criss-crossed their lower legs and they each held a knife. Sunlight glinted on the blades.

Wells was at the rear of the group, his face leaner than the previous versions.

Sophie looked over her shoulder. Their front door was bolted shut. In the time it would take to bang on it, they'd be dead—

'Flee!' shouted Tarchon.

'Charlotte, run away,' yelled Sophie. Charlotte was too brave for her own good. The dogs sped off.

Sophie sprinted as fast as she could. She didn't slow by the front door of their villa, kept running, level with Hugo and Freddy. The thugs were chasing, their heavy, hob-nailed sandals pounding on the hard pavement.

'Split up, and head for the main road,' said Aelia.

'Charlotte, go around, then double back to the villa,' gasped Hugo. 'I'll meet you there.'

The dogs ran faster and though her lungs were burning,

Sophie kicked harder, and focused. Reach the main street. Reach the crowds.

They all sprinted round a bend. Sophie stumbled on a crooked paving stone. She hit the ground, wincing as her bulky satchel slammed into her stomach. She rolled over and met Wells' eyes.

'Kill her,' he said.

But the men bearing down on her hesitated, glancing at each other, unclear who should deliver the blow. Sophie opened her satchel. 'I have money.'

Anger twisted Wells' mouth. 'You don't need her—'

Sophie had slipped on the pendant, total silence cutting off his words. Though they couldn't touch her, any more than she could touch them, she scrambled backwards.

Wells and his thugs were sepia, shadow-men, gawping at the spot where she'd been. She caught her breath. Preoccupied with her, everyone else should have got away.

She got shakily to her feet. Her hair hung about her face and her shawl was creased and dirty. She tied it on her waist and looked back up the street. To shout the house word by the villa door and be heard, she'd have to remove the pendant. No, hide. Then take it off.

But there was nowhere to hide. Sophie stepped into the shade of the olive tree.

Wells marched along the road, agitated, and mouthing something. He banged on the door before theirs. Buffoonish. A comedy actor in a silent movie.

The neighbour's door didn't open, and Wells whirled around and mouthed again. Probably cursing. He gave orders, gesticulating, and strode off in the direction everyone had fled. Four of his men stayed, watching the wrong door.

Sophie ran in the opposite direction to Wells, the pendant bouncing on her chest. Just past the corner, she stopped and scanned the next residential street. Deserted. Hugo would double back soon with the dogs. She had to warn them about the goons.

She stayed on the corner, watching the thugs and waiting for Charlotte and Hugo to race into view. If the thugs spotted them, she'd do the ghost routine to scare them off. The familiar, isolated feeling from the pendant grew stronger, until she felt like a lost soul, trapped between the underworld and the living.

Where were they? As soon as Hugo and Charlotte had realised she wasn't with them, they'd have stopped running, risked their lives to help her. And if they'd hadn't noticed in their dash to escape, as soon as he could, Hugo would have kept with his plan, returned with Charlotte. Something bad must have happened. She had to find them.

She stepped back round the corner and took off the pendant. Everything was in technicolour and a hot-pavement smell assaulted her nostrils. She stored the pendant in her satchel.

If Hugo and Charlotte couldn't return to the villa but were still ... okay, where would they go? The gardens of Augustus, to steal the walking staff. And Freddy and Jack would go with them.

Half a mile from the Villa Fullia and Wells' thugs, Sophie paused in a picturesque street where slaves were watering hanging baskets and delicate trees. In the middle of the thoroughfare was a fountain. Water poured out of bronze, wide-mouthed fishes and, supervised by women in fancy shawls, toddlers were laughing and splashing. Sophie smiled at them, her ache for Bella hitting her anew.

Keep going. Only a mile to the Gardens of Augustus. Find Hugo and Freddy and the dogs.

Further up the road, a play was in full swing. Young men wearing white masks were lamenting, while other men in red masks were giggling. Strange.

Outside a popina with a gilt-edged awning, a woman was giving out free goat wraps. The next store sold over-the-top shawls, more gold than fabric. In front of another swanky shop, children and teenagers were posing as classical statues, their pink pretend togas arranged in elegant folds. An art exhibit? Sophie peered at a notice on the shop wall. Going by the names on each line, they were reviews, but she couldn't read them. She turned her back to the store and scanned the street. No sign of Wells, or of Hugo, Freddy and the dogs.

A scuffling noise came from the shop behind her, and heavy footsteps. Someone grabbed her shoulders, their fingers digging in, and Sophie gasped in shock. What the hell? Passers-by hadn't noticed she was being assaulted. 'Let go of me!' She twisted to escape but was held fast. The man had arms as big as hunks of ham. She couldn't kick and, in any event, was wearing flimsy sandals. She relaxed her body to make him think she'd given up, then slammed her head backwards. Her skull hit his chest and he just grunted.

Her mind raced. A mugger? A rapist? A murderer? Once she was off the street, she'd be finished. She had to attract attention. 'Help!'

No one gave her a second glance.

The guy manhandled her into the store, and she was helpless to stop him. Sophie swore and spat and yelled. A curly-haired woman serving at the counter looked up, then resumed her conversation. Behind her, on a shelf, were pots of pink geraniums. The shop smelled of spicy perfume and too-sweet strawberries.

'Fetch the watchmen!' Sophie shouted, but the shop assistant continued chatting.

Sophie's assailant kicked open a door and threw her into a gloomy room. She put out her arms to break her fall, slammed into the floor, and cried out. In response, laughter came from the counter. Sophie jumped to her feet and spun to face her attacker.

He was dressed in a pink tunic, the same as the togas in the art exhibit. He marched over and seized the strap of her satchel. Sophie gripped the satchel tight.

The guy slapped her, stinging her cheek, and Sophie hesitated. He snatched the satchel and made off with it, shutting the door behind him. A key turned in the lock.

Sophie stared at the door. She'd been kidnapped, robbed, and when she'd screamed at the top of her lungs, not a soul had intervened. She thumped on the door with both fists. 'Let me out *immediately*. My husband, Lucius Veranius, will make you pay dearly. You'll wish you'd never been born.'

The door opened, and the man who'd grabbed her strode in. Sophie backed away and her legs met a bed. 'What do you want? I have money.'

He guffawed. 'The few coins in your satchel?' He held out a length of rope and loomed over her. She saw her chance and punched him, landing a clean blow on his jaw. His eyes registered surprise but he hardly flinched. 'If you don't stop this nonsense, I'll score your pretty skin like meat.' His fleshy lips pouted, and he tapped a small knife on his belt.

Disbelief, and horror. She couldn't fight her way out. Her best hope was to find her satchel, use the pendant. She gave a slight nod and let him tie her wrists in front of her.

He pulled a rag strip from his belt and forced it into her mouth, fastening it with a sharp jerk behind her head. His face was inches from hers and she felt sick. He reeked of pork and cheap wine.

Her jailer shoved her, so she fell on the bed. He wagged a finger. 'That's better.'

He left, and Sophie didn't move, shock making her shiver. Eventually, she sat on the edge of the bed. All the furniture was pink: the bedframe and headboard, the cotton sheet, the side table, and under the bed, a chamber pot. The walls were a plain, dull cream, except for an empty recess which matched the furniture.

High up under the roof was a narrow gap, the only source of light. On the ceiling was a fresco, an enormous grey swan looming over a plump, naked woman on a couch. A scene from a myth… The details weren't coming to mind but was sex involved?

Her stomach turned over. The teenagers and children outside weren't part of an art exhibit. They were soliciting for business.

She was in a brothel.

CHAPTER 38

Curled up on the bed in the brothel, a rope binding her wrists, Sophie tried to sleep. Her arms ached from her fall and her lips, constricted by the gag, were crusty and dry. The light from the tiny window above her was fading. How long had she been here? Nine, ten hours? What had happened to Hugo and Freddy, and Charlotte and Jack? Would she ever know?

She closed her fingers around her necklace. Hugo had said that for him, the cylinder appeared to be base metal with little monetary value, like her key-rattle. The cylinder was a crucial survival tool but losing Bella's rattle would be immeasurably worse. Hopefully, the pimp would think the necklace not worth stealing, though he might throw it away, force her to wear something flashy—

Click. The door was unlocking. She sat up.

The pimp sauntered in and shot her a smug smile. But for the gag, she'd have spat at him.

'I'm Tacitus, discreet by name, discreet by nature. Screaming can be good for business, angry shouting not so much. If you promise to keep quiet, I'll remove the gag.'

Sophie nodded. Play nice.

He untied the gag.

'Could I have some water, please?' She'd smash the glass into his sweaty face.

'Nice manners. That's better.' He gave her a greasy smile. 'You'll have your water. We want those lips all plump and moist.'

The woman from behind the counter came in and laid a pink robe on the bottom of the bed. She set a glass of water on the table.

With her hands still tied, Sophie managed to pick up the glass and swallow tepid water.

'She's definitely one of Thorgrim's.' Tacitus chuckled. 'He'll lose it when he realises we have her.'

'She's too old,' said the woman. 'Must be at least twenty.'

Did 'too old' mean they'd let her go — or something worse? 'I'm seventeen,' lied Sophie.

'Allow me some credit, Paulina,' said Tacitus. 'She's a catch.'

Paulina grabbed Sophie's hands, turned them over, and stepped back.

'Show your teeth,' she said.

Sophie responded with a forced, sarcastic smile.

'You're right,' said Paulina. 'She's his type.'

Sophie swore.

'Now listen here, Missy,' said Tacitus.

'I'm not *Missy*,' said Sophie. 'I'm married. I'm wearing a wedding band.'

'Do you think I'm stupid?' Tacitus' large face loomed close to hers. 'All the girls wear them. Matron-rings add an extra *frisson*.'

This was a misunderstanding, likely based on her being alone, and the state of her clothes. 'We were robbed outside our house. There was a fight, and I was separated from my husband. If you let me go, I'll persuade him not to prosecute.'

For an instant, Tacitus' expression wavered, revealing a flicker of doubt.

'We need to crack on,' said Paulina. 'The best client will be here within the hour.'

'Whoever your best client is,' said Sophie, keeping her tone even, 'he's not as important as Lucius Veranius.'

Tacitus rolled his eyes.

'Fetch Domitia,' said Paulina, 'and the wash boy.'

Tacitus left and returned, accompanied by a child carrying a bowl of water and Domitia, a short woman with brassy hair secured in a neat bun. She emptied the contents of her satchel onto the bed: a comb, a tin, gold hairpins, a ball of thread, and blonde hair extensions. More alarming was a giant needle.

'What's that for?' Sophie pointed.

Domitia set her mouth. 'To sew the extensions and tie them on your head.'

Tacitus placed a lit candle in the recess in the wall. The candle was scented, tangy, reminiscent of cheap aftershave.

She could push away the wash boy, and Domitia was tiny. Tacitus, though, was a different matter. If she could just surprise him...

'Good evening.' The deep male voice came from reception.

Paulina hurried out, closing the door behind her.

Domitia dragged sour-smelling wax through Sophie's hair and Sophie pushed her away.

Domitia put her hands on her hips. 'Suit yourself.'

'Remove your clothes.' Tacitus snatched up the pink robe.

Sophie folded her arms.

'You little—'

The door swung open. Tacitus bowed to a tall, lean man

in a white toga. The stranger's short hair was flecked with grey. His eyes narrowed.

'Sir, she's not ready,' said Tacitus. 'I sincerely apologise.'

'No matter.'

The client met her gaze, and a shiver of pure fear ran through Sophie. This man might be dressed posh, but he was a street fighter. He didn't blink, reminded her of a crocodile, but she didn't look away.

She was rewarded with a slight frown.

Domitia and the wash boy scurried out. Tacitus followed them, bowing, a human bobbing-pigeon. If the situation hadn't been so dire, Sophie would have laughed.

The door shut with a click, and she met the man's gaze again. Seize the initiative. 'Who are you?'

He raised an eyebrow. Prostitution was legal, but maybe the 'best' clients remained anonymous?

Sophie stood up from the bed. He gave off vibes of calculation and arrogance. Offering him money would be pointless. He held himself like he owned half of Rome. But powerful people believed they were good guys. Well, usually. And they valued their reputation.

She cleared her throat. 'I am Hortensia, wife of Lucius Veranius. This afternoon, I was kidnapped off the street. Please help me return to my family's house.'

Puzzlement, annoyance, then curiosity flashed across his face. 'You're not willing?'

'I'm married and I'm in love with my husband,' said Sophie. 'So, no, I'm not willing.'

He smiled. 'Ah, this is the foreplay, to spice up the act.'

Sophie's heart rate sped up. 'No. It's the truth!'

He stepped towards her, and Sophie held her breath. If this man didn't believe her, being 'not willing' wouldn't matter. She desperately cast her mind back to modern London, to Freddy practising Latin. He'd learned a quote about Roman attitudes to virtue, how high-born men should conduct themselves. 'Virtue should be guided by reason and self-restraint.' Yes, that was the gist.

His lips twitched. 'In order to *gain* virtue, reason should guide thought and action, with appetite suppressed.' He studied his feet, so she did too. His sandals were gold, the straps decorated with tiny crescents.

He glanced up. 'You have due respect for my upbringing?'

His upbringing? Presumably, rich Roman men were respected as soon as they drew breath. Like everywhere. Remind him about behaving honourably. 'I have great respect for your upbringing but later actions, as an adult, reveal character.'

He rubbed his patrician chin and Sophie assessed her options. If she fought him, he'd do this anyway and, depending on what he was into, he'd give her a nice or a critical review. If she lay stiff and unresponsive, the review would be bad, and Tacitus would beat her up. If she pretended to be into him, that could increase her brothel-value, but then she'd surely be even more closely guarded?

No good choices. She sat on the bed and hugged her knees.

His eyes crawled from her sandals to her hair. 'Where is your family home?' The authority in his voice delivered another frisson of fear.

'Villa Fullia, on Barollo Street.'

He strode over to her. She steeled herself, but he gently tugged her arm, making her stand up, and guided her out of the room.

'Sir, is everything in order?' Paulina asked from the counter.

'No,' said the client.

Paulina paled.

'Call my escort.'

A young boy grabbed a wooden tab off the counter, ran towards the front door, and a burly man unbolted it. The child jumped out into the night. Moments later, the boy returned and disappeared down a corridor.

The front door remained open. Sophie ignored Paulina who was glaring at her and assessed the bouncer. She couldn't get past him. Her only chance was to leave with the client. He was still holding her arm.

A rangy youth came in from the street, sporting a uniform similar to Tarchon's. His hand rested on the hilt of his sword.

The client strode out of the brothel, taking Sophie with him. On the pavement was a litter. Eight uniformed slaves surrounded it. Other slaves with flaming torches stood in a circle, a formidable, security ring. There was no moonlight and across the city, there were few points of light.

A line of watchmen with shuttered lamps were on the road. The lead man, carrying a crook, waved in greeting as he passed.

The client spoke to a slave, his voice too low to hear, then he gestured at the litter for her to get in.

She'd be riding in the litter? It took a moment to gather her wits. 'The brothel people stole my satchel, including my pendant. It has great sentimental value.'

He snapped his fingers and a slave darted into the brothel. The slave reappeared with her satchel over his shoulder and resumed his place behind the litter.

Right. She wasn't getting the satchel because rich people were wafted about in litters and didn't carry stuff. She ground her teeth. The client took her hand, and she was obliged to climb in.

They set off at a quick pace, the open litter curtains waving in the night breeze. Two slaves were touching distance from Sophie on either side and their owner was walking level with her. His attention was mostly on the street, but when his eyes flicked to her, he looked annoyed.

She shifted her sitting position. Underneath her was the tab from the brothel. Scratched on it was LAPPIUS MAXIMUS. Were they going to Lappius' house? Had she just exchanged one prison for another? But he'd return the satchel once they reached Villa Lappius. If she was lucky, before she was taken inside.

Light cast by the torches occasionally flitted across boarded-up shops but most of their route remained mysterious. She made a mental note of when they turned left and right but soon lost track. Stay calm. Once she had the pendant, she'd escape, and in daylight she'd find her way to Villa Fullia.

Finally, the litter stopped and lowered. In the gloom, Sophie could make out a wall and a door. She climbed off the litter and stared right, then left. Down the pavement was the solitary olive tree. They were outside Villa Fullia!

If Wells' goons were around, Sophie couldn't see them. In any case, they wouldn't take on Lappius' guards.

'House word?' asked Lappius.

'Arbor flore,' whispered Sophie.

A security slave knocked on the door. There was no response. Who knew what time it was? Everybody must be asleep.

'Knock louder,' said Lappius.

The slave's fists, banging on the iron door, echoed across the deserted street. Lappius folded his arms.

Sophie held her breath. This was Villa Fullia. She was sure it was.

Eventually, Melissa's voice said, 'House word?'

'Abor flore,' said Lappius, his tone authoritative.

'We only admit family.' Drusus' voice.

'It's me,' said Sophie. 'Arbor flore.'

Drusus and Melissa whispered to each other behind the door. Finally, there was a scraping noise from the bolt being moved, the key turned in the lock, and Drusus peered out. Lappius' slave handed Sophie her satchel and Sophie smiled at Lappius.

To her surprise, he returned the smile. 'Goodbye.'

She wanted to kiss him, but having played the respectable matron card, probably unwise. She slipped through the door and as Drusus drew the bolt closed, she sagged in relief.

Melissa hugged her. 'Where are the others?'

The villa was silent. Charlotte and Jack weren't here…

No one else had made it back.

CHAPTER 39

Six hours after Sophie returned to the Villa Fullia, George Wells reluctantly accompanied Ishtar and her team to the riverbank. He'd have preferred more sleep and a leisurely breakfast, but following Janus' instructions, he'd feigned interest. However impressive the Janus-golem might be, these dawn preparations were just tedious.

Ishtar's machine had made him a pale green tunic with gold etching on the neck and sleeves. Far more practical than a toga. But his tunic was damp from summer rain. He shivered.

The disappearance of the girl on Barollo Street had shaken him and he couldn't stop reliving it. One moment she'd been there, the next … gone. Not magic. Presumably, some advanced technology. An unfair test. How could he kill a woman who could vanish at will?

A young chap tapped his transparent page and grinned. 'The weather will be favourable.'

What they hoped to achieve with the Janus-golem and why was unclear, but he was no academic. 'Academic' had

241

two meanings: a scholar but also an irrelevance, of no concrete use.

Ishtar's team beavered away near the river with individual tasks. The Tiber stank of rotting meat and mould and George kept his distance. Ishtar released mechanical insects from a box. They flew across the river, tiny red lights flashing on them. George gasped. 'What do they do?' he asked her.

'They carry instruments that check the underwater barriers. Assess levels of structural integrity, their tolerance to heat.'

None the wiser.

The insects turned in an arc, glided back in a line, and dropped into the box.

Ishtar shut the lid. 'All is in order.' She opened a long leather bag, its brown contours shaped around the device inside. She eased out a smooth, metal column, the length and width of a sturdy walking staff. On top of the column was a ball. The ball was flat on one side, the upper half transparent.

George moved closer, but Ishtar tutted. 'No touching.'

Janus had told him not to touch it and to prevent the girl and her lovers from stealing it 'at all costs.' As it only summoned an illusion of the god, what attraction it held for Janus' enemies was a mystery. Something else Janus had omitted to tell him.

Ishtar set the device upright, holding it as if it were a fragile vase. Anything that was coveted was usually valuable. If the opportunity presented itself, he'd take the device. A unique trophy of this adventure.

A young woman handed Ishtar what looked like a powder compact. Ishtar waved it over the device, and foreign writing appeared under the see-through cover. 'Face number seven,' said Ishtar, and her team clapped.

Apparently, the face of the Janus-golem was selected at

random. George was playing the role of an historian, so should pretend to be curious. 'What is face number seven?'

'From the figure the locals sculptured out of marble,' said Ishtar. 'The warrior god displayed in their temple.'

George hadn't visited any temples, but he nodded.

It was fully light now and the drizzle had returned. Ishtar and her team set off back to the residence, and George strolled in the opposite direction.

After the girl had vanished, he'd lost his dagger and three guards in the street fight. Then, he'd had to pay an extra fee to retain the rest.

It took him ten minutes to reach Dagger Row. He marched into the nearest shop. Knives of all sorts were displayed on the wall, but he ignored them. 'I'm after a sword.'

The shopkeeper bent down and, from under the counter, brought out a weapon in a black leather sheath. 'Army issue.'

The blade gleamed.

CHAPTER 40

At first light, Sophie stumbled into the kitchen of Villa Fullia. She made tea, found a honey cake in the pantry, and sat in the pool room. Had she slept, or just laid on the bed with her eyes shut? She had to believe that Hugo and Freddy, and the dogs were alive, or she'd go insane.

Pitter-patter. Soft rain was falling through the gap in the ceiling into the pool. Out in the courtyard, birds were chattering. Sophie rubbed her temples. The final day of the festival was here. She had to come up with a plan to steal the staff, to get back to Bella. But she couldn't focus. Instead, her thoughts resonated with Aelia's voice, how she'd described being snatched off the street. *People disappear all the time. Never seen again.*

Sophie bowed her head.

The gentle smack of flip-flops made her look up. Drusus and Melissa were in the pool room, and Sophie managed a weary smile.

They sat down. 'Please accept our apologies,' said Drusus.

Sophie squinted at him. 'What for?'

'I feared to open the front door.' Drusus cleared his

throat. 'In case you'd said the house word...' He hesitated. 'Under duress.'

Sophie took in his serious expression. 'There's no way to see who's on the street without opening the door?'

'No,' said Drusus.

Big design fault. 'So, what made you open it?'

'Your tone of voice,' said Melissa. 'You sounded ... like yourself.'

Sophie told them about the brothel.

'You were fortunate to return safely,' said Melissa.

Sophie hugged her knees. 'Lappius Maximus is an honourable man.'

Melissa's mouth dropped open and Drusus' eyes widened so much she worried he was having a heart attack.

'Doubly fortunate,' said Drusus, when he'd recovered himself. 'Lappius Maximus is the second most powerful man in Rome.'

Sophie stared at him. 'He knows the emperor?'

'Lappius Maximus will outlive the emperor and his fellow senators.' Drusus looked around the pool room as if someone was listening. 'His enemies drink poison rather than challenge him.'

Sophie ate her honey cake, beyond thankful the man had believed her. 'Drusus, can I ask a favour?' It felt good to be asking, not ordering. 'I must find the others. Would you come with me?'

Drusus avoided her gaze.

'Of course, you don't have to.'

'I'll accompany you, though I fear the search may be long.' He didn't have to say, 'and fruitless.' That was clear from his frown.

'But at the first sign of trouble, please leave,' said Sophie. 'I can handle myself.'

He said nothing, obviously thought she was bluffing.

Understandable. He wasn't aware she had the pendant. 'They might have sought refuge in a villa, where, um, colleagues of ours live. I have the location marked on a map.'

'I'll stay here,' said Melissa, 'in case the others return before the festival.' She smiled at Drusus. 'I'll join you at the feast later.'

Sophie got to her feet. She'd forgotten about Wells' men. Were they back, waiting outside? She could sneak past them, using the pendant, but when Drusus and Melissa left, the thugs might interrogate them — or worse. Opening the door to check the street, even for a moment, was a risk, but with the pendant, a small one.

She retrieved the pendant from her satchel beside her bed and when she returned to the pool room, Melissa and Drusus weren't there. Good. The way was clear. She didn't want to scare them witless with her disappearing act.

Sophie walked the short distance into the gloomy front corridor and listened for any sounds from the road. Hearing nothing, she pulled aside the bolt, wincing as it made the scraping noise and she waited, to ensure the ex-slaves hadn't heard. She turned the heavy key in the lock, then inched the door open towards her. She could do this. By the time the goons spotted it opening, she'd have time to bolt it again. They'd be watching the wrong house.

She threw on the pendant and scanned the deserted, sepia street. Surprise and relief. Wells must have deployed them somewhere else. Or maybe Lappius scared them off?

Half an hour later, Drusus led the way to the builders' headquarters, navigating winding side streets and unexpected short-cuts. Sophie's hair was in a neat bun, courtesy of a spare woollen band, and she'd rinsed the mud from her shawl.

Drusus pointed at an iron door. 'I've never delivered messages or parcels here, but I believe this is Villa Acilius.'

Sophie remembered the smooth door, but there were similar ones in the road, and the cross on her map was an approximate guide at best. 'You've memorised all the villas in the city? Their names and locations?'

'Only those in central Rome,' said Drusus. 'Learned over many years. Incentivised by beatings.'

Sophie winced. 'I'm sorry.'

He shrugged.

'Can you wait for me outside?' She deliberately didn't say his name. If Drusus saw the builders' futuristic base, he'd freak out. 'When I go inside, I'll seem to disappear into thin air, but don't be concerned.'

'Tarchon said this villa is guarded by an invisible fence.' Drusus hesitated. 'What should I do if you don't ... reappear?'

'Return to the Villa Fullia and keep safe.'

Drusus moved his mouth to reply but changed his mind.

'I won't be long.' Sophie stepped through the prickly barrier and unclipped the brooches that secured the annoying shawl. She tied the shawl on her waist, stored the brooches in her satchel, and waited for Ishtar to come out.

She didn't, so Sophie cautiously walked up the drive and touched the opaque glass wall. A door slid open.

The false window encircling the reception area was showing the satellite feed, but the silent view of Rome was playing to a deserted room. Ishtar and her team must be out, preparing for the final day of the festival. The walking staff's field test, yesterday in the Gardens of Augustus, was done and dusted. Had it passed? If not, it was already beyond reach, stored in the team's ship.

The silence was oppressive, ominous. The dogs weren't

here. They'd have sensed her on the drive, would have run to greet her. But if Hugo or Freddy had been hurt and somehow found their way to the base, they could be recuperating in a bedroom?

She dashed along a corridor, almost colliding with the local girl she'd seen before.

The girl looked mildly surprised. 'Do you require anything?'

'Did any historians visit yesterday? Are any in the villa now?'

The girl shook her head and scurried off.

Disappointment soured Sophie's throat and changed into dread. Where were they? She turned to leave but curiosity made her pause. She knew so little about the builders. Couldn't hurt to have a quick nose around.

Her sandals tapped on the white floor, loud in the quiet. She peeped into a cubicle, then another. Utilitarian wardrobes and beds that had been slept in, but no personal items. How she imagined a military barracks. The builders resembled regular humans, but they really weren't. They had a home world, somewhere, but she'd only ever met their anthropologists, a tiny group from what was presumably a multi-layered, complex society. Sophie pushed at a cubicle door and froze. The wardrobe was ajar, a white toga too long to fit inside. The research team didn't wear togas. This was Wells' room. Right now, he was somewhere in the city. How was he dressed?

Time to go. She hurried out of the headquarters and stepped through the barrier.

Drusus shot her a relieved smile. 'Can you still conclude your business at the festival?'

She supposed she could, but all her energy had drained away. She couldn't think about dodging Wells, or stealing the staff, or even about Bella, not while everyone else she loved could be gone.

'You seek the magic artefact.' Drusus was trying to keep her on track.

'It might not be there.' She threw the shawl over her head and fiddled with the brooches.

'The bravest men have the clearest vision of what is before them, glory and danger alike, yet they venture out to meet it.'

'A rousing sentiment.'

'My friend from Britain liked the work of Thucydides,' said Drusus.

'What happened to him? Not Thucydides.' She mangled the name. 'I mean your friend?'

'Drowned. He threw himself into the Tiber.'

That last info detracted from the inspirational quote. 'I'm sorry.'

Drusus acknowledged her sympathy with a nod. 'Your family was set on this endeavour. You may yet find them at the festival.'

'You're right.'

Drusus put his arm through hers. 'We should make haste to the Forum of Domitian and Janus' temple.'

CHAPTER 41

In the Forum of Domitian, near Janus' glittering third temple, Sophie paused, looking for tall men. None of them were Hugo or Freddy. She couldn't see Wells either, but that didn't mean he wasn't here. Short, clean-shaven, and not wearing a toga, he'd be easy to miss in this crush.

Musicians were weaving through the crowd in a single, fluid line, blowing on flutes and trumpets and banging drums. Pop-up shops edged the square, including one that sold buckets of live eels.

Sophie pointed at the wriggling fish. 'Getting those home for dinner would be a nightmare.'

'They're not for eating,' said Drusus. 'They're for court-yard ponds. Many men love them like children.'

And yet the Romans murdered animals and people in the arena for fun. Irrationally cruel as well as irrationally kind.

Drusus shaded his eyes and squinted at the temple. 'Good. We haven't missed the sacrifice.'

'I'm not staying to watch a ram being killed—'

'Three rams.'

'I'll throw up.'

'Only the priests witness the sacrifice,' said Drusus.

She should have remembered. Hugo had told her that. A fresh lurch of fear and worry, and she fought an irrational urge to search the city, every building, even if it took the rest of her life.

'If anyone unworthy sees the ceremony, Janus won't respond.'

She dragged her mind from Hugo. 'Do you worship Janus?'

'I do. I was found, only hours old, on his festival day, so he has a special place in my heart.'

'Found?'

'On a rubbish heap.'

Sophie didn't reply. Though Drusus didn't seem upset, more questions might distress him. And as he drew comfort from worshipping a benevolent Janus, she wasn't going to enlighten him.

The tumbling acrobats from the talent show were performing in the centre of the square in a roped-off space, eliciting enthusiastic clapping from revellers. A temple slave offered them free, watered-down wine. Drusus accepted a glass, but Sophie declined. It wasn't yet ten in the morning, and she had to stay sharp.

The show finished and all eyes were on the temple. A man dressed in a long, green robe emerged from the private entrance. On his head was a close-fitting, round cap with a wooden spike sticking vertically out of the top.

'What's the spike for?' Sophie whispered to Drusus, not wanting to broadcast her ignorance.

'The bottom symbolises the beginning of time, the middle is now, the top's the end.'

More priests in identical clothes came out. As they made their way down the steps, their lit lanterns swayed to and fro.

'Janus spoke to the priests.' Drusus grinned. 'We'll have good luck for another year.'

'How do you know?' whispered Sophie.

'Their lamps are lit.'

The priests advanced towards the altar where three flames burned, reeking of sulphur.

'The fires represent the past, the present, and the future?' said Sophie.

Drusus nodded. 'They burn until dusk.'

The people around them were all girls and women in emerald dresses, honouring Janus. Sophie scanned the rest of the crowd again. There was a private bodyguard in armour. Too gangly to be Tarchon. She turned her attention back to the altar. 'How do they keep the fires going?'

'They're stoked like the braziers in the baths. Fed with balls of fat.'

The priests filed out of the square into a side road, and the crowd followed, applauding and clapping. Now surrounded by raucous families and a haughty woman with slaves, Sophie tried to calm down. If Wells was here, she'd see him coming.

They reached the Gardens of Julius Caesar, and the remorseless crush of revellers, freed from being hemmed in by narrow streets, melted away across the park. Drusus flopped onto a stone bench that was shaded by a tall bush and waved his fan. Sophie sat next to him, dearly wanting to pull off her shawl and her dress and sit in a fountain. No. She was blending in. She should keep with that.

Drusus drank water from a small metal flask. He was red in the face from the walk. Finally, he stood up and Sophie matched his laboured pace up a hill. At the summit, parasol pine trees were silhouetted against a perfect blue sky. Young parents with children, couples, and fancy litters were all headed in the same direction.

Beyond the trees, on a flat plain, were identical green pavilions, too many to count. Carts were delivering food and wine, wending through a rippling sea of people, and there were hundreds of serving slaves. The sound of trumpets and tambourines echoed over the valley.

Sophie gave a low whistle. 'Half of Rome must be here.'

A slow walk later, they reached the first pavilion. Going by the age of the revellers, reserved for the elderly or the infirm. There were around twenty tables flanked by benches. Every table had a giant, three-tiered cake-stand in the middle, surrounded by water jugs, wine bottles and glasses, and lidded dishes. The prevailing cooked-food smell was hot and fishy, likely from the ubiquitous sauce.

Drusus selected a honey wrap from a cake-stand and sat on a bench. 'Melissa will be here soon. We were on this table last year.' He poured himself a glass of water and added white wine. Then he rummaged in his satchel and, from a tiny, draw-string bag, added a pinch of seasoning. The pepper with a hint of saffron was his favourite.

He hadn't had a coughing fit today. Hopefully, his lungs would gradually clear. 'When did you leave your job at the baths?'

'Eighteen months ago.'

His face was less red, but he wasn't up for searching the pavilions. 'If you see me again today, or the others, don't come near us, unless we wave at you. The brother who tracks us is very dangerous.' He looked conflicted and Sophie patted his shoulder. 'Enjoy the festival.' She ensured her shawl was over her hair and marched off.

Over the next two hours, grateful for the shade provided by the pavilions, she methodically searched the feast tables. To her relief, she didn't come across Wells, but there was also no sign of Hugo, Freddy, and the dogs, or of Tarchon and Aelia.

Sophie paced herself, conscious that if she ran or even walked fast, this relentless heat would do her in.

The revellers in previous pavilions merged in her mind: senators' wives in gold shawls, families loading food into satchels, high-spirited slaves enjoying a rare day off. The current pavilion, though, was uniquely memorable. The pet tiger from the Forum was here, held in check by a heavy chain, while nervous dogs curled up on laps or dozed under tables. A pet ostrich was making rhythmic hissing noises, accompanying a talented flautist.

Time for a break. Sophie topped up her water flask, picked up a cheese wrap, and joined a table of female slaves.

'I can't wait to see her by the riverbank again,' said a skinny girl. 'Janus as a woman was wonderful.'

Her companion munched on an olive. 'She seeks you out, delves into your soul.'

Sophie finished her wrap and got to her feet. Was she wasting her time here? Should she go to the riverbank? No, she'd searched most of the pavilions. She should check the rest.

When she reached the final one, there were only a few revellers. Most had already joined the grand procession moving south. This lot wouldn't make it to Juno's arch, though. They were wine-swaying.

Sophie touched her fancy shawl, ensuring it was covering her hair, and retraced her steps. She kept close to a tipsy group of teenagers. If there were brothel-keepers lurking in the procession, they'd assume she owned them, was filthy rich, and off limits.

The slaves were giggling, telling saucy jokes, and Sophie tuned out their happy voices. The despair she'd managed to ignore, searching table after table, was now so intense she felt faint with it.

She reached the road. Trundling through the crowd were decorated cart-floats drawn by donkeys. Actors posed on the floats, dressed as Janus in mock armour, holding wooden walking staffs and keys. Some wore grey cloaks.

Sophie plodded behind a float and on impulse, climbed up and sat on the back. She leaned against the raised side of the cart, cushioning her head with her hand, and pictured Hugo and Freddy, and Charlotte and Jack. They faded, and Bella took their place. Sophie shut out the laughter around her, and the creaking of the wagon wheels, but she couldn't escape the relentless, savage sun. Her quest was coming to an end.

If she died today, so be it.

CHAPTER 42

Someone was licking Freddy's chin, their tongue warm and rough. Bemused, Freddy registered Charlotte's anxious golden eyes. Jack's earnest retriever face was staring at him too.

His leg! Freddy felt it and found a bandage. The injury ached. 'Don't worry,' he said to Charlotte. 'I'm all right.' But it was horribly hot, and insects were buzzing, insistent and loud. He was lying on the floor on a thin mattress.

The dogs scampered away through a gap in an emerald curtain that hung across a door, and Freddy sat up. He was in the dusty back room of a shop. There was an old table with a set of friezes, and shelves were stacked with gold and green statuettes. Janus souvenirs.

'Customers report feeling better just hours after leaving this offering.' A woman's voice from beyond the curtain. 'It may work faster, being a festival day.'

Freddy touched the outline of the cylinder under his tunic, glad he still had it. How was he here? They'd been running from Wells' thugs, getting away, but then they'd met more. An ambush. Tarchon and Aelia had kept them at bay

"

and Charlotte had mauled at least two, but they'd been hopelessly outnumbered. He remembered charging the nearest chap in a terrifying blur of slashing knives. The watchmen had waded in with their axes... What had happened after that?

Freddy felt the bandage on his calf again and tried to make sense of the fractured, flashes of memory. He'd been in agony, and Hugo had been on the ground—

The doorway curtain swished aside, and Hugo came in holding a glass of water.

A wave of surprise and relief. Freddy took the glass, and it was sweaty in his hand. He drank greedily. 'Where are we?'

'Two streets away from the third temple.'

'You were knocked out.'

'Clever move on my part to avoid the worst of the fight,' said Hugo. 'How's the leg?'

'Sore.'

'The stallholder, Silvina, she's a medic.' Hugo opened a tin of white paste. 'The girl from the Forum gave this to Silvina to treat Tarchon's injured hip, and she's used it on your leg. I think it's an advanced antibiotic.'

'Where's Sophie?'

Hugo's expression darkened. 'We don't know.'

'She might have used the pendant?' Freddy wiped his brow with his fingers.

'If she's … okay, she'll be down at the riverbank.'

'Why?'

'It's the last day of the festival.'

Freddy swallowed, disorientated. 'I've been unconscious since yesterday?'

'Silvina gave you something to make you sleep.' Hugo pushed his fringe off his brow. 'You're going be fine.' The dogs ran in, and Charlotte pawed at Hugo's leg. He strode with them towards the green curtain.

'Where are you going?'

Hugo turned. 'The riverbank.'

Freddy pictured Sophie by Juno's arch. Wells would be there. Freddy's heartbeat sped up. 'I'm coming with you.'

'You can't walk.'

'I have to.' Freddy pulled himself up, using the rickety friezes table. Dear God, his leg hurt. 'Did the walking staff pass its field test?' He was panting with the effort of keeping upright.

Hugo steadied him. 'Who knows? I've been here since the fight, ensuring you didn't die.'

Freddy shot him a grateful glance.

Charlotte was watching them. Agitated, keen to go.

'Good to see you awake.' Tarchon's bulk filled the door-way. A shout came from behind him. He barged back through the curtain and returned with Aelia. Her face was damp with sweat and her hair messy.

'My sincere apologies for leaving my post,' she said. 'I saw Calpurnia and took my chance.'

Freddy trawled his sluggish brain. Calpurnia... 'The woman who sold you into slavery?'

The corners of Aelia's lips lifted in a satisfied smile. 'I offered her to the river.'

'What do you mean?' Freddy couldn't keep the shock from his voice.

Aelia gave him a hard stare. 'I punched her unconscious, so she didn't suffer ... which I half regret.'

Charlotte raised a furry eyebrow, and Hugo looked at the floor.

Freddy opened his mouth to speak but thought better of it. Aelia lived by a warrior's code. She prized honour and duty, and in a peculiar way, exacting her revenge was part of that.

'If you hadn't bought me,' said Aelia, 'I could have been starved, beaten black and blue, or worse.'

Freddy frowned. 'When Calpurnia's body is discovered—'

'It won't be,' said Aelia. 'The water's thick with every kind of filth. And the current runs strong to the sea at Ostia. Takes everything.'

'Is it possible to buy a walking stick?' Freddy gingerly stepped forward and regretted it.

'Silvina uses one,' said Hugo. 'I'll ask if we can borrow it.'

Tarchon shook his head. 'We need a litter. How much coin do we have?'

Hugo rifled through Freddy's satchel and his. In a rush, he put fistfuls of coins on the table beside the friezes.

'Plenty here to buy Silvina a better walking stick, and another one.' Tarchon's lips moved in a grim smile. 'I can buy a gladius, for me and for Aelia.'

She gave him a curt nod.

'I won such a blade in battle, and it served me well.' Tarchon addressed Hugo. 'There's enough for a third sword.'

CHAPTER 43

Two young men joined Sophie in the procession float. They sat beside her, their lower legs dangling over the end of the cart. One took a swig from his amphora bottle. 'I'll give you double odds Janus appears as a man.'

'Nah.' His companion hiccupped. 'It'll be the woman.'

The float trundled on until they were almost at the river. The procession's slow progress at the hottest time of day hadn't been the best preparation for stealing the walking staff, but Sophie had gathered her wits. If the staff had passed the field test, Ishtar's ship would be inside Juno's arch by now, and to summon out Janus, her team would be close by. Sophie squared her shoulders. She had the pendant. She could do this.

Sophie jumped off the float and headed to the arch. Litters carried by uniformed slaves weaved around teenagers lounging on the grass, drinking and laughing. Souvenir stalls were doing brisk business and, despite the free feast laid on earlier, so were pop-up shops selling food and wine. Many families had brought picnic rugs. The sharp scent of alcohol mixed with a riot of other smells, from sweet honey to spicy wraps, steeped in strong, fishy sauce. But there was another odour, something sour. She recognised the stench and its origin. The river.

Pushing through the jolly revellers was a slog and it took her fifteen minutes to reach the arch. When she did, she only took a single step inside, in case the ship took up the entire space. So far, so good. She blinked in the relative gloom. A few feet ahead of her was a rundown shed. That had to be the ship, camouflaged until someone opened it.

At least she was in the shade. Sophie turned on her heel and peered out of the arch, watching the crowded riverbank. No sign of Wells. She had time to marshal her courage. Be brave. For Bella.

All the floats were stopped on the road, the donkeys that had pulled them corralled into a tent to be fed and watered. Sophie's breath hitched. Ishtar was strolling past the floats towards the arch, the strap of a long, narrow bag over her shoulder.

The walking staff.

Her team was bringing up the rear. Sophie squared her shoulders and walked out to meet them. Ishtar gave Sophie a polite smile and, though her heart was banging loud in her ears, Sophie smiled back. She acknowledged the guy they'd met on the temple steps, and he shot her a friendly grin.

Ten yards from the arch, level with the entrance, the team sat on the grass, and each of them took a pale, plastic tube from their satchel. With one tap, the roll became flat, a rigid, transparent page. Symbols appeared as holographic images in the air, moving like scrolling computer code. The locals showed no surprise or interest. The pages and projected letters must appear as something else to those without the gene. Maybe just wooden tablets, or sheets of papyrus.

A tipsy youth wandered up and chatted about Janus. Ishtar shooed him away.

'Couldn't you put up a barrier?' asked Sophie. 'So you can't be seen?'

'Not in this temperature. A remote barrier wouldn't be stable.' Ishtar sighed. 'Drunks and pickpockets are a minor nuisance.'

Explained why her team only carried small knives.

'What happens next?' said Sophie, half an eye on the staff in its bag.

'Wait and see,' said Ishtar. 'You'll enjoy it more if you don't know the programme.'

'You're right.' Now she'd see if Janus really did have two — or four — heads.

Out of the corner of her eye, Sophie caught a movement, and she held her breath. That man, how he walked, was familiar... Hugo? She leapt up and ran. It *was* Hugo, and Charlotte and Jack were with him, and so were Tarchon and Aelia! Sophie flung herself at Hugo and burst into tears.

Hugo hugged her, shaking with relief. 'We thought... We didn't know what to think.' After a long, precious moment, he let her go.

'Cool sword.' The weapon hung from his belt.

'Sorry,' said Hugo. 'I wasn't thinking. We should have got one for you.'

Sophie kissed him. 'I've got the pendant.' She hugged Charlotte and kissed Jack, but then her stomach clenched. 'Where's Freddy? No, *no*.'

'He was stabbed by Wells' thug, but he's okay,' said Hugo.

'I'm perfectly fine.' The curtain of a litter parted, revealing Freddy looking regal and, more importantly, alive.

Sophie hugged him too.

Freddy eased himself gingerly off the litter and leaned on a black, polished walking stick. 'I knew you'd be all right.'

'I almost wasn't,' said Sophie.

Tarchon paid the slaves who'd carried the litter, and they jogged off with it.

Freddy's eyes flicked to Ishtar and her bag. He drew a calming breath. 'The staff?'

'It has to be,' said Sophie.

'Did you finish off Wells?' asked Hugo.

Sophie shook her head. They all followed her back to Ishtar. None of the research team glanced up, entirely focused on their transparent pages.

On the river, a green mist was tumbling and twisting, confined to the water but lengthening and obscuring the surface. The locals stood up. Small children were hoisted onto shoulders and Sophie was glad Bella was in Shorten. Whatever happened today, Wells would try to finish them here.

Gliding through the mist were pale, ghostly figures. They wailed and the spectators clapped. The mist and the figures faded away, and gilt letters glowed high above the river. Even in the bright afternoon sun, they were clear and vivid: EGO SUM PRINCIPIUM ET FINIS.

'I am the beginning and the end,' translated Freddy.

'Fireworks in broad daylight. Amazing,' said Hugo, squeezing Sophie's hand.

The letters in the sky turned dark green, then changed into a circle of spinning heads: old, young, male, and female. A clean-shaven male face swirled bigger and obliterated the others. A square jaw with faint stubble, that straight nose... Sophie recognised the features. Taken from the statue in the temple by the crossroads. The statue, like the temple, created by the locals.

The mouth on the face opened wider and wider, and the roar of a terrifying predator rolled across the sky. The gaping mouth swooped low over the revellers, appearing to swallow people whole, then vanished. Children screamed, Jack barked in alarm, but most of the crowd clapped and whistled.

A new image sparkled in the sky: a simple cottage with a front door and windows. Sophie squinted at it. The childish image reminded her of something. But what?

Identical cottages fell towards the original one, settled beside it, and on top of it, until there was row upon row.

'A tenement block,' said Freddy.

Hugo shaded his eyes. 'Representing the Roman family?'

Yellow, orange, and red flames leapt and danced on the tenement roof, and there was a collective gasp. The blaze was twice as tall as the building, and the crackling and fierce heat rolling in waves across the riverbank was horribly realistic.

The face that had seemed to swallow the crowd shimmered next to the tenement block, and out of its mouth spewed blue water, extinguishing the fire. Everyone erupted into delighted clapping.

A rumble of thunder.

Though there wasn't a cloud in sight, another thunderclap, nearer and much louder. Lightning dived in a dramatic fork into the Tiber, followed by a second flash, this time striking Juno's arch. The structure's impressive columns and roof shimmered, became gold, appearing to glow, and Janus strode out.

Eight feet tall like his statue, this was the warrior defending Rome. His armour shone, the blade of his sword glinted, and his limbs were toned and muscled. He'd been created by technology, but the god looked human. Flesh and blood.

He only had one head, which should have been reassuring, but the way he walked, how he turned that head, sent shivers down Sophie's spine.

'Greetings,' boomed Janus. 'Who dares disturb my peace?' His blue-green eyes swivelled, scanning the revellers.

Sophie whispered, 'Not sentient,' but terror had her by the throat, and she couldn't move.

Hugo was squeezing her hand, hard enough to break bones. 'He's coming for me.'

'He's not,' said Sophie. Janus was striding away from them, cutting a swathe through the awe-struck crowd.

Hugo was breathing hard. 'I swear, he was hunting *me*.'

Sophie had felt a jolt of atavistic terror, but those who lacked the gene experienced a personalised delusion? Charlotte was leaning against Sophie's legs, her heart racing. Sophie stroked her and checked on the walking staff. Her breath caught. Standing upright beside Ishtar was a grey cylinder, half as tall as her. On top of the cylinder was a ball. Flat on the bottom where it was sealed to the cylinder, the ball's upper section was transparent. Inside was a line of three grey buttons. Which button had summoned Janus? Sophie swore. Instead of watching the show, she should have been watching Ishtar. 'Freddy,' she whispered, 'which button did Ishtar press?'

Freddy patted Jack who was close to his legs. 'I was distracted. I won't be again.'

'Do you see a wooden walking staff?' Sophie whispered to Hugo.

He nodded.

'While I protect you, Rome will endure.' Janus had reached the river. The green mist and ghosts were back, and the figures rose in steady lines into the sky. They vanished in a burst of white light and the crowd whistled and cheered.

'Fill your glasses,' thundered Janus. 'Salute the might of Rome.'

CHAPTER 44

Half an hour after the first toast, the crowd on the riverbank was still drinking with gusto, paying tribute to Janus and to Rome.

'The display was wonderful,' said Sophie.

The research team was taking a break, standing up and stretching, and Freddy's eyes darted to the walking staff.

Hugo squeezed Sophie's hand. His palm was sweaty. 'It'll be okay,' she whispered.

The team settled on the grass again and opened their transparent pages. 'All is going to plan,' said Ishtar.

Tarchon was following the gist of the conversation. 'These people control Janus?' he asked Sophie, under his breath.

She hesitated. Tarchon worshipped Mannus, a German god, not Janus. She should be honest. 'It's just a show.'

Standing beside the Tiber, Janus raised his right arm, and the crowd fell silent. The river rippled, lapping at the banks. The ripples became bubbles, spreading out from the centre. They gathered pace, until the whole expanse of water was frothing like a hot tub. A veil of scalding, volcanic steam hissed across the surface and an acrid, cooking smell wafted into the crowd, a bitter taste that lingered on the tongue.

The Tiber was boiling, and so was everything in it.

After an awed silence, the revellers applauded.

'Cool trick,' said Hugo, catching Sophie's eye. 'And he's only boiling water, not anyone's blood.'

Sophie looked at her sandals. In some universes, women with the builders' gene could boil all liquids, merely by wishing, and to survive in medieval Georgia she'd done exactly that.

Freddy dragged his gaze from the river. 'Isn't it dangerous for the boats and barges?' he asked Ishtar.

'This section is cordoned off. We'll return tomorrow before dawn and remove the underwater barriers. The locals know not to use the river until then.'

The bubbles on the water were subsiding. Janus held his sword aloft and the crowd cheered.

The research team remained focused on their pages, but Ishtar's attention was on the walking staff. She opened the transparent cover, pressed the last grey button in the line, and it glowed black. She closed the cover with a click.

Janus turned on his heel and strode away from the river towards Juno's arch, the crowd parting before him. Was he a hologram or solid? If the latter, one misstep and he'd crush any stragglers. But he had a clear path to the arch and was soon lost to sight.

Sophie pictured him vanishing into the builders' ship and, despite knowing he wasn't yet sentient, felt a powerful surge of relief. She glanced at the staff. The black button returned him. That left two others. One did the summoning, the other reset the ship — and Janus. Both were grey. Which was which?

Right now, the reset button was merely a handy repair option to sort technical glitches. But way in the future, it would reset a *sentient* Janus back to factory settings. He'd no longer be alive. And the mindless software running his ship would take them smoothly to Shorten and to Bella. Sophie frowned. Crucial to know which button reset him. Otherwise, even if everything went to plan today, when they used the staff on a sentient Janus, they'd have to guess what button to press. If they guessed wrong, summoned the god for real… The stuff of nightmares.

'I'm very glad your device was repaired in time.' Freddy patted Jack who was keeping close. 'Which button summons him?'

Ishtar pointed to the middle one. 'Flashes red.'

Sometimes, a direct polite question worked a treat.

Charlotte stared at the staff, committing the info to memory, and Sophie made a mental note: middle button for summoning, last one on the right does the returning, so the first is the reset button.

The festival floats were trundling back up the road, surrounded by locals, giggling and singing. Most people were leaving, but some were opening more wine bottles, reluctant to go home. The research team tidied away their pages and Charlotte moved nearer to Sophie. This was it. The moment to steal the staff.

Ishtar gestured at it. 'Can you assist me?'

Sophie swallowed. 'Of course.' She lifted the metal base and helped to feed it into the bag. The device was lighter than she'd expected.

Ishtar closed the bag with a sturdy buckle and secured the strap over her shoulder.

Sophie fished the pendant out of her satchel, breathing hard. The distraction would only last an instant, and she'd have to reappear to grab the staff—

'Wells is here,' said Hugo, his tone urgent. 'Two o'clock.'

Wells was by the floats, elbowing through the crowd. His

pale green tunic ended above his knees and outlined his wiry legs as he walked. His eyes were hard, and his lips were fixed in a determined line. Behind him were a big group of thugs.

Inspiration struck. 'Mr Wells means to kill you and all your team,' said Sophie.

Ishtar viewed the oncoming men with alarm. 'Why didn't you mention this before?'

'We thought we'd stopped him,' said Sophie.

Ishtar registered the pendant and her face tightened. 'Who are you working for?'

What? 'Nobody.' The thugs were brandishing daggers, and Wells had a freaking sword. Sophie cast around to give Wells a motive. Ishtar believed he was an historian. 'Wells thinks your work with the Janus myth distorts history,' she said in a rush. 'He's obsessed with the purity of timelines. He's a psychopath and a killer. We'll distract him and his thugs so you can reach your ship inside the arch.'

'The locals cannot see our vessel,' said Ishtar. 'To the villa! Roundabout route.' She marched off in the direction of the riverbank, taking her team and the walking staff with her.

Up on the road, Wells shouted something, and his thugs broke into a run. Uninterested in Ishtar, they headed for Sophie, Hugo, and Freddy. Tarchon and Aelia drew their swords. Charlotte snarled but beside her, Jack just barked.

'Flee!' ordered Tarchon.

Freddy limped towards the arch. He wouldn't make it. Sophie sprinted, threw the pendant over his head, and he vanished.

'Sophie, go after Ishtar,' shouted Hugo. 'Get the walking staff!'

She hesitated. How could she leave him? They were heavily outnumbered.

Hugo tightened his grip on his sword. 'Go.'

Yes. She had to do this. And it wasn't too late. Though

Ishtar and her team weren't hanging about, they were walking, not running. She gave chase, gaining on them, but some instinct made her look back to the road. *No.* Wells was racing after her, waving his sword.

Sophie sped up, her heart pounding. If she was quick, she could still grab the staff and out-run him. 'He's coming!' she yelled to Ishtar. 'He wants the summoning device. Leave it and he won't attack.'

Ishtar stared at Wells, her face rigid with terror, and her team cast about in a panic. Ishtar laid the cylinder on the ground by the river, and ran, along with her team.

Sophie checked on Wells. He was still ten paces away, arguing with a lean man with greying hair. She did a double-take. Wells was engulfed in a dense, round patch of white light, so bright, she had to shade her eyes. What the— The light snapped off, and the lean guy calmly took Wells' sword and headed off with it.

Wells made no attempt to follow him. He didn't move at all, like a stick insect set in amber. Then he slowly moved his arms and legs, as if performing Pilates.

Whatever was going on, this was her chance. Sophie picked up the staff and secured the bag strap across her shoulders. She turned to run to Hugo and the others, but Wells had covered the ground between them. He was right in front her.

His lips curled in a cruel smile. 'Hand me the staff and I'll spare your life.'

He wouldn't. She scrambled backwards.

Wells advanced, calm and focused. His eyes, that distinctive cobalt blue, were granite-hard, and bore into hers. He grabbed at the staff, and though Sophie kicked and twisted, it was no use. He hauled it from her. Then he slammed the base into her stomach.

Sophie doubled over in pain, lost her footing, and

dropped down into thin air. She hit the surface of the river and yelped, the shock of the fall snatching her breath as she was swept under water. Detritus floated by her face, and a ferocious current dragged at her legs. Her feet found something hard near the bank, and she pushed up, flailing towards the light. But the current was too powerful. She kicked harder, her arms straining, pushing apart the water to find the surface.

Keep going, hold on.

Her lungs burned, and memories rolled around her head. Her mother kissing her goodnight, Charlotte curled up on the bed as a puppy, Hugo smiling as she walked down the aisle, Bella sleeping in her cot…

Sophie kicked and kicked, but the current was stronger. No good, can't hold on.

She gave in to the agony, and just before she blacked out, it felt … right.

CHAPTER 45

The woman sitting on the park bench looked up. Gentle sunlight played on her blonde hair and on her green medic's scrubs. The lawn in front of her was smooth and the smell of cut grass was fresh and rich. Birds chattered in a nearby oak tree.

'Hello, Mummy.'

Her mother smiled and Sophie sat beside her. 'Where's Dad?'

'He's here, somewhere.' Her mother took her hand. Her palm was warm and smooth. 'Bella's formidable. Well done.'

'You're just in my head, aren't you?'

'We taught you better than that—'

Agonising pain tore through Sophie's lungs, and her mother and the sunlit park snapped off. Sophie heaved and spluttered and vomited water. *No.* She didn't want this. She wanted her mother, wanted to be safe and happy…

Shivering, soaking wet, and lying on a hard, smooth floor. And something smelled foul. But the pain was easing.

Kneeling next to her was the girl in the grey tunic.

'You brought me back.' Sophie's voice had a raspy, rough edge.

'Forewarned is forearmed.'

The girl and this place seemed less real than her mother in the park, as if time and reality were suspended. She was inside a bubble. She couldn't see beyond its pale, curved boundary, and there was an eerie silence except for water dripping from her satchel and her shawl. Plop, plop onto the floor. Yuk. The disgusting stench was coming from her clothes.

This made no sense. If she'd been resuscitated, why was she inside a weird bubble? With a groan, she sat up. The man who'd disarmed Wells was wringing out his tunic, smelled as bad as her. He'd pulled her out of the Tiber...

She struggled to her feet. 'Where's the sword?'

'In the river.' The girl took a black bottle from her satchel and unscrewed the top.

She offered it to Sophie. 'What's in it?'

'Counteracts waterborne infections. Without it, you'll die. Again.'

Sophie relived struggling underwater, the fragments of who knew what scratching at her hands and her face. She poured the liquid down her throat. Tasted as bad as the Tiber. She handed back the bottle and tried to spit out the taste of the river and the medicine, but her mouth was too dry.

The man pulled a translation cylinder off a chain around his neck and spat out a single word. From his frown, probably a curse. Sounded French. The girl tapped her bracelet. Gold and adorned with green and red gems, it was like a builders' bracelet, the one worn by the guy on the temple steps. No. Scrap that. It was identical, with the same unusual jewels: round, oblong, square, and oval.

'Request for your new enabler received and accepted,' said the girl.

Enablers … that's what Ishtar called the translating cylinders. Right. The guy's cylinder had broken in the river, and so had Sophie's. Luckily, the girl's cylinder was working fine. Why she could understand her.

The guy took off his bracelet and dropped it in his satchel. The girl gave hers another tap. 'Request for your new security band received and accepted.'

The builder had called his bracelet a 'security band.' These people might not be connected to Ishtar and her team, but their bands might operate in the same way. The builder had confirmed that his colleagues used his band to track his location, to keep him safe, but then he'd clammed up, only saying it had *several functions.*

This girl might be more helpful. 'The security bands stop you being tracked by others?' Sophie asked.

The girl nodded, seemed surprised. In the Forum, when they'd thought she'd been talking to herself, she hadn't been tapping her wrist. She'd been tapping the bracelet.

'You use your security bands to communicate?'

The girl's lips twisted. 'When they both work.'

Sophie wrung out her shawl and the bottom half of her dress, water pooling on the floor. These bracelets appeared to be regular jewellery. No local would realise their true purpose. 'Why do you wear long sleeves to conceal the security bands?'

'They overheat in direct sunlight.'

The girl's partner spoke. Sounded like an order.

'Broken heart-stopper. On it.' The girl gave her bracelet a sharp tap.

'What's a heart-stopper?' said Sophie.

The girl shot her a shrewd look. "For someone who almost died today, you ask a lot of questions.'

'This isn't my first rodeo.' Sophie adjusted her wet satchel strap across her chest. 'What's your name? Who are you?'

The girl shrugged. 'Travellers. We protect innocents when we can.'

Her answer sounded rehearsed. A slogan. And Sophie eyed the girl's partner, unconvinced. They had a professional air, as if they were on duty. She hadn't seen the girl since she'd rushed up with the translation cylinders, but she could still have been following them. 'Why have you been spying on us?'

Her partner folded his arms, not understanding the conversation.

Sophie pressed on. 'That first day, it was you watching us from the crossroads temple.'

'Private shrines with offering windows are good for surveillance.'

She must have realised that Wells had trapped them in Janus' third temple. Sophie met her eyes. 'Why didn't you rescue us from the cellar?'

'If your bodyguard had died, we would have. Interference should be minimal.'

Sort of logical. 'What is this place?'

'Temporary protection sphere. I need to switch it off.' The girl tapped her bracelet.

The bubble vanished. Sophie was on the riverbank. A clash of steel and frenzied shouting assaulted her ears.

Near the arch, Tarchon and Aelia were battling Wells' thugs. Charlotte and Jack were darting in and out of the fight. There was no sign of Freddy. Presumably, still wearing the pendant. Yards away from the main struggle, Hugo was wrestling with Wells. Hugo no longer had his sword, or his knife, and his left arm was bloody. Beside them, on the ground, was the walking staff in its bag.

Sophie sprinted, quickly closing the distance between

them, and punched Wells in the face, her momentum strengthening the impact. He staggered. She found the kitchen knife in her satchel and gave it to Hugo. He was quicker and stronger. She grabbed the walking staff and secured the bag strap across her chest.

Wells circled Hugo, his eyes on the knife, then pounced. They wrestled and Wells gripped Hugo's wrist, forcing the knife from his hand. It fell on the grass.

'Mannus!' Tarchon's shout sounded clear and anguished.

Unlikely the German god would help... Sophie rushed to retrieve the knife.

'Call Janus,' panted Hugo. 'Now!'

Oh, she'd been stupid! She controlled a god, for pity's sake. Sophie tore open the bag, raised the transparent cover, and hit the red button.

A moment later, Janus strode out of the arch. 'Greetings. Who dares disturb my peace?' His voice reverberated and his blue-green eyes swivelled, scanning the scene.

Still wrestling with Wells, Hugo didn't react, but Sophie had to push down the wave of familiar, overpowering fear. She focused on breathing, in, out, and the illogical reaction to the builders' puppet faded.

Janus marched forward. His pre-programmed route would take him straight through the main fight. Would he crush everyone in his path, including the dogs, and Tarchon and Aelia?

In the nick of time, everyone fighting abandoned the battle and backed away from Janus. Wells glanced over at them, and Hugo landed a clean punch, putting him on the ground. Hugo picked up the knife with his right hand, his left arm hanging limp by his side.

'You're wounded!' said Sophie.

'Looks worse than it is.'

'Where's your sword?'

'Lost in the scrum.'

Sophie checked on Wells, who was lying stunned on the grass, and Hugo took in her damp clothes and hair.

He frowned. 'You fell in the Tiber?'

She nodded. The riverbank had fallen silent, the festival stragglers and the thugs watching Janus.

Wells, though, got to his feet, and cursed. 'Do the job you're paid for. It's not Janus. It's not real. Kill them!' Though his order was shrill and loud, his men made no move to obey him.

Aelia and Tarchon lowered their swords, seemed bemused, and the dogs ran towards Sophie and Hugo. Both had bloody jaws but were unhurt. Sophie exhaled in relief.

'An inauspicious day,' shouted a thug. His words galvanised his mates and they all ran up the road. Wells stared after them, his face a mask of fury.

Janus had reached the river. 'While I protect you, Rome will endure.'

Freddy materialised beside Wells. He dispatched him with one thrust and twist of his sword. Wells' eyes bulged, his mouth went slack, and he crumpled.

Hugo averted his eyes. 'Tarchon and Aelia showed us how to do that.'

Freddy stored the pendant in his satchel and cleaned his blade on the grass. He limped over to Hugo. 'This is yours,' he said, offering the hilt. Hugo took it.

'We can send Janus back now.' Freddy's voice was faint with relief.

Sophie was still carrying the walking staff, the opening at the top of the bag hanging open. She flicked up the transparent cover, but her brain was scrambled. 'Which button?'

'The last one.' Freddy pressed it.

Janus turned on his heel and marched to the arch. He strode in and vanished from sight, safely stored away in Ishtar's ship.

Sophie shut the cover with a click and fastened the bag. They'd done it. She wiped her eyes and rested her hand on it. Such a light, strange thing. She was cradling all their futures, including Bella's.

Freddy stroked Jack, who leaned against him. 'I expected Charlotte to hold her own, but Jack was just as plucky. Biting and not staying long enough to get stabbed.' Jack enjoyed the caress, the gentle retriever once more, and Charlotte watched him, a proud gleam in her eye.

Freddy straightened. 'Sophie, why are you so wet?'

'I went for a swim.' Too raw, too unpleasant an experience even to summarise.

The girl and her partner were walking towards them. They'd stayed by the river this entire time, watching Janus and the end of the battle. The guy's expression was blank. So was the girl's. Something was … off.

'Sorry about this.' The girl took a pen from her satchel, pointed it, and the next moment, Sophie, Hugo, and Freddy were engulfed in a blinding light. So were the dogs.

Tingling and numbness invaded Sophie's body, and she couldn't move or speak. Her feet were fixed to the ground. The girl's partner pulled the staff bag off her shoulder. Sophie strained every sinew to stop him. Her body didn't respond. And she couldn't make a sound, though inside she was screaming.

The guy jogged with the staff, heading for the river. Looked to be in his forties but as fit as a greyhound. Sophie knew with a throb of despair what he would do. Sure enough, he threw the staff as far as he could into the Tiber. It landed on its side, and in a blink of an eye, it sank.

As he strolled from the bank, retracing his steps, Sophie found she could wiggle her fingers. Rage consumed her. The staff was gone, and with it, their way back to Bella. Sophie could shift her lips and tongue, though they were numb. 'Why?' she managed.

'If Janus' ship were to be made safe,' said the girl, 'many more travellers would cross universes.'

No, no, no. How did this couple know about their plan?

The girl's eyes softened. 'Timelines would change, innocents would suffer, and chaos would destroy ... countless worlds.'

Hugo opened his mouth, but no sound came out.

'We only want to reach our daughter,' said Freddy, his words jerky.

The girl's face shuttered, carefully expressionless. She wasn't a traveller who helped people. Neither was her partner. They were cops who guarded timelines. The guy spoke, and the pair walked off up the road.

Feeling was returning to Sophie's legs, but her utter despair about the staff eclipsed any relief. Bella, her dear, darling baby. Would she ever see her again?

Hugo shot Sophie a bleak look. He took a wobbly step forward and patted Jack who was blinking and whining. Charlotte nuzzled Sophie's legs.

Aelia hurried over, sheathing her sword. Tarchon had a vivid gash across his brow. Otherwise, uninjured.

'What was that terrible light?' said Aelia in Latin.

Her cylinder broken, Sophie struggled to understand but caught the gist. 'We don't know.' She wiggled her shoulders, made stiff by the light-weapon or her fight with the Tiber, or both.

'The staff might wash up against the bank?' Freddy limped towards the river.

How likely was that? But Sophie went with him, and Hugo and the dogs came too.

Sophie shielded her eyes, scanning the water. 'I don't understand why it sank so fast. It wasn't heavy.' Charlotte leaned against her legs, trying to comfort her.

'The river water might be different from home,' said Freddy. 'We can test that.' He slipped his satchel strap off his shoulder. 'Does the staff weigh less than this?'

Sophie held his satchel and nodded.

Where the drop to the river was shallower, Freddy lay on his front and swung his satchel down to the water, keeping hold of the strap. The satchel met the surface and floated. Water seeped into the bottom and the inside, and it slowly sank. Freddy yanked it out. 'Entirely what I would expect.'

Sophie wanted to scream. 'So why did the staff sink like a stone?'

Hugo stared out at the river. 'Ishtar carried it with ease. So did you. What if that was because of the gene? Perhaps I couldn't have lifted it, let alone used it as a walking stick?'

Sophie remembered picking up the base with Ishtar. 'I was surprised how light it was.'

'Over the last thousand years, by accident or by design, there must have been occasions when the locals managed to touch the walking staff or tried to move it,' said Hugo. 'The builders would have ensured that the locals found what they expected.'

Freddy drew a long, shuddery breath. 'The walking staff of a god. Awe-inspiring and immensely heavy.'

'Even for us, finding it underwater will be near impossible,' said Sophie. 'Trust me, I know.'

A muscle worked in Freddy's jaw. 'We should wade in. We have to try.'

Sophie hauled off her shawl, but Hugo clamped his arms

around her. 'If a drop of moisture could break the staff before, under all of that?' His voice cracked. 'It's destroyed.'

Freddy sat down abruptly on the grass and sobbed. Charlotte rested a paw on his shoulder.

Sophie couldn't cry. Her body was no longer frozen, but her soul was numb.

The locals still on the riverbank were muttering. They didn't seem bothered about Wells' body or the dead thugs. They were staring at the arch, maybe expecting Janus to come out again.

Sophie watched them, not caring. Not caring about anything.

Aelia addressed Freddy, asked something about the pendant.

Freddy's shoulders were slumped, and he just nodded.

Tarchon asked Hugo something and Freddy translated. 'This was your first battle?'

'Yes.' Hugo looked sheepish. 'I stayed behind him.'

The festival stragglers continued to watch the arch. At the edge of the group were a couple holding hands. Drusus and Melissa. They'd done as instructed. Kept their distance, out of harm's way. Sophie waved them forward, their signal it was safe. As they drew nearer, Melissa dropped Drusus' hand, seemed embarrassed.

Behind them, from the top of the road, came a shout. 'Vigiles,' said Aelia. She and Tarchon drew their swords.

'Don't kill the watchmen.' Freddy's eyes were red-rimmed. 'They're simply doing their job, investigating the fight.'

'Retreat to the arch.' Sophie's voice was quiet. Not an order, more an admission of defeat.

'Freddy, put your arm around my shoulder,' said Hugo.

'And mine,' said Sophie.

Supporting Freddy made for quicker progress than him limping with his stick, and they soon reached the arch. The interior was empty. The shed — the ship and Janus inside it — gone.

Janus' over-sized footprints had pushed down the hard earth and Sophie stumbled on the uneven ground. Like his walking staff. The weight of a god, not a man.

Hugo looked back through the arch at the watchmen. 'Call for Juno.'

'Regina, Curitis, Moneta,' yelled Freddy.

Nothing happened.

'Juno, you promised,' shouted Sophie.

'We call you to be reunited with our daughter,' said Freddy.

Still nothing.

'Appeal to her as the queen of the gods in Latin,' said Sophie. That had worked before.

Freddy spoke slowly but Sophie only caught Juno's many names. With her cylinder broken, she was side-lined and useless. Hugo had been a complete hero, learning and speaking Latin.

He was by the entrance to the arch. 'The watchmen have finished examining the bodies. They're searching the area.' Hugo drove his hand through his hair. 'Freddy, try again.'

'Rogamus te,' shouted Freddy. 'Moneta, Caprotina, Tutula…'

Charlotte barked.

A faint humming, and where the shed had been, a black void. Then the darkness dissolved, replaced by the wall of red bricks. The bricks rippled, separated, and fused together at the summit, forming the arch into the ship.

Hugo ran over to Sophie. 'What's happening? All I see is grass and cow poo.'

She said, loudly, 'Hugo.'

He rolled his eyes. 'Juno doesn't reveal herself to the lower orders, remember?'

'She's here,' said Sophie.

The ex-slaves were looking at each other, bewildered, and Sophie ushered them into the ship. They gawped at the courtyard illusion. 'We're safe in here. The watchmen can't see us.' Courtesy of Juno, Sophie's English also came out in Latin and German. As Freddy limped inside with Hugo, Charlotte herded in Jack, pushing at him like a sheep dog.

Sophie put her satchel on the floor and took off her damp shawl. Surprisingly, her necklace with the broken cylinder and Bella's key-rattle was still around her neck.

Tarchon waved his hands in Juno's fountain. 'Why is there no water?'

'The courtyard's not real,' said Freddy, his voice flat.

The ex-slaves perched on the long stone seats. Hugo laid his sword on the paving stones, then sat with Freddy, who'd rested his walking stick across his knees. Jack was by the exit, quiet, copying Charlotte. In case he got spooked, Sophie held onto his collar.

The watchmen strode into the arch. Their eyes glided over Juno, but Sophie held her breath until they left. She turned around. Freddy was studying his lap, all the fight gone out of him.

'How did you fall in the river?' asked Hugo. 'I was avoiding being cut to ribbons, so missed it.'

Sophie dearly wanted to lie down and embrace sleep.

Instead, she summarised and added, 'I don't recommend the Tiber for a swim.' Banter would never drive away the memory, but it helped. Drusus handed her a flask, and she gratefully sipped the clean water.

Freddy looked up. 'Resurrection is a terrible honour to share.' After his drink had been spiked, he'd 'died' in modern London.

Sophie gave him a sympathetic glance. 'After the girl resuscitated me, she said "Forewarned is forearmed." That confirms what I thought before. She'd visited a similar universe where it was 95 AD, one where she couldn't save me. Well, another version of me.'

'When you were dead, did you have horrid dreams?' said Freddy.

'No, I saw my mother. She knew about Bella.'

Freddy blinked rapidly and Sophie pretended she hadn't noticed.

'Our eyes stung like hell after we were hit with that light.' Hugo patted Jack and sighed. 'I am so sorry about the staff.'

Sophie's despair would soon consume her, and there'd be nothing left. She tried to picture Bella, but her memories seemed hazy, her baby even further away.

'I'll check on the watchmen.' Hugo left the ship and soon came back. 'They've thrown Wells' body into the Tiber, and the dead thugs.'

Sophie put her hand to her mouth. How many corpses ended up in there?

'They're heading off,' added Hugo.

Freddy got to his feet, leaned on his stick, and addressed the ex-slaves. 'Thank you so much for your help. We'll always remember it. It's safe for you to return to Villa Fullia.'

Despite his despair, Freddy was being polite and kind. She should be too. Sophie hugged Melissa, and Melissa hugged her tighter, despite Sophie reeking of the river.

'Let's leave Rome a little kinder than we found it,' said Hugo. 'Freddy, do you have the key to the heavy chest in the study?'

Puzzled, Freddy rummaged in his satchel.

Hugo gave the key to Tarchon. 'There's enough money in the chest to buy a home for you and Aelia, and for Drusus and Melissa.' Juno translated Hugo's English.

Tarchon opened his mouth, but no words came out.

Melissa turned to Drusus. 'We can buy our own slaves.' Her face was a picture of joy.

Slaves? Sophie cleared her throat. 'No, on condition—'

'No conditions.' Hugo shot her his warning look.

Sophie bowed her head. She hadn't the strength to argue, or do anything else.

CHAPTER 47

Drusus and Melissa held hands as they left the ship, and Tarchon and Aelia departed with a spring in their step. But when Juno's exit shut, Sophie sighed. 'I hate that we'll never see them again.'

Freddy faffed about, getting comfortable on a long stone seat, ensuring his bad leg was elevated.

Hugo glanced at his own bloody arm. 'I hardly noticed this before but it's really hurting. And I feel dizzy.'

'It's not a competition,' panted Freddy.

Quoting back at Hugo his own banter. One of Hugo's favourites. A good sign. Freddy wasn't broken. He'd recover from this.

Sophie steeled herself and examined Hugo's arm. A jagged blade had left an ugly slash, and the skin around it was red and swollen.

She bit her lip. 'Juno, show me supplies that will treat an infected knife wound.'

'Done.'

Sophie hurried out of the pretend courtyard towards a

light some way down the ship. The light was illuminating a steel box. Inside were just scissors, rolls of bandages and what looked like baby wipes in a transparent bag. 'Juno, we need antibiotics.'

'The dressings release remedial paste.'

Sophie carried the box into the courtyard. She cleaned the injury with the wipes, cut off a long bandage and tied it firmly around the injury. The bandage was slimy and sticky. Didn't need tying.

'Juno, please review all the variants of London in 1889,' said Freddy. 'Choose the universe with the highest probability that we'll survive.'

Charlotte shook her head, and Sophie frowned. 'Juno, delay that.' They were in no state to start a new hunt for the walking staff. Might not be for a while.

'We know Wells' address in the 19th century,' said Freddy, 'and that he has the staff.'

'You can barely stand up,' said Sophie.

'We must go home.' Hugo was wincing in pain. 'Regroup.'

'Your home, you mean?' said Freddy.

'In the 21st century, we can thoroughly research 1889 online,' said Hugo. 'We can't do that in Shorten. We don't want to miss anything.'

Freddy's brow creased. 'The odds of surviving might not change with every trip, but even a single extra crossing's not worth the risk.'

Sophie hesitated. A sliver of doubt. At least one version of them had died in this ship, attempting a first crossing. If they returned to modern London, that would be their second. Crossing to 1889 would be the third. Abandon this mad quest. Go to Shorten and be done with it. She might be with Bella within days. What had the girl in the grey tunic said would happen if they ended Janus? *Chaos would destroy count-*

less worlds. No, that was ridiculous. A lame attempt to justify her partner's actions, destroying the staff. Who knew what their motivation was? The girl hadn't even shared her name. Hardly a sign of honesty.

'The ultimate prize is more important. Guaranteed, reliable travel.' Hugo nursed his bandaged arm. 'I'm being practical.'

'*I'm* being practical.' Freddy glared. 'We should go straight to the 19th century.'

'Speaking of practical,' said Sophie, 'we've no money. We've just given it all away.'

Freddy briefly shut his eyes, defeated.

'Juno, take us to universe 666,' said Sophie. 'The best version for me, for all of us.'

The courtyard became the cargo bay. 'Secure yourselves,' said Juno.

Freddy struggled to his feet from the metal bench. Hugo strapped Jack into a flip-down seat, Sophie fastened Charlotte's seatbelt, and everyone else belted up.

'We were so close,' said Freddy. 'So close—'

The cargo bay dropped and spiralled and Sophie blacked out like she had before. When she came to, she focused on not being sick.

Finally, the ship stopped spinning and made its steady humming sound, and Sophie breathed in the sterile air. In, out. When she'd recovered herself, she undid the dogs' straps and her own.

'I'll never grow accustomed to that,' said Freddy.

'Ambient temperature is twenty-two centigrade,' said Juno.

'I'll get us some water,' said Sophie.

She and Hugo walked along the ship with the dogs. Charlotte gave a single bark. Up ahead, there was only one trolley.

In it was a slab of water bottles and a solitary carton of protein bars.

Sophie stared, hoping she was hallucinating. 'Juno, where are the other trolleys?'

'No longer required.'

'Where's the rest of our supplies?' asked Hugo.

Silence.

Sophie ground her teeth. Juno had remembered their preferred temperature. It sucked they had to confirm Hugo's status on every crossing. 'Juno, answer Hugo as you would me.'

'Your supplies were consumed by other travellers.'

'I told you it was for us,' said Hugo.

'You said to keep your supplies safe.' Juno's matronly voice was annoyingly unemotional. but she was just a machine.

Hugo's mouth thinned into a frustrated line. 'I meant *safe* as in *untouched.*'

'The items weren't categorised as private property.'

'We're lucky there's anything left at all.' Sophie unclipped the straps that secured the trolley and trundled it back to the courtyard.

'Juno broadcast your conversation.' Freddy eyed the trolley. 'We'll need to restrict ourselves to half a protein bar and half a bottle of water, per person, per day.' His jaw clenched. 'And even then, there may not be enough.'

Their survival holdalls were also gone, so was Charlotte's page-turning machine and paperback, but their modern clothes were where they'd left them. They changed into shorts and T-shirts, but Sophie was still smelly. Couldn't be helped. Even if most of their water hadn't been taken, she wouldn't have wasted any on washing. 'Juno, can we have the room with the five beds, please?'

The illusion appeared with the same frescoes as before,

decorating the wall and the ceiling: the goddess Juno, dressed in her blue robe, a loving mother with her children.

Freddy's bench became a bed and Charlotte and Jack jumped onto beds. Freddy emptied the contents of his damp satchel on the floor. The gem of the pendant was dull, looked like cheap glass.

'Leave the device for disposal,' said Juno.

Sophie sat on the edge of the nearest spare bed. 'What's happened to it?'

'Destroyed by water.'

Sophie relived Freddy lowering his satchel into the Tiber. How it floated, then half sank. She frowned. 'Juno, why wasn't the pendant waterproofed?'

'It couldn't be sealed because it drew power from elements in the air, including oxygen, argon, hydrogen, neon, helium, xenon, and radon.'

Right. The cylinders, the security bands, and the walking staff... They all had the same flaw. 'I forgot to say,' said Sophie, 'my translation cylinder's as dead as the pendant.'

Charlotte touched hers with her paw. 'At least, ours still work,' said Freddy.

'When we do find the staff in the 19th century,' said Hugo, 'we'll know to keep it away from water.'

Sophie shot him a rueful glance. 'And to avoid the time police.'

Hugo sat back on his bed, holding his arm. 'How did they know about our plan for the staff?'

'They were spying on us,' said Sophie. 'Maybe they somehow tapped into our conversations?'

'More to the point,' said Freddy, 'how did they know we were there? In that Rome, on those dates? With countless universes, and other versions of us trying to steal the staff, they'd need a truly vast database.'

'Perhaps they just protect the most important timelines,'

said Hugo. 'Otherwise, they'd have stopped Sophie in the medieval realm from wiping out an army.'

Sophie winced. Change the subject. 'I think the light-weapon's called a heart-stopper.'

'It didn't stop our hearts.' Hugo touched his chest.

Sophie sat fully on the bed and hugged her knees. 'Maybe they used a non-lethal setting?'

'Rome wasn't *that* similar to the ancient city in my universe. Janus didn't boil the Tiber.' Freddy lay down, fidgeting to get comfortable. 'Although the Sabine women and Janus setting off a scalding, volcanic spring isn't that different.'

'I'm guessing Janus was programmed with the builders' female ability to boil liquid,' said Hugo, 'whatever his outward appearance.'

Charlotte jumped onto Jack's bed and the dogs high fived.

'I needed to see that,' said Hugo.

'Jack's learning from her. Every day something new.' Sophie plumped up her firm pillow. 'The locals who saw Janus a second time must realise he's on a loop.'

'I'm not sure they will,' said Freddy. 'They've no TV shows or films that can be played again, and stock repeated phrases are a common feature of many religions.'

'The crowd seemed to enjoy the fear, as if they were watching a horror movie,' said Hugo. 'Many of them must have seen a similar show before.'

Seen before... 'The firework display,' said Sophie. 'The single cottage before it became a tenement.'

'What about it?' said Hugo.

'It was the same image I saw on the lift doors, on Janus' ship, that first day in the students' union with you. Huh. The cottage on fire was a destination after all.'

'Or a choice?' said Hugo. 'We didn't have to go to Rome.'

'I can't believe *any* versions of me wouldn't have tried to acquire the walking staff there,' said Freddy.

'I'd like to think the same.' Sophie touched the shape of Bella's key-rattle under her T-shirt.

This wasn't over. Not yet.

CHAPTER 48

Ten minutes after Sophie poured the last of the water into Jack and Charlotte's mouths, there was a soft click. 'Juno has landed at your destination.'

'Thank God,' said Freddy.

The crossing had taken five long days. And all the while, they'd feared they'd never reach home, that their search for the walking staff, for Bella, had been for nothing. The dogs high fived, and Hugo sagged in relief. Sophie hugged him.

The blank wall transformed into the arch, revealing the students' union beyond it. They picked up their satchels, leaving their Roman clothes behind. Someone might have use for them. Sophie had already taken the eternity brooch off the shawl, storing it in her satchel.

Hugo fastened his sword belt over his shorts and ensured the gladius' blade was secure inside its scabbard.

Sophie rolled her eyes. 'Why are you keeping that? You'll give the university security guard a heart attack.'

'I'll store it in our basement with the medieval sword.' He tied her shawl around his waist, concealing the blade. 'We may never need it but, hey, just in case.'

They hurried into a deserted students' union. Outside the institutional windows, it was dark, and the security door which led to Elliot and Lorna's flat was locked.

'If it's the early hours,' said Hugo, 'we'll be stuck out here until Elliot and Lorna wake up.' Without watches or phones, they had no way of knowing the time.

They sat on the floor, but only a few minutes later, they stood up, hearing footsteps from across the hall. Charlotte cocked her head and Jack barked.

'I'll convince the guard to let us through,' said Freddy. 'I've done it before.'

But it wasn't a security guard. A student with an untidy mop of fair hair tottered towards them.

'Hello,' said Sophie.

The boy giggled and gave her a lazy wave.

'Do you know the time?' asked Freddy.

The boy stared, his eyes unfocused. 'Um...' He fished a phone from the pocket of his jeans. 'Nearly midnight,' he slurred. He passed them and fumbling with a card, opened the security door.

After he'd gone through, Freddy held the door open, and everyone trooped into the gloomy passage, illuminated by a single bulb on the ceiling. The boy was stumbling up the stairs at the end of the corridor.

Freddy knocked on the plywood door to Elliot and Lorna's flat. Numbered 0001, the first 0 was loose, about to fall off.

'Apologies for the late hour,' said Freddy, when Elliot opened the door. 'Could we trouble you for glasses of water?'

Elliot smiled. 'Good to see you.'

In the kitchen area in the sitting room, Sophie filled a bowl and put it down for Charlotte and Jack. 'Drink slowly or you'll get tummy ache.' The dogs took no notice.

'I'll take the risk.' Hugo untied the shawl and dropped it

with his sword and belt on the floor. He filled three mugs and drank one in a fevered gulp. Sophie tried to sip but then just drank. So did Freddy.

'Before you ask,' said Elliot, 'it's Friday, the 18th of September. Three weeks since you left.' He stroked Jack and straightened. 'You've all caught the sun.'

Sophie looked down at her tanned legs. She couldn't face telling them about Rome. She glanced up at Hugo and he nodded, reading her face. 'I'll tell them.'

Lorna came into the sitting room. 'Feel free to use the shower.'

'Thank you,' said Sophie, conscious she was smelly.

'Elliot, if it's not too much trouble, could you give us a spare card?' said Freddy. 'For the door to the passage?'

'First thing in the morning.'

'And I'll sort you a key to the flat.' Lorna stroked her guide dog and in response, Fudge leaned against her legs.

The following afternoon, in Hugo's kitchen in London, Sophie made tea. 'It feels surreal being back.'

'We need to decompress,' said Hugo. 'Adjust, like soldiers returning from a war zone.' His phone bleeped. 'My parents are having a great time in Scotland.'

While they'd been crossing universes, engrossed in their quest to reach Bella, family here were happily living their lives. The holiday photos would be on the Harrington chat group. She glanced at her phone, charging by the fridge, but couldn't muster the enthusiasm to switch it on.

Jack was snoring under the table and Charlotte was pacing by the window. Sophie went over to her. 'What's up?' Charlotte shrugged. She didn't know.

'The dogs of legend Drusus mentioned, Bran and

Sceólang…' Hugo tapped his phone. 'They're hounds from Celtic mythology. Fought alongside mighty warriors.'

Charlotte stopped pacing. Sophie set down a bowl of Earl Grey tea for her, and she lapped it up.

'*They hold a special place in Irish hearts,*' read Hugo. 'Extraordinary how these stories have survived.'

Freddy was also scrolling on his phone. 'Ha! Listen to this. From a tombstone in Rome. *Tiberius Claudius Secundus. To the Spirits of the Departed. Baths, wine, and sex destroy our bodies, but only baths, wine and sex make life worth living.*' Freddy's lips lifted in a rueful, half smile. 'I can enjoy two of those things.'

Sophie studied her flip-flops, irrationally guilty. Freddy wasn't hinting. He'd be loyal to Clarissa, even if he never saw her again.

Freddy was still scrolling. 'Goodness. It's them!' He turned the phone around. On the screen was a stone inscription, built into a bridge.

'What is it?' Sophie asked him.

'A tombstone. Preserved in a modern viaduct. It says, *Tarchon Finius and his beloved wife, Aelia.*'

'The first names must be a coincidence,' said Hugo. 'Our Tarchon would have called himself Tarchon Veranius, after you, his former owner.'

Freddy peered at the photo. 'Don't you see what this means? In this universe, two thousand years ago, Tarchon *Finius* was freed by someone else. Another version of us who chose a different surname, or someone else entirely.'

'A nice idea,' said Hugo.

Sophie stirred the teapot. 'They got lucky twice.'

'Hopefully, they were lucky more times than not.' Freddy pinched the photo to make it bigger. 'This confirms it's them. *Supplier of renowned German guards to four emperors.*'

Sophie gave a low whistle. 'Tarchon said he'd rather die than serve his tribe's enemy.'

'Perhaps settling down with Aelia, he changed his mind?' said Hugo.

'I hope Melissa and Drusus were okay.' Sophie wiped her eyes. Sometimes, time-travel sucked.

Hugo hugged her. 'Memento mori. Remember you must die.'

She scowled at him. 'Not helping.'

'Drusus and Melissa may be long dead in this universe,' said Freddy. 'In many others, right now, they're safe and well.'

'I'm calling Lucy and Tiana,' said Hugo.

Sophie poured tea into their mugs. 'What happened to decompressing?'

'It will be nice to chat,' said Freddy. 'Might help.'

The couple were veterans of crossing universes, albeit just to Shorten and back, but Lucy had been heavily pregnant before they'd left for Rome. She was due to give birth in less than a week.

Lucy picked up and Hugo put her on FaceTime and speaker. She was cradling a tiny baby. 'Janet arrived early.'

'Mother and daughter both doing fine,' said Tiana, in her drawling Californian accent.

'Wonderful,' said Sophie, beyond pleased for them.

'We'll be up for crossing universes in no time.' Once Janet was old enough, Lucy dearly wanted to return to Shorten. 'Did you get the walking staff?'

'Not yet,' said Freddy.

'We know where it is.' Sophie tried to sound up-beat.

'Send us dates when you can visit,' said Tiana. 'You'll be most welcome.' She smiled and ended the call.

A moment later, Hugo's phone bleeped. 'It's my mother.

Returning from Scotland early evening, 23ʳᵈ. Emily says call her. No idea who Emily is.'

Sophie yawned and stretched. 'I'm going to sleep for a week.'

Hugo chewed his lip. 'I feel … unsettled.'

'As do I,' said Freddy.

Sophie tramped upstairs with the dogs. In the bedroom, she opened her satchel and took out the eternity brooch and the Janus frieze wrapped in its green doily. They needed to be kept somewhere safe. She stored them in a drawer before lying down on the bed.

She'd hardly closed her eyes when Hugo burst in and put her phone on the bedside table. He was panting from running up the stairs. 'What was your mother's first name?'

The question threw her. 'Milly.'

'Was that her birth name or a pet name?'

Sophie rolled over and half sat against the pillow, her mind muzzy from sleep. 'Her real name was Emily.'

Hugo placed the phone in her hand. 'Prepare yourself for a shock.' He sat on the edge of the bed. 'You've new messages.'

'So?' While they crossed universes, messages stacked up. But she stared at the screen and so did Charlotte. *Are you still coming round tomorrow? I'm making your favourite veggie lasagne. xxx*

Even after so long, Sophie recognised the number and felt sick. 'What a nasty scam.' She went to delete the message, but Hugo snatched the phone away.

Freddy limped in carrying a bottle of brandy and a shot glass.

Sophie frowned at him. 'It's four in the afternoon.'

Hugo clicked on another text and held the screen in front of her face. *I've made chocolate cake. xxx*

Precious memories tumbled through her mind, but Sophie pushed them aside. 'Stupid texts from a troll.'

'What if they're not?' said Hugo.

I've made chocolate cake. xxx A quiver of doubt. Her mother had made the best chocolate cake, and she'd always packed one into Sophie's school trunk. Her mother standing on a blustery platform waving goodbye… The last time she'd seen her… 'No.'

'When you gave the destination to Juno for here, my arm was sore and I wasn't thinking straight,' said Hugo. 'If I had been, I'd have dug out my notebook so you could read the final digits of the universe's number.' He hesitated. 'Perhaps that was a lucky mistake.'

'I … I can't take this in,' said Sophie.

'You set the destination in Juno, saying something like, Universe 666, a good version for me, for all of us,' said Hugo.

'Juno would have tried to identify 666 universes using that criteria.' Freddy poured brandy into the shot glass. 'There were probably a lot, so she randomly assigned one.'

After dying in the Tiber, seeing her mother in that idyllic park had only strengthened closure, reinforced her acceptance that her parents were gone. Was that why she was struggling to react, why she wasn't dancing with joy? Sophie drew a calming breath. Think this through. 'If my parents had joined the main road a few seconds earlier or later, the accident wouldn't have happened.'

Hugo put her phone, screen-down, on the bedside table.

'Okay, say they're alive…' Sophie shook her head. 'Presumably my mother's sent other texts? To another phone with the same number? *I* haven't been here. I've never been here. Who was receiving the texts?'

'A different version of you,' said Hugo.

'So, where's the other me? Are we talking about the version that *did* drown in Rome, or that died in Juno, or another version? And if this isn't *our* universe, where's the other Hugo, the other Freddy … the other Charlotte, the other Jack?'

'I don't know.' Freddy handed her the brandy.

Sophie stared into the glass and gave in to hysterical tears. 'Why aren't I happy?'

'Because it's overwhelming,' said Hugo. Charlotte nuzzled close, and so did Jack.

Sophie downed the brandy.

CHAPTER 49

The following morning, Sophie opened her bedside drawer to take out her necklace. Keeping Bella's key-rattle on the chain, she slid off the broken cylinder and as she did, her fingers brushed another necklace, a precious gift from her own mother. The single stone had spiralling shades of blue, like a wondrous galaxy. Stored away for keeping, not wearing. But now the past had changed, altering the present.

She added the opal to the chain and put it on.

After breakfast, Sophie fed her parents' postcode into the satnav of Hugo's car and, over the next hour, heading to Buckinghamshire, her sense of unreality splintered. Fear and hope warred inside her head. Other people had gone through this. Traumatised after wars or natural disasters, many survivors must have unexpectedly returned home. And been happily reunited, or not.

They came into a residential road. The semi-detached houses were identical except for the occasional extension and doors painted different colours. Sophie pointed. 'That one.'

Hugo stopped the car. He leaned down and released Sophie's seatbelt.

'Call us, day or night,' said Freddy.

'You're not coming with me?' Sophie gulped. She couldn't do this on her own.

'We might never have got married here,' said Hugo. 'It'll be tough enough unravelling all that. And a lot of other stuff might be different. Your aunt might never have adopted Charlotte, not to mention where Freddy fits in.'

'You've … all decided,' said Sophie.

On the back seat, Charlotte gave a solemn nod, and Freddy patted Sophie's shoulder.

'1889 is the last roll of the dice and you'll need to be physically and mentally strong,' said Hugo. 'Adjust to your parents, to this reality. Then you'll be ready.'

'How will I know when I'm ready?' Tears pricked her eyes.

Hugo kissed her tenderly. 'You'll know.'

Sophie made herself get out and shut the car door. Fallen leaves were blowing across the pavement, a swirl of yellows and reds, releasing a faint scent of mildew. She still associated autumn with the start of the academic year, a fresh beginning. Why was this so hard?

Freddy blew her a kiss, Charlotte and Jack pressed their muzzles against the car window, and Hugo gave her a mock salute before driving off. Sophie watched the car until it disappeared.

When she turned to open the gate and walked through it, her mother was standing on the doorstep. She looked older than in Sophie's death-dream.

Sophie took a tentative step, then another, her heart a worried drumbeat in her ears. Then she ran and gathered her mother close. Bella's key-rattle was between them, unyielding and angular, but Sophie didn't stop hugging. This *was* her mother. Her cotton shirt smelled exactly as it should, of cooking, of home.

'Is everything all right?' Her mother held her at arm's length and searched her face. 'Where's Hugo?'

'He, um, sends his apologies. A last-minute work trip.'

Her mother nodded. If she'd sensed her daughter wasn't the same, the thought had been fleeting.

Sophie came into the hall and closed the door. She embraced her father, savouring the aroma of coffee on his cardigan and old mints in his pocket. 'Can I stay over, just until Hugo gets home?'

Her father smiled, his eyes crinkling at the edges. 'Any progress on the grandchild front?'

She'd forgotten how blunt he was, and she hesitated. 'Not yet.'

'You always say that.' He went with her into the kitchen. 'Don't leave it too long.'

'We won't.' Sophie bit back what she longed to share. You have a granddaughter, and she's formidable.

Over lunch, her parents chatted about their friends, and Sophie resolved that in a fortnight, she'd visit Lucy and Tiana, and welcome a new soul into this world.

The conversation shifted to organising a sale to mend the church roof, and her parents' voices enveloped Sophie in a familiar soft blanket of love and contentment. A brittle knot of regret loosened and started to unravel. Ironically for a time-traveller, she couldn't make up for lost time, but she could cherish every moment now.

Hugo and Charlotte, and Freddy and Jack would wait for her, and at the right time, they'd be ready.

And so would she.

~

Historical Note

Most of the portrayal of everyday life in ancient Rome in this novel is as historically accurate as I could make it, but artistic licence has been used in some instances. These include the value of Roman money, the bridge of the four heads, the Roman god, Janus, and playing fast and loose with the splendid uniforms of bodyguards. It's unclear whether there would have been estate agents trading in the Forum as property was sold privately, but hey, this is an alternate Rome.

Please, classical professors, don't judge me too harshly...

I hope you enjoyed *Hunted*.

If you did, let people know.

Reviews are the most effective way of building awareness of a book you've enjoyed.

While I love telling people about the *Shorten Chronicles,* honest reviews bring the books to the attention of other readers.

If you didn't buy *Hunted* direct from my Fantasy Bookshop, I'd really appreciate it if you'd leave a review (short as you like) where you bought it.

Thank you!

Book Six is the last novel in the first *Shorten Chronicles* series.

Sophie must retrieve Janus' walking staff from London in 1889 to reach her daughter.

Sophie's last chance, and the most deadly.

Check release dates, special offers, discounts, and more: *www.rosalindtate.com*

Buy direct: *https://bookshop.rosalindtate.com*

About the Author

Rosalind Tate lives in Gloucestershire, England, and holidays on the Cornish coast. She served in the British military, then worked as a journalist and a lawyer.

Rosalind enjoys talking about publishing and encouraging new authors. When she's not behind her computer, you can find Rosalind reading her favourite books, walking her dogs, swimming, or watching sci-fi and fantasy shows.

Rosalind has three grown up children, a tolerant husband, and two utterly gorgeous dogs.

Acknowledgments

To my husband, Ian. Thank you for your patience, support, and sharp, proofreading eyes.

To my mother, who many years ago showed me how to be a writer.

To my editor, Debi Alper, and my fabulous readers in Team Charlotte, particularly Carla Mortensen, who realised how much H. G. Wells would shape this story.

I must also acknowledge a debt to T. R. Burgess for sharing her detailed knowledge of Ancient Rome, and to L. J. Trafford's book: *How To Survive in Ancient Rome*. A boon to every time traveller!

Thank you to our labradoodle, the wonderful Bella. You inspired the Shorten Chronicles after all. And thanks also to Bella's goldendoodle kid sister, for her author guarding skills. She's called … Sophie. What? Okay, when we adopted her, I was obsessed with Sophie Arundel, and our energetic puppy has some things in common with her literary human counterpart. She's sassy, runs fast and is far too impulsive.

Finally, Toby deserves a mention. He was our first labradoodle and is no longer with us.

Well, in this world.

Rosalind Tate
Gloucestershire 2024

HUNTED
BOOK FIVE OF THE SHORTEN CHRONICLES
First published in Great Britain in 2024
by TOB Publishing
Copyright © Rosalind Tate 2024
® The Shorten Chronicles is a registered trademark

A catalogue hardback record for this book is available from the British Library:

ISBN: 978-1-7395073-4-3
Cover Design by 187 Designz
Website by sprkdesign
TOB Publishing

www.ingramcontent.com/pod-product-compliance
Lightning Source LLC
Chambersburg PA
CBHW030800210726
48290CB00002B/349